Designs by Margie Lucas
www.margielucasarts.com

Written by Stephen Richard Echols, Roanoke, Virginia
dorseywhitlock@icloud.com

Special acknowledgement: The World's Best Golf Jokes.
Russ Edwards and Jack Kreismer. Red-Letter Press, Inc.
Saddle River New Jersey "www.Red-LetterPress.com"

Acknowledgement:

Titanic Thompson. The Man Who Bet on Everything. By Kevin Cook
W.W. Norton & Company.
New York London

Virginia Golfer
Golf Digest
The Roanoke Times-Dispatch

And:

Bulldog Adams – Jackson, MI and Boynton Beach, Fl

Bunny – good friend, matchmaker par excellence

Carol Demarco – "Be Creditwize"    BeCreditWize.com
2015 Dog Ear Publishing  Indianapolis IN

C. David Gelly – @Fancy Gap -  2011 Create Space

David E Black DDS – Roanoke Va

Luisa- she makes it all happen

Emma Stark – my hero

Nicole Kovacs – a born teacher

Mike Wilson – Bohemian Robot Media Group, Roanoke

Victor Clarke "The Marketing Quarterback", Clarke Inc, Lynchburg
Va.  www.bebetterdomore.com

A portion of proceeds from sales of this work will be donated to the
Alzheimer's Association

# Dorsey's first rules:

- If you can CONSISTENLY hit your drives over 250 yards, you can CONSIDER playing the Black Tees

- If you can CONSISTENTLY hit your drives 225-250, you can CONSIDER playing the Blue Tees

- If you hit your drives over 200, you can CONSIDER playing the White Tees

- If you hit it under 200, even if it's straight, play the Gold Tees

# According to the National Golf Foundation:

Assuming No Mulligans, "Play them as they lie,"
and no "Gimmes", and taking appropriate penalties:

5 % of Golfers can shoot under 80

21% of Golfers shoot from 80 to 89

29 % of Golfers shoot from 90 to 99

24 % of Golfers shoot from 100 to 109

10 % of Golfers shoot from 110 to 119

11 % of Golfers shoot over 120

This book is dedicated to the 95% of those of us who have made peace with our games and play anyway.

## Prologue - the Rules of Golf and related Topics

**"Income tax has made more liars out of the American people than golf has" - Will Rogers**

**The Rules of Golf** are governed jointly by the "Royal and Ancient" (R&A), based in Scotland and The United States Golf Association (USGA) of Far Hills, New Jersey. Anyone can receive the **Rules of Golf** by contacting the USGA; www.USGA.org, The book is free. Or join the USGA annually and get a free hat as well.

There are 34 rules. The first twenty-eight concern playing the game and the additional six address various forms of competition, the ruling body and complaints. Twenty-eight basic rules don't sound like a lot for a game that may be 500 years old, but the book takes two-hundred-thirty-one pages to explain them.

There are rules for arriving at a tee time on time, how many clubs you can use, and their specifications. There are rules describing eligible balls a player can use, what to do if the ball moves, what debris you can move out of the way, how to assess penalties on yourself, how you must tell your playing partners and so on.

There are several key rules watched closely by the Greater Roanoke Invitational Tour for Seniors (GRITS), often ignored in casual golf;

**Rule 13 "Ball Played as it Lies" (p.77) indicates that you cannot move the ball at all.** GRITS offer a concession, allowing a ball in the fairway to be "rolled over" or moved one club-length. This is very practical, as it allows golfers to move from a hole or bare patch of grass onto a spot a little easier to hit from. Pros and serious competitors do follow Rule 13.

**Rules 26, 27 and 28 (pp.113-118)** cover the things that most golfers do, which are hit it in the water, out-of-bounds, or up against a tree or in a bush. These rules are complicated, and most casual golfers will revert to a mentality of recording strokes as; 1 in (into the trouble), 2 out (drop it out of the trouble) and hit away. Again, the Pros are held to the higher standard,

**"Mulligans"** and **"Gimmes"** are not mentioned in the Rules of Golf but are among the most common occurrences in casual golf. A "Mulligan" is the allowance to hit another shot (without penalty) if you have hit one in water, out of bounds, etc. A "Gimme" is granting a fellow player the luxury of not having to hit a reasonably short putt, but "giving it to them" as if they would automatically make it and dispensing with the formality of taking time to putt it.

Unless you are playing for a lot of money or in a formal competition, these concessions can lead to greater enjoyment and faster play. Golf is hard enough to not allow ourselves a little slack sometimes. It should be emphasized that the GRITS Tour does not allow Mulligans or Gimmes, which is only fair, as players do take the competition seriously and enforcement ultimately rewards the better golfer. Serious golf does not allow for either of these.

Note: **"Par"** is the stated number of strokes it takes a golfer to play a given hole. **"Bogey"** is one shot over the stated Par. **Double Bogey** is two over, **Triple Bogey** is three over, etc. Per hole.

Note: The GRITS Tour limits players to Triple Bogey. In other words, once you reach Triple Bogey, take that score and move on. This is a very positive way to play, with many friendly groups limiting players to Double Bogeys or even Bogeys. It leads to faster rounds.

# HANDICAPPING

In a nutshell, one's handicap is the number of strokes over Par that one normally takes to complete a round. Most golf courses are Par 72. A golfer regularly shooting an 80 would be an 8 handicap. A golfer regularly shooting 90 would be an 18, and so on. There is more to it than that, but this definition will suffice for our purposes.

Scores can be recorded as **"Gross"** meaning the total actual score, or as **"Net"** meaning the score after the handicap has been deducted.

A SECOND TYPE of handicap has to do with which tees a player plays from. Professionals may play from **Black Tees** (7000+- yards). A good golfer may play from **Blue Tees** (6300+-), or **White Tees** (6000+-), while the GRITS (Seniors) play around 5500 yards. Women will most often use a separate designated set of **"Red"** Tees (5000+-). These do not seem to be great distances that separate the Tees, particularly spread out over 18 holes. But they matter. Pros hit their Drives 300+ yards. A good golfer may hit it 250 yards or more. Better than average golfers may hit it over 200 as well. Seniors can be lucky to hit it 200 yards. The variety of tees allows for compensation among the skill (and age) levels, allowing the game to be enjoyed by all. At the end of the day, these handicapping scenarios should make the game more enjoyable, as long as everyone is careful about who they bet against, how valid their Handicap is, and which Tees each are playing.

Note: Each course will designate on their scorecard the relative handicaps (difficulty) of each hole on their course. This helps players set expectations as they move through a round.

# PACE OF PLAY

For 2019 the USGA has adopted several new rules specifically geared to increasing the **Pace of Play**, or the average time it takes to finish a round. Individual players have a major impact of **Pace of Play** not only for their group, but for an entire course. Playing from the proper tees, limiting oneself to Double or Triple Bogey, taking one-in-one-out all have a positive effect across the entire course.

**Tips:**
- Don't leave the cart without a club in your hand, you are going to have to walk back to the cart to get one.

- Park the cart where you can move ahead, not have to go back to get it

- Hold the flag for your playing partners, rake the traps for them, bring their putter to the green.

- Don't take too many practice swings.

- Walk to your ball (with a club or two) while your playing partners hit their shots. But don't hurry, be deliberate, not slow.

- Tally the strokes on the next tee, not while next to the green.

- There are a multitude of little tips like these that can make the game more enjoyable for everyone.

- Be alert. Think of what you are doing NEXT. Get Ready to Play, Get Ready to Hit your next shot, don't stand around being a spectator shooting the breeze when you are supposed to be playing golf.

- And a big one – LEAVE YOUR CELL PHONE IN THE CAR.

# DEFINITIONS

*(Notations reflect Chapter references)*

1.1 **"Muni"** – Public courses, often managed by local governments, or municipalities. Accessible, inexpensive with their own flair and history. The United States Open is played on a "Muni" to remind us of the democratic foundation of the game.

**"Semi-Private"** clubs wish that their membership could support them without opening up to daily players, but they need the revenue. These courses are a step up the ladder and afford everyone a chance to play a little better kept course.

**"Private Courses"** Their grooming, staff attentiveness, status and exclusivity is commensurate with their fees. The top of the heap, the #1 option if one wants to make this kind of commitment.

1.2 **"Ready Golf"** allows for the spirit of Pace of Play among players. For example; if you are ready, hit, don't wait for the next guy. Walk to your ball, get ready. It is a lot of little things without some of the formalities while allowing for a better Pace to be enjoyed by all.

1.3 **"Local Rules"** Those factors that are specific to that course, or even to that days' conditions as far as wetness, maintenance or other temporary day-to-day adjustments to that course.

1.4 **"Cart-path-only"** A Local Rule that may be instituted on a daily basis, asking players to keep their carts on the paths so as to not damage wet fairways, which could take a long time to recover.

**"Divot"** Indentation left by prior ball in fairway or on green

**"Fairway"** groomed target area for most shots. As opposed to

**"Rough"** which is in play, but deeper grass or **"Green"** which is shortest cut, closest to the hole.

**"Dogleg"** – A hole that goes straight out one way, then bends another way. Like a dog's leg. Can go left or right.

**"Drop Area"** or **"Drop Zone"** Normally on Par 3s with water in play. Saves the frustration and humiliation of re-hitting more balls in the water. Take a one-stroke penalty and hit again.

**"False front"** The front of the green slopes steeply back toward the fairway so that a ball not hit solidly will roll back into the fairway rather than staying on the green.

1.5 **"Ground-under-repair"**; Temporary maintenance - you can move your ball to a nearby spot to not have to hit from the torn-up area.

1.6 **"Front Nine / Back Nine"** Eighteen-hole courses are generally divided into two equal segments, most often looping by the clubhouse as players "make the turn" and proceed to the "Back Nine" or "Second Nine"

**"Lag putt"** A long putt where you don't expect to make it, you just want to get it close enough to make the next one.

2.1 The player's ball "Lying" one or two, or three, etc. This refers back to "playing the ball as it lies". It's the number of strokes hit on a given hole to that point. "After his drive, he was "lying" one."

**"Pin High"** – the proper distance to the hole but left or right. Not a bad thing, indicates proper distance / good club selection.

2.3 **"Sandbagging"** A player overstating his handicap to gain an unfair advantage. Indicating needing more strokes than appropriate.

2.4 **"Scramble"** Most often indicates "Captains' Choice" or "Best Ball" competition. Each foursome hits their drives, picks the best one, all hit from that point, hit the next shot, picks the best one, all hit from that spot, etc. until the hole is completed.

**"Shanked"** For no apparent reason, shots start to go off at a 90-degree angle. A dreaded condition that can set in and repeat itself. Very difficult to diagnose and correct. A golfer's nightmare.

2.5 **"Comebacker"** Hit the initial putt too far, made the "comebacker".

2.6 **"Babied"** Hit it tentatively.

2.7 **"Skulled"** Hit the top half of the ball, leading to low ball flight, loss of distance. Similar to "looked up", or "bladed it".

2.8 **"Chumped it"** Hit behind the ball, more dirt than ball. Ball doesn't go desired distance. "Drop-kicked" is similar reference and result. Or "hitting it fat".

2.9 **"Flighting"** Sorting players in a competition into brackets of similar handicaps so that similar skilled players compete among each other.

# SAMPLE OF GOLF EXPRESSIONS;

*(Note that golfers almost always tend to encourage playing partners)*

**After tee shots;**

"That won't hurt ya" – (if you hit the next one better)

"It opens up over there" – (optimistic that it's not in the woods)

"That'll play" – (at least we'll find it)

(Silence) – not a good shot at all, other players turn and walk to carts

"did a Linda Ronstadt on you" - "blew by you" (Blue Bayou)

**Approaching the green;**

"Chip and a putt" – you should have hit the green from there.

"In the beach" – in a sand-trap. Potentially "buried"

On the "dancefloor" – on the green (maybe can't hear the music)

**After a putt;**

"Had the line" / "Good line" – (but short / long)

"Never up, never in" – (you left it short)

The high (or low) side – hackers often leave putts short. Pros don't. Missing on the high side is what the pros do.

"short-armed it" – (didn't hit it hard enough) also "Alligator Arms"

Above / below the hole – many greens slope from back to front to assist water runoff. The back (above) the hole means you are likely to have a downhill putt, which are harder to control than uphill. The ones going downhill are harder to stop and the dang things can actually roll all the way off the green – (maybe down the false front).

"South-American putt" – needed one more revolution

Readers are encouraged to send their favorites to:
dorseywhitlock@icloud.com

# CHAPTER 1

## Opening Day

**"Give me golf clubs, fresh air and a beautiful partner, and you can keep my golf clubs and the fresh air."**                                        Jack Benny

April 23 – 8:05 AM
London Bridges
Par 72
5650 yards from Senior Tees
Slope 67.6 / Rating 126
Approximately 60 degrees at Tee time, winds gusting to 10-15 mph

Dorsey made his way onto the edge of the Practice Range. He had come around the Clubhouse through the parking lot, having changed his shoes leaning on the open trunk of his car. He was early and had parked close to the cart return area, which would allow for a quick getaway once the time came. The other early birds had arrived in a wide assortment of pickups and sedans, noticeable for the absence of Lexus and Benz. He was almost an hour early and appeared to be midway in the group that would ultimately show up. Several of the other guys catcalled to each other across the lot, some slang, some profanity, usually followed by too-loud laughter trying to show it was funnier than it really was.

He carried his bag over his shoulder, clubs clanking as he walked. Dorsey's clubs clanked because he didn't use headcovers, thought they were silly. He had a bunch of them acquired from various venues, famous and not, but found that they were a nuisance to keep up with and easy to lose. After all, the clubs were made of titanium. What sense did it make to cover them up with little booties?

His bag wasn't much to look at either. Years before he had tried to buy a bag that was classic, with little adornment. From ten feet the bag could be leather. Or it could be pleather? He didn't care because it did the job. The bottom zipper was broken, and the linings of the pockets were ripped but none of that was a big deal to Dorsey. The reason he kept the bag was that he could slip a soft-sided cooler with four Mountain Lite beers and ice into the side pocket without it being noticeable. He always tried to place the bag on his cart himself so that the cart guy wouldn't notice how heavy it was with the beer and ice. Itt might be wet from draining since the ice had been put in the cooler at home, maybe an hour earlier.

Dorsey moved hesitantly onto the range. He really didn't know anyone here. Oh, a few he had met, a few he knew a little better, and a very few he knew well. Of the one-hundred twenty golfers spread out across the range, he really didn't know many of them. He located the makeshift sign-in table at one end, occupied by an earnest guy with a clipboard. Must be Manny Proudfoot, the Tour Director. There were several other guys queuing up in front of Proudfoot, taking turns having their names checked off his list, receiving sheets of paper, shuffling away. Dorsey observed Manny as he waited, taking him in as the line moved. Very average overall. Probably 5'11", 175, dark hair that had once been darker. Fit, simply dressed, rimless tinted glasses. Proudfoot made eye contact and smiled as he shook Dorsey's hand in welcome. "So, you're Dorsey Whitlock. I've been hearing your name around. Welcome to the Tour. Glad you could join us." Despite the great name, Dorsey couldn't detect any Native American features. More like your average Mid-Atlantic German or Scotch-Irish background.

Proudfoot checked Dorsey's' name off and handed him the printed rules sheet for the Tour. At the top of the sheet "11-A" had been scribbled with a Sharpie. "Your name will be on a cart, and the carts are lined up by hole order. Find your cart and introduce yourself to your playing partners. We have some time before we tee off, range balls are free, so loosen up, stroke a few putts and have a great day. Pay George over there your $30 entry fee for the day, and you'll be off and running."

Dorsey waited behind a few others in front of "George" and studied "George." Once Dorsey focused, he could barely take his eyes off of "George." George George was a cross between Mister Magoo, Elmer Fudd or Popeye. Dorsey couldn't decide which one he favored the most. Bald as a cue ball, with his left eye slanted shut Dorsey expected any moment for him to bump into something, start looking for a "pesky wabbit" or pull out a can of spinach. He had an air of a serious character but the look of a cartoon figure. Dorsey handed him the $30 and went looking for 11-A.

The range area was peopled with one-hundred twenty Senior Peacocks. It was a full field of fashion faux-pas. Golf clothes, particularly in warmer weather, brought out the best and worst fashion trends among Senior men. Most men over 55 had lost the shape of their best years but retained the fashion sense of their worst years. Sans-a-belt slacks, too long shorts, knee length socks, plaids, tartans, and pastel combinations screamed for attention. Keeping it simple was not necessarily part of the mix. Those that had been railroad men, linemen, foremen or supervisors now sported the pent-up look that they had once shunned. Far from the mottled blues, grays and black colors of their pasts, they now expressed themselves with Crayola colors and Stay-Dry fabrics. It was hard on the eyes to take it all in at once. Dorsey avoided vertigo by keeping his head down, focusing hard on the lineup of carts and the numbering system that would lead him to his group for today's event.

It was the opening round of the 16th season of the "Greater Roanoke Invitational Tournament for Seniors" (GRITS for short), run by Proudfoot and his wingman Randy Ridgeline. Dorsey had not laid eyes on Ridgeline yet. To this point he had been the silent partner to Proudfoot, referenced but unvoiced. Plenty of time for that. "George" who had collected the money was a complete unknown. Undoubtedly part of the hierarchy, so far unfamiliar to Dorsey.

The GRITS would be played on an irregular schedule at nine different venues spread around the Blue Ridge Valley over the next seven months, mid -April to late October. Dorsey had signed up since he had recently returned to Roanoke after a fifty-six-year hiatus. He thought it would be a good way to meet people and see some pretty places. The courses were mostly "semi-private" as opposed to Private courses or "Munis". They were all pretty, the natural beauty of the Valley making them spectacular without major improvement needed. This was the first event of the Tour, April 23, at a "semi-private", London Bridges, between Bedford and Lynchburg.

Dorsey had played the best of the best and some of the worst. To him, it was all pretty much still golf. He had never wanted to fork over the bucks to join the big-time clubs and had never seen the justification either. To Dorsey, other than the bucks, the primary difference was that at the Munis' or the Semi-Privates, players put their shoes on leaning on the trunks of their cars. At Private Clubs, players put their shoes on sitting in front of their lockers. Dorsey had never had a locker.

GRITS had made arrangements for participants in the next outing to be able to play a practice round at the host club a week before the event. Dorsey and his buddy Junior Loaf had come over the previous Tuesday to check it out. They had to tell a white lie to get Junior the reduced GRITS rate, since he wasn't actually on the Tour. Tuesday had been the only day available, and the weather had been awful. It never got above 40 degrees and for a lot of the round, winds blew at 30+ miles per hour.

The weather had been an unpleasant reality of Dorsey's' return to The Blue Ridge. After thirty-three years in South Florida, the Valley weather had been more complicated than he remembered. Through March and April, it could be 80 degrees one day and snow two days later. Layering clothes became an art form. His trunk had extra jackets, windbreakers and sweaters. Regrettably, no shorts had been needed to this point. Today was a little bit of a toss-up, hovering around 60 degrees. The wind was the big variable. Without it, layers could come off. With it, there was almost no defense.

The truth of it was that he hadn't planned to be here for the winter. He had spots lined up where he could go back and spend at least January and March in Delray Beach. Out of the blue Dorsey had met Luisa Parker, an amazing woman. He didn't want to screw things up with her, so Florida was scratched from the itinerary and Dorsey had toughed out the winter. It was brutal, but once the decision was made, he promised himself that he wouldn't bitch. And he hadn't. The only tough spots had been watching the Honda Classic on TV and the occasional time he had inadvertently watched some other sort of broadcast from the warmth of South Florida.

As for the practice round, Dorsey hadn't learned a lot about club selection, but he had seen some of the tricks of the course, starting at Number 1, listed at 402 yards, but playing more like 350 since the tee shot was straight downhill aiming right at a lake. He did pick up some of this type of intel from playing the practice round, so it wasn't a complete loss of a day.

Junior Loaf was a buddy from way back. Over the years they had been able to connect whenever Dorsey came through Roanoke to visit his parents. As guys can do, they always simply picked up where they left off. They had been through some scrapes together, and the bond was strong. Dorsey had been willing to call the practice round off at multiple points, but Junior had been steadfast that they push on, that they didn't have anywhere better to be. When the winds picked up as they made the turn, Junior finally acceded to playing best ball, and they finished the last six holes that way. At least they got to see the course.

Dorsey wound his way through the lined-up carts until he found the one with his name on it, marked "11-A". There was another cart marked "11-A" with two more names on it. This was his foursome. Since none of the other guys were there, he grabbed his 9-iron, 6-iron, 4-iron, Rescue club and his Driver and looked for an empty spot on the range. Once he had hit 15-20 balls, he thought that was enough and looped back to the cart. Standing near his cart were the two riding in the other cart, who introduced themselves as Maynard Ferry and Dooley Hopper.

The fourth of the foursome, Marvin Pharratt, showed up a few minutes later. He was huffing and puffing that he had forgotten his shoes, had to go back, didn't have time to warm up, hadn't even had time to putt. Dorsey studied Pharratt closely as he fussed over his clubs, his glove, his tees and his ball markers. He was a little guy, grey in the temples and the face. He looked to be maybe 5'7" and 140 pounds. Dorsey himself wasn't a big guy, but Pharratt was pretty small, tucked into his golf hat and windbreaker. He had an uneven caterpillar of a mustache, and shifty grey eyes.

Dorsey wrote the three first names down, a habit he had picked up from many a round at many a Muni. Better to have a fighting chance to remember their names than to fumble and be distracted all day. Dorsey had often returned from afternoons of golf to be asked by a girlfriend or spouse what the foursome had talked about. Women apparently talk about stuff. Men do not. Men talk about the sun, the wind, what club he hit, how good or bad he hit it and how he wished he had hit it. But men don't actually talk about anything real like wives, kids, jobs, politics or religion. It's mostly "Good shot", "nice putt" or complete silence as a matter of diplomacy. For variation it could be "that'll play", "it opens up over there", or "that won't hurt you". That was about all that passed between them for four hours or more. Sure, they would exchange "Where you from?" "You Retired?" "Where did you work" ... But that was about it. This round would be no different.

Dorsey had had an experience during his first divorce when he had to make himself scarce for a while and retreated to his condo at PGA Village to hide out until things cooled off. The retreat had worked and allowed him some time to decompress. He had played a round with a really nice, distinguished older guy and they had followed the man regime, not really talking about anything until maybe the 10th or 11th hole, when the gentleman had opened up about his family. Dorsey had shared what was going on with him, his laying low, abandonment of a prior life, and that he had made the move that he felt he had to make. The small talk generally dissipated after that until the 17th tee, (Two hours later!) when the guy broke his silence to admit that "Damn! I wish I had had the guts to do that fifteen years ago! I'm miserable and it's too late." Dorsey had always felt bad for the guy.

Since he had been early, Dorsey had attempted to get a Bloody Mary but the girl working at the inside snack bar had been underage and couldn't make him a drink. The guy who ran the place was too tied up glad handing and taking care of last-minute details, so Dorsey finally gave up. It would have been nice to have the Bloody to take the edge off. "Aiming Fluid" had been a big part of the South Florida golf experience. There were times after a round that he definitely shouldn't have driven home. Valley golf was different, and he had had to learn to play sober, which somehow should have been factored into his handicap. So, no Bloody to start this round.

Having grown tired of waiting for Pharratt and almost thinking that he wouldn't make it, Dorsey had strapped his bag to the driver side and set his water on that side, tossed in his sunglasses and sat. Dorsey didn't like to drive the cart. Number One, the guy driving the cart, since he had the steering wheel with the card clipped to it, had to be the scorekeeper. Number Two, Dorsey liked to walk some to keep loose and he also liked to play "ready golf". He would often grab several likely club choices and strike out towards his ball while his partner or the guys in the other cart were lining up to hit theirs. That way, when his time came, he was most often ready to hit and move on. Pace of play was critical to Dorsey. Driving wasn't a big deal. Someone had to do it.

Proudfoot stood on the back steps of the Clubhouse and greeted the Opening of the Tour. He welcomed new members, introduced the London Bridges Pro, mentioned "Jeanette" would be around the corner at the tent with snacks to sell and Raffle Tickets. Dorsey perked up at this. He loved Raffle tickets and he wanted to win something. A new Golf Bag would be his first choice. "George" would be grilling hot dogs and hamburgers at a grill set up behind the Clubhouse.

The Pro talked about the Local Rules, how #10, #14 and #16 were cart-path-only since the grass had been slow coming in. It was the players option to hit out of "ground-under-repair" areas (there were a lot of them), There were "drop areas" at each of the Par 3s over water. No need to re-hit, simply move up to the drop area and hit your third shot from there (1 in, 2 out, hitting 3). This was good for the Pace of Play and a relief to Dorsey who had put one in the water on #2 during his practice round, and two in the water on #15. Wind or not, this was unsettling. Hole #2 wasn't as worrisome, slightly uphill over water, but with a backdrop. He could just hit more club if he was worried about it. But #15 was another matter. It was an island green with very little green in the front, and not much more in the back. Both holes would play around 140 to 145 yards, which should be a 6-iron. Three 6-irons last Tuesday had found the water. He would have liked to blank that out, but it was there. At least the drop zones might prevent a total collapse.

At Proudfoot's go-ahead, the carts began snaking off to their assigned holes. Dorsey's group cut the back way toward the second nine. Winding down the cart path past the 10th green around the back and to number #11. The two carts pulled onto the grass next to the tee box, making room for other carts to pass on the way to their holes. The group for 11-B pulled in a little way behind, expecting to wait their turn while 11-A hit and moved down the fairway, and played their second shots before 11-B could hit.

Once Dorsey and the others stretched, picked clubs and meandered to the tee box, somehow collectively they all nodded at Dooley Hopper to go ahead, lead it out. Hopper was a sight to behold. Maybe 5'11", Grisly Adams beard that had probably once been brown, but now matched the thatch of grey on top of his head. He had to be 325 pounds, maybe 350. In true man tradition, he was wearing shorts that probably were no more than 42 at the waist, even though he could have used 52's. To make this work, the shorts had to be slung way below what might have once been his waist line. The shorts were then left to droop past his knees. Even the 4X Blue Bells logo shirt couldn't cover all the real estate that was his belly. A mildly hairy, flat and extended belly button completed the look.

After a waggle or two, Hopper wound up and cranked a drive that was pushed to the right. It was hit hard, and not fading, but definitely pushed. As the other three (and the four from 11-B) stood and stared, the ball stayed straight and true toward the fence and the road. Since it was hit pretty good it was a little hard to follow in the morning sun, but the delayed sound of a noticeable "crack" was pretty clear. Quickly they looked at each other asking, "Did it hit the fence? Did you see where it went?" Speculation reigned until they noticed the silver Toyota slowing to a stop on the apron of the road, now abreast of the tee box. Hopper slunk toward the fence with the offending Driver still in his hand. The 11-A group turned to the 11-B group and waved them onto the tee box so that they could play ahead while Hopper and 11-A sorted out the Toyota. The 16th season of the Greater Roanoke Invitational Tour for Seniors (GRITS) was underway with one broken windshield under its belt.

# CHAPTER 2

## London Bridges First Tee

**"Ninety percent of putts that are short don't go in."** Yogi Berra

April 23, 9:00 AM

After the 11-B group moved through, 11-A had a few minutes fun with Hopper, then hit. Since Dorsey was the new guy to the tour, the group elected him to hit first on the restart. The broken windshield had diverted everyone sufficiently that he really didn't feel the jitters that he might have expected for his first swing of the formal season. He kept his head down, took an easy cut, and got a nice result. His favorite flight path, a high fade, climbing the hill, not great, but good. He felt relaxed as he waited on the others but didn't pay much attention to what they did. He had already told himself that what they did didn't matter. His cart partner Pharratt hit it short and to the right, not great but in play.

Hopper hit last and though he kept it in bounds, he was lying 3 with a broken windshield in the back of his mind. His consolation was that the woman driving the Toyota was a golfer, didn't give him too hard of a time, and it turned out that they shared the same insurance company (Farmers). Hopper circled across the course looking for his original ball, just in case it had gotten a favorable kick off the windshield, but no such luck. He was still lying 3.

Much had been made throughout the runup to the season that handicaps were important. The GRITS Tour played by the "Rules of Golf";

- "Play the ball as it lies". No turning it over, no moving it.
- No Mulligans. If you hit a bad shot, you must play it.

- "Putt them all out". No friendly "gimmes". Putt it until it goes in.

There was a tiny concession; Triple Bogey was the maximum on any hole. This was in the spirit of "Pace of Play". Keep the game moving.

Since Dorsey had come in from out of town, Proudfoot told him he had assigned him a 22 handicap. Proudfoot also indicated that the lowest score Dorsey could record was a 68, just in case he had been sandbagging and 22 were too many strokes. Dorsey had played the requisite ten rounds at the home course, Blue Bells, and was tracking closer to an 18 handicap. By that time Proudfoot had assigned him the 22, and there wasn't a lot of protesting to be done. The higher handicap gave him some wiggle room, but the lower handicap would have allowed him to net out lower if he shot a good score. It didn't much matter. Winners got trophies and maybe a gift certificate from the pro shop. After the first four events, his handicap would be reset based on whatever he scored in them. Better to keep quiet, play on and see how things developed. In his mind, 90 was the score he was shooting for (90 – 22 = 68). That was the lowest he could get for a while anyway. If he shot a 90, he would be maximizing his opportunity. Play on.

Proudfoot had assigned players handicaps from 4 to 37. There were implications; Someone with a 4-handicap shooting a 72 (par) would record a 68. Someone shooting a 104 with a 37 handicap would record a net 67 and win the tournament. Good golfers hated this arrangement. Proudfoot had assigned himself 26 strokes. After all, it was his tournament.

To a good golfer, talk of this level of handicapping was just plain irritating. Dorsey had friends who had quit the game since they couldn't break par. To Dorsey's mind they had it wrong. He had stopped practicing years ago, preferring to enjoy the game and the camaraderie rather than sweat it. He knew he wouldn't get much better, particularly after losing 20-30 yards on his shots when he turned age 65. As a Senior, he was enjoying the idea that he could play at all, favoring the fresh air and personal competition as opposed to being stuck inside.

Since Dorsey was driving the cart, he would be keeping the second card, with the other cart keeping the "Official" score that would be attested to and turned in. As the round went on, or at the end, the two carts would compare cards. Each player would sign a final version and turn that in to Proudfoot and Ridgeline.

As his group moved off the 11th green, each player announced his score. Dorsey said "6", Ferry said "6", Hopper said "8", since the highest score allowed was a triple bogey. Dorsey did an inward double take when Pharratt said "5". He hadn't paid that much attention, but knew the drive had been short right, then the second shot had been to the top of the hill, the third shot had stopped short of the green, and the chip had been to the right of the cup…. Did he make that putt? Dorsey couldn't actually remember, he hadn't been watching that closely, but he didn't think so. Dorsey was pretty sure it was a "6". But he had only known these guys for a half hour, was the new guy on the Tour, and he couldn't be sure… Bottom line, it was up to Pharratt to record his own score, not up to Dorsey to challenge him. Play on.

The next few holes unfolded with a random set of Bogeys and Double-Bogeys, with a few Pars thrown in. Bogeys were good in this group, that's what was to be expected. Pars were to be celebrated and a Birdie was the Holy Grail. Double and Triple Bogeys were always looming out there and came with the territory.

Dorsey was playing about as well as could be expected. Ferry was struggling with his back but putting up a good fight. Hopper appeared to be a better golfer than he was showing, so maybe the windshield incident had stayed in his brain. Pharratt couldn't seem to hit it out of his shadow, but had demonstrated an uncanny ability to scramble, something Seniors had to show if they were going to score at all. It was a good start.

The 15th was listed on the card as a 138-yard Par 3. In his Practice round, Dorsey had put 2 in the water with his 6-Iron. That was a lot of club for 138 yards, but the practice round had been windy, and it had knocked both shots down short of the green area. There wasn't much green area. It was essentially an Island green with water on three sides and a little peninsula at the left rear. Short shots would be wet. Long ones did have a bunker long right to catch shots, but long left behind the pin was only water. It was a generous green but ran side to side. Distance was key. He had to hit first since he hadn't lost the Honor. He would have liked to see the others hit, but what the hell.

Dorsey hit the 6-iron easy, keeping his head down and focusing on a clean hit, getting it airborne. He had learned to hit a high ball while he was in Florida. He couldn't generate enough club speed to spin the ball, so hitting it high was his only was of stopping it once it hit. This shot stayed in the air a long time but landed with a satisfying thud 30 feet to the right of the pin, a little long, but dry.

Ferry was next and couldn't control his low burner. It hit on the front of the green and kept going, into the water behind the green. Once he made his drop and missed his putt, he would end up with a 5. Hopper hit a nice shot inside of Dorsey and Pharratt made it to the far-right side. Both of them 3-putt for 4s. Dorsey nursed his downhill slider to just below the cup and made the 4-foot comebacker. Another Par. Amazing stuff. He was playing well.

Then the wheels started to come off.

The 16th is a 355- yard dogleg left. For whatever reason, Dorsey convinced himself that the road on the left was a problem and babied his drive. He chumped his second shot and had 89 yards to the green. Still no problem, #16 was the #2 handicap on the course. But then he didn't commit to his wedge, left it in the trap and by the time he was done had his first Triple Bogey of the day.

Dorsey hit a good drive on #17 but his (well hit) approach trundled down to the left in the fringe above a trap. A skulled pitch sent him across the green and led to a Double Bogey. Another good drive on #18, but a weak 2nd shot out of the fringe. Ran the pitch past the hole and short-armed the comebacker. Another Double. At least 2 or 3 wasted shots in 3 holes.

Dorsey managed a half-decent Drive on #1 and a nice long second shot to the right fringe. A good bogey on the #5 handicap hole. Really nice 6-iron tee shot on the Par 3 2nd, with a solid approach on a long curling downhill putt. (Ferry putted from the same angle and ran it off the green). Dorsey made his putt for a nice Par. Stupid approach chip from the back fringe on #3 led to another braindead Double. Really good par on the uphill 481-yard Par 5 4th.

Dorsey knew that he always lost focus around the holes that made up his 12th, 13th and 14th holes. It didn't always help to know that, he did it anyway. The 6th only plays 287 yards but has a narrow landing area that funnels everything down to the creek running on the left. He hit Driver anyway. Mental mistake, he didn't see it bounce into the water. Lying 3. Chumped the approach into the greenside trap and was rewarded with another Triple Bogey. The shots were there, the mind wasn't.

Parred the Par 3 7th over the water (another 6-Iron) Then went Double Bogey, Triple Bogey, Triple Bogey.

Really lost consciousness, focus, and finished very poorly, cursing himself the whole way. It all added up to a 97, 7 strokes more than his target. His mental game had cost him the Triple on #16, the one on #6 and definitely the one on #10. He had kind of quit the round too soon.

With handicap, Dorsey had finished with a 75, tied for 72nd. Four strokes better would have put him at 25th, almost 50 spots up the leader board. The 90 that he knew he could shoot would have put him in 10th place and based on the flighting system, might have won him some sort of recognition. Golf is a game of ifs. He wasn't totally devastated, knew that he could be competitive, hadn't really had the jitters as much as made mental mistakes. He could play better. No golfer has ever finished a round without knowing he could have played better.

# CHAPTER **3**

## London Bridges Scoring Tent

**"Golf is a game in which you yell fore, shoot six and write down five."**
Paul Harvey

Tuesday April 23, 2 PM

Even though he was disheartened by his round, Dorsey stayed afterward and wandered into the Pavilion where scores would be tallied, and awards presented. He wanted to see how the scores shook out overall. The scores were high. With all the strokes given, the outcomes weren't so bad, but some of the gross scores were over 100, and yet these could still win something.

As Dorsey moved under the metal covering, he ran into Dana Blades, a guy he had known from days past, but hadn't seen in years. Dana was a much better golfer than Dorsey. Dorsey had always been intimidated by Dana. He was only maybe 6'1" and 180 pounds, but he was really fit. He was nice as hell but in his mind, Dorsey still deferred to Dana. He was just a cool guy. Dana sometimes rode a Harley, still played League hockey and drank hard. He could knock off a twelve-pack and not show it or do shots without missing a beat. Over the years, Dorsey had played golf with Dana multiple times. They had some buddies in common, all of them better golfers than Dorsey. They thought Dorsey was funny and he drank a lot, so they asked him to play in their group when they needed someone to fill in. On every occasion Dorsey had played with Dana, Dana had always been the first one to the course, usually chipping or putting as everyone else slid into the parking lot, putting their shoes on as they came in moments before their tee times, often with little or no time to warm up. They all joked that the more Dana practiced, the luckier he got. Golf was like that. Dana was a good golfer. He could hit it long and straight, and he had a good short game.

Dorsey nodded to Dana and grunted, as he always seemed to get tongue-tied around Dana. It was Dorsey's fault. Dana couldn't be nicer, it was just that Dorsey had him on a pedestal. Dana offered him a beer from a six-pack next to him and Dorsey settled into an adjacent chair to take in the results. Dorsey immediately checked the big board and looked for the best net scores.

Not many guys had hung around after the round, which surprised Dorsey. After all, he played for the camaraderie, keeping the game itself in perspective. Proudfoot, Ridgeline, George and a couple of other guys that appeared to be semi-official were tallying the scores on a big cardboard spreadsheet kind of thing, divided into the three Flights. It was a little confusing at first, but as his eyes adjusted to all the numbers, he could begin to see the pattern.

The best golfers of the day were Chandler Hoffman with a gross score of 71, net 68 Dana with his gross score of 73, net 69 and Briscoe Sisson with a gross of 79, net 73. These guys handicaps were 3, 4, and 6 respectively. As Dorsey continued to absorb what all the scores actually meant, it was easy to see why the better golfers hated Proudfoot's handicapping system.

The trophy winners had more fluid scores let's say. Dallas Grandin shot a 104 but had 37 strokes (!) to net out at a 67. Manny Proudfoot shot a 90 but had 26 strokes (!) to net out to a 64 for second place. And Marvin Pharratt, Dorsey's cart-mate had shot a 93, but had 30 strokes (!) for a net 63!

Dorsey looked on in amazement. Had Pharratt made that putt on the first hole for a par, as he had claimed? It was the stroke that decided his win. Dorsey hadn't watched him that closely the rest of the way, were their other places he might have shaved one or two? With 30 strokes, Dorsey hoped that he had counted them all. Would a retired 77-year old postal worker cheat to win a little plastic silver cup and a $25 gift certificate to the Pro Shop? Dorsey wondered and walked away muttering. Strokes aside, Dorsey wondered just how realistic it was to think he could win under these odds, deciding to keep his head down and play on.

"Jeanette" had been introduced before the round from the steps by Proudfoot. Dorsey hadn't quite figured out who she was, but when the teams made the turn, she was at the pavilion selling snacks and Raffle Tickets. She was an attractive woman, mid-fifties, and kept herself up. She had most likely been a knockout in her younger days. The Raffle Tickets had been a 50-50 for Alzheimer's.

Since Maynard Ferry had been in pain, he had mentioned early in the round that he had already had a couple of pills and several shots of booze before they teed off to try and get the situation under control. Dorsey had given him a couple of Advil, which was all he had but by the time they made the turn Ferry sprinted into the clubhouse telling Dorsey he would buy a six-pack and Dorsey could have a couple. To offset his gesture, Dorsey bought 20 Raffle tickets and had given Ferry 10.

In the pavilion after the round, Ferry introduced Dorsey to his wife Carlotta. Carlotta had a look similar to a certain set of the Valley wives. A little thicker than her younger version, hair piled a little higher than her age, makeup a little thicker than the bright sunlight would do justice to. She had layers of eye shadow and when she was introduced to Dorsey, gave a practiced look of nonchalance as a greeting. Her face was orange and Dorsey had trouble making eye contact. Dorsey thought that even though he hadn't been back in the Valley that long, he knew the type. He slotted her into one of the two types that a lot of these women seemed to fall into. One of the types were kind, genuine and interested in your well-being. The other type ... not so much.

Maynard offered that Carlotta had been concerned about him and had made the half-hour drive to make sure he got home. Apparently, he had started with the pain pills and alcohol shots before leaving the house and had ridden with Dooley Hopper to the course. Carlotta had just come to collect him and make sure the pills and alcohol didn't springboard Maynard into a scenario where he had too much fun before he made it home.

Carlotta looked accusingly at Dorsey "Maynard says you gave him all them Raffle Tickets. It ain't like him to buy Raffle Tickets." While saying this she was looking sideways at Jeanette.

Dorsey stammered back "Well, he did me a little favor, so I was just trying to do him one."

"Well, it ain't his normal thing to do favors for others or buy Raffle Tickets. Buy a drink maybe, but not Raffle Tickets." Somehow Dorsey wasn't following where she was leading and was pretty sure that either way, he and Carlotta might not turn out to be best buds. Oh well.

There were a handful of other wives, girlfriends and significant others at the pavilion. Since London Bridges was a little bit of a trek from Roanoke, the afterparty was sparsely attended, with a lot of the players cutting out to make the drive home before encountering what passed for "rush-hour" in the Valley. Traffic here was a joke compared to what commuters dealt with in D.C., Atlanta or even Charlotte. But everything is relative, so four cars waiting for a light in Roanoke still provoked modified road rage. To Dorsey, everything in the Valley was fifteen minutes, even the longest errand. These folks didn't always remember how good they had it.

Dorsey was introduced to Beth Martin and Halle Hopper, Dooley's wife. Halle and Beth seemed to fit more into the nice, genuine group. He was glad to meet them and told them so. They all waved at the husbands pointed out at the other side of the room. By the time he was halfway through introductions Dorsey had already lost track of who was who and hoped for name tags the next time. He answered the usual small talk about yes, he had just moved back from Florida, yes, he knew everyone usually went the other way and yes, he was really, honestly enjoying being back in the Valley. He took their interest as genuine but had been back long enough to know that sometimes it came with a velvet glove hiding the dagger. On the surface they seemed like nice folks.

Off to one side, murmuring to themselves were Fawn Ridgeline and Jamie George, (it turned out that George's name was actually George George). The George family was quite an extended clan across the Valley with a wide variety of branches of cousins. George George was the guy cooking the hot dogs and burgers. After staring at Dorsey for a minute, Carlotta Ferry joined these two. She made a statement by turning her back to Dorsey, chomping on her gum and sipping from what looked like a wine cooler.

"Jeanette" was Jeanette French. Dorsey later pieced together that Jeanette's husband Tom had played on the GRITS but had died at an early age from Alzheimer's. Jeanette's Mission had become raising money for the Alzheimer's' Foundation. Not just at the golf tournaments, but at just about any gathering where she could post herself or stake out a spot to try and do what she could to raise a buck to pass along to the Alzheimer's Foundation. The whole idea made Dorsey sad, but just as bad was that Jeanette was pretty much the only woman volunteer on the entire property that day. There were a few clerical types working off to the side in the Clubhouse, and at least one underage cutie in the snack bar. Dorsey blamed her for his having to play the front side cold sober. He had welcomed the jumpstart of the Mountain Lites from Ferry.

Dorsey was also amazed that there were no women as participants. If this were Florida, as much as 20% of the field would be women. That was a common occurrence there. In the Valley men were men and didn't mingle with other women outside of their own. To Dorsey this was a throwback to his days in grade school. Just because men and women mingled or played golf together didn't mean they were going to score or run off with each other. This was a disappointing aspect of the Valley social life that Dorsey had already noticed and wasn't impressed with. At most gatherings, even the nice ones among the more civilized groups, the men and women more or less adjourned to their neutral corners until it was time to go home. Dorsey knew they were missing something but also knew that the Valley women were very protective of their menfolk.

Before the trophies and prizes were given out, Jeanette was introduced to announce the Raffle winner. Since the crowd had thinned considerably, and Dorsey had bought a relatively large share of tickets, he knew his odds were pretty good. After a few numbers were called, with no winners present to accept, one of his numbers came up. He walked up to Jeanette, shook her hand, gave her a chaste hug and handed the money back to her. It was $57. Which meant that the entire pot had been $114. Out of 120 golfers, they had managed to buy $114 in tickets. Dorsey was disappointed for Jeanette, and glad he had given his $57 back. He was disappointed in his fellow man's lack of Philanthropy. There were still some other social lessons that he had yet to get used to in the Valley and they weren't all flattering to the home folk.

After Dorsey handed the money back to Jeanette, he pivoted to leave and ran smack into Pharratt standing half a step behind him, so close they almost butted faces. Pharratt leaned past Dorsey waving a pack of Raffle Tickets in his hand. He spoke through Dorsey to Jeanette "Hey Jeanette, with all of these tickets, I was hoping I would win and get a hug."

Jeanette's face screwed up into a fake smile and her words came out "Aw Marvin, that's just so sweet. Maybe next time".

Pharratt was still standing in Dorsey's way and chimed back. "You bet Jeanette, I'll take you up on that."

Dorsey wasn't sure that he understood these people. He hadn't seen a display like that since passing out Valentines in fifth grade. This on top of Carlotta's cold shoulder had him shaking his head. He maneuvered himself around Pharratt and walked purposely to his car. He wasn't there to see Pharratt awarded his Silver Cup. He did see the picture of him holding it in the GRITS online newsletter the day after the tournament. The whole day had been a little unsettling.

# CHAPTER 4

## Draper Mountain

**"Learning to play golf is a lot like learning to play the violin. It's not only difficult to do, it's very painful to everyone around you."**

Hal Linden

May 15 – 8:10 AM
Par 72
Yardage from the Senior Tees 5550
Slope 67.2 / Rating 117
Weather at Tee Time Around 65, winds gusting to 10-15, light intermittent drizzle

Dorsey drove the 40 minutes to Draper Mountain by himself. He had plans to meet Junior Loaf in Floyd after the round, then take the long way home. Luisa was looking after their beautiful rescue dog Anya, so he had the time. After London Bridges, Dorsey hadn't been all that confident in his game and had not had a chance at a practice round, so had never seen the course. That, plus the weather made him anxious, so expectations were not high.

One odd thing had happened the prior week that really got Dorsey thinking. Out of the blue, Marvin Pharrratt had called him and asked if he wanted to play a practice round at Draper Mountain. Dorsey explained that he couldn't make it, but really appreciated the gesture. He hung up confused and couldn't shake the call. Was Pharratt a nice guy and not a cheat? Dorsey chewed on the call for a long time.

Dorsey arrived in plenty of time to get loose and figure out the landscape. It was a beautiful country spot, even if it was a little damp and chilly. From the practice area all you could see were rolling hills and trees, no houses. It was a magnificent view. He found the cart for 6-B and noticed that he had been paired with Randy Ridgeline, who already had his bag on the cart and would be doing the driving. He thought that this was cool, riding with a rules official and scorekeeper. He would be able to walk when he felt like it.

Dorsey took a look at Ridgeline when Ridgeline wasn't looking. He was a tall guy, maybe 6'2", and he was ramrod straight. He was all bones and right angles and his eyes moved under his brow slowly from side to side. Ridgeline withheld offering a full smile and his handshake was a crusher. When he looked at you from under his golf hat, behind his reflective glasses, his gaze lingered just a little longer than the average introduction required. He was a 9-handicap. Pretty decent golfer.

Dorsey strapped his bag onto the passenger side and checked the names on the other cart. Dallas Grandin and Briscoe Sisson. Hmm didn't know them either. That was good. Anonymous meant not having to do too much small talk. Grandin was a squat, square 22-handicapper. Sisson was an open, smiling, sincere 6-handicapper. Both seemed nice enough.

Dorsey tried to stay quiet, stay within himself. He took his usual 9-iron, 6-iron, 4-iron, Rescue and Driver and found a spot on the range. After 15-20 balls, he came back, put those clubs in, grabbed his putter and rolled a few. By the time he made it back to the cart, they were all there, mounted up, ready to go. Proudfoot muttered some stuff, Jeanette curtsied, and they were off.

Golfers from other places scoffed at the distances on these courses until they got a look up close and personal. There was tons of mounds and swales on the fairways, not to mention the greens. Tee boxes were dramatically elevated, and greens were often straight up, on the crests of hills. Dorsey had checked out the website and noted some of the descriptions "… open and challenging…A player is able to hit every club in their bag…. Greens undulating…water on 7 holes." It wasn't all about distance. A 340-yard par 4 straight up hill played like 390. A 450-yard par 5 that started off uphill and required a long downhill carry over water was a 3-shot hole. These courses weren't that easy. You could get into trouble at any moment.

Dorsey had seen a quote from Gil Hanse in Golf Digest that he agreed with and felt summed up the future for golf. Since Tiger Woods had arrived on the scene, golf had gone crazy for hitting the ball a mile. Dorsey had read that over seventy players on the PGA Tour averaged over 300 yards on their drives. This was unrealistic for most golfers and had led to hitting from the wrong tees, slow play and a misdirection of what good golf looked like. Gil Hanse is possibly the hottest golf course designer on the scene today. His team designed the course in Rio that was used for the Olympics, as well as other prominent courses. The quote that rang true with Dorsey was:

*"Shorter actually is the answer, not longer. I don't think the everyday male golfer appreciates how brutal a 5,500-yard golf course is for women, children and even some men. What we propose-and what you'll see more of in our future designs-is a forward set of tees that play less than 5,000 yards. The 5,500 set will remain for more skilled women and also seniors, who can play that yardage without having to say they play the forward tees. And then you'll have the more traditional white/blue/black sets for the avid club players. By the way, none of these tees will have gender-or-age-related names. This approach isn't a lark. It's really a necessity to keep this game alive."*

Early golf courses measured 4600 to 5300 yards, just like the distances that the GRITS was playing. Players still had to make shots to score. Dorsey found it ironic that the game had come full circle this way, away from pure "Grip it and Rip It" and back toward the finesse of shot-making. Playing behind a bunch of 30-something Bankers hitting from the Black tees was not his idea of fun. It mostly lent itself to a long boring day.

Starting from 6-B was a good break. Holes #6 - # 12 had some reasonable distances and some of the easier handicap holes. True, the number three handicap hole was in there too, but all in all a fairly gentle way to start. Dorsey Parred the 347 yard #6. Two good shots, two good putts, good start. His 6-iron found the green on the 147-yard Par 3 #7. He made an aggressive run at it, and made the comebacker, two Pars to start. Sloppy Bogey on #8, good Bogey on #9, the number 3 handicap.

Bogey on #10 (it was only 279 yards, yikes!) and a not-bad Bogey on the
Par 3 11th. A really, really dumb Double Bogey on #12. It went on like
this throughout the round, no real fireworks but no real bad stuff either.
He made Pars on #15 and #16.

Halfway in the round, conversation had begun to flow a little and
Ridgeline had even offered a few words of encouragement. He was
playing well and seemed tolerant of Dorsey's game. On the tee box
as they were waiting for the foursome ahead to move out, he said
something totally unexpected "You might want to tell your girlfriend to
be mindful of Carlotta."

Dorsey woke from his inner thoughts and took a moment before
answering "My girlfriend?"

"Yeah, Ms. Jeanette"

"She's not my girlfriend. Why would you think she's my girlfriend?"
was all Dorsey could offer.

"You buy a lot of Raffle Tickets. And when you win, you give it back.
A lot of guys thinks you're showing off. And since you give the money
back, they thinks you two must have somethin' goin' on."

Dorsey shot back "I did that once. And she's a nice girl, working hard.
Who is Carlotta to say something about it?"

"Carlotta, my wife Fawn, and Jamie George thinks they've got it
figured out pretty smart. You and Jeanette may not be a little couple,
they can see that. But they really thinks Jeanette is after Maynard Ferry."

"What are you talkin' about? Jeanette and Maynard Ferry?"

"Yeah, Carlotta was plenty agitated when Maynard had all them Raffle
Tickets. She's pretty sure he's too cheap to buy Raffle Tickets. They may
not know what exactly is goin' on with you and Jeanette but they figure
the two of you are in cahoots to get Jeanette closer to Maynard," With
this, Ridgeline's top lip curled over his teeth and his gaze stayed fixed
on Dorsey.

"Well, you, Carlotta, Fawn and Jamie have pretty good imaginations.
For me, I don't see Jeanette with Ferry. She seems pretty smart. He's
probably not her type." Dorsey felt good about phrasing that one.

"Hmph." Was what came from Ridgeline next, and then. "Just let your
girlie-girl know that these women aren't to be trifled with. They keep

a close watch on their men. And single gals should keep to themselves around married men. That's all."

As they moved to the tee, Dorsey's head was spinning. What had just happened? What were these people thinking? To this point his game had been a little wobbly. Now the wheels officially came off. Doubles on #17, and #18. A slew of Bogeys, another couple of Doubles. They finished on #5, the number 1 handicap hole which Dorsey saved to make his only Triple of the day. He had stumbled down the stretch again, not being able to finish strong. It all added up to a 94, which under the conditions wasn't bad, but nothing to write home about either.

It may have been the weather, but other than the weird exchange between Dorsey and Ridgeline, his cart mates were pretty quiet throughout the round. Also, with the up and down terrain, everyone was often huffing and puffing to climb to their next shot, wiping off clubs, dealing with the cover over the club, towels, and trying to walk around or steer the cart around puddles. It wasn't a bad time, but a little sun might have brought some cheer and made it a little nicer. Dorsey vowed to come back and play the course again on a nicer day. They all shook hands and commenced to fussing with their golf bags, tees, wallets and cell phones. Since the exchange on the tee box at #17, Dorsey and Ridgeline hadn't said a word. Ridgeline seemed to attempt to break Dorsey's fingers with his parting handshake and made some evil eye contact.

Dorsey took his clubs to his car rather than leave them exposed to the misty rain that had begun to fall. He took off his golf shoes, threw the rain jacket in the trunk and headed around the clubhouse to find the Scorer's Tent. Overall wet and rainy, and the hilly course had played hard. Scores were high. Chandler Hoffman slipped up to 78, but with only 3 shots, netted 75. Dana Blades shot a 79 and since he only got 4, tied Hoffman with a 75. As for Dorsey's foursome, Briscoe Sisson shot an 80, and with 6 strokes had a net 74. Ridgeline had a respectable 87, but with only 9 strokes, net to a 78. And Grandin shot a 104, with 22 strokes, 82. Everybody in Dorsey's foursome was out of the money.

The Third Flight was a wide-open affair again. Dorsey first checked

Pharratt's score. 104. Even with 26 strokes, his net was 78 – out of the money. Too much ground to make up with a few foot wedges, or was he being falsely accused by Dorsey's inner mind? Proudfoot won it with a 94, minus his 26(!) strokes, net 68. Maynard Ferry's back must have lightened up on him, as he shot a 91, (-22), net 69, second place. And Dorsey was pleased to see a rebound by Dooley Hopper, who apparently kept in the course and shot a respectable 93 (-23) for a net 70 and third place.

There were the usual pictures of the winners and a nice shot of Jeanette presenting the 50/50 winnings to Deuce Acton. Pharratt had actually "photobombed" the picture with Acton and Jeanette, sticking his mug up next to her and throwing an arm around her shoulder. She did not appear amused, ducking under his embrace with a nice pivot to get away from him. Acton didn't appear to give his winnings back, so Dorsey assumed Jeanette worked another long day for maybe $50 for her cause. It wasn't his business, but it really bugged him.

Draper Mountain was even more off the beaten track than London Bridges, a place not really on the way to anywhere. Due to the weather and the long drive none of the female support group had made it. Things broke up pretty quickly and everyone started wandering toward their cars. Dorsey walked with Maynard Ferry and Dooley Hopper toward the parking lot. Dorsey looked over at the two of them and asked, "How'd you play?".

Hopper just looked at the ground and scuffed his feet at the gravel, shifting his bag on his shoulder without saying anything. Ferry chimed in "I played well. But my day was a trainwreck." Dorsey tilted his head and looked at Ferry, waiting for a follow up. Ferry continued, "Well, at the beginning of the season I had replaced my 3-iron with a Chipper. Then last week I went to the range and hit the 3-iron since I had heard that this course could play long. I started out here pretty good but on my 4th tee box I noticed that both the Chipper and the 3-iron were in my bag. So, I had 15 clubs, one over the limit. That means a penalty of 2 shots per hole, or 6 shots total for carrying too many clubs. The very good 90 I shot turned into a 96 real fast. So I was out of the money. Dorsey kept his thoughts to himself, inwardly noting that golf could get to you in a million ways.

Dorsey was thinking of the proper response when Ferry leaned over and said "Man you almost got me killed with Carlotta! She didn't really believe you gave me all of those Raffle Tickets at London Bridges and really went off on me! She accused me of having something going with Jeanette!"

Dorsey was dumfounded. "C'mon man, really? She got that ramped up over something that simple? She has some imagination."

Before Ferry could say anything, Steve Martin came up behind them and said; "Guys I need a favor."

They all stopped and looked at him while he explained "Jeanette rode with me, but I have to go to Blacksburg. I need one of you to take her back to her car at the park-and-ride in Salem."

Ferry just looked at the ground. Dorsey piped up "Not me, I'm expected in Floyd so I'm not going that way."

Ferry and Hopper exchanged a glance and Ferry's shoulders slumped. Quietly he spoke up, still keeping his head down. "I drove. She can ride with Dooley and me and we'll drop her." His face was stern, very stern.

Martin waved a hand to Jeanette, so that she came over to where they were next to Ferry's car. She hopped in the back with her Raffle Ticket bag in one hand and a set of muddy tennis shoes in a plastic bag in the other hand. She had come prepared, so she had on cleaner sandals when she got in the car. Ferry and Hopper took their seats, Ferry fired it up and they pulled away. Dorsey shook his head, once more perplexed at the way men and women interacted in the Valley culture.

The 25-minute drive from Draper Mountain to the park-and-ride next to I-81 was pretty quiet. Ferry pulled his car up to Jeanette's, she climbed out with a "thank you" and started fumbling for her keys. Only when she had gotten the door open and put her Raffle Tickets in the backseat did she realize she had left her muddy shoes tucked under Ferry's driver side front seat, since she had sat in the back behind him. She tried to yell and wave, but they were gone. She didn't have his cell phone number on her since all of that stuff was on the GRITS website. Oh well, she could live without the shoes for a few days. She was sure Ferry would drop them off at Blue Bells one day and she would pick them up there.

Dorsey had gotten in his own car and began the winding trek over the mountain to Floyd. He filed Draper Mountain away for a future outing with Junior Loaf. Junior worked up that way sometimes, maybe they could rendezvous some afternoon. It would stay in the back of his mind until they could work it in.

Dorsey wasn't that bummed out about his day. It was more mediocrity but there were still two weeks before the next event, June 5 at the Home Course, Blue Bells. A large percentage of GRITS played out of Blue Bells, so he figured the scores should be pretty good. But rain set into the Valley and practice rounds were limited. Dorsey got one round in and shot an easy 87 that could have been better. He was left pondering why he couldn't score better when it counted, in tournament play.

# CHAPTER 5

## Blue Bells

**"Gimme. An agreement between two losers that can't putt."**  Jim Bishop

June 5 – 8:05 AM
Par 71
5411 yards from Senior Tees
Slope 65.0 / Rating 111
Weather at tee time. Perfect. 76 degrees breeze 5 mph

On Tuesday, June 5, GRITS was at Blue Bells, home course for most of the players. It was a spectacular "Chamber of Commerce" type of day. Dorsey had forgotten his phone and had to go back to the house but since he was early, made himself a Bloody Mary to see if it might help soothe any jitters. He drank most of it in the car, leaving the rest for later if he wanted it on the drive home.

He found the signup desk and located a cart with the placard; "15-A". His cart-mate was Jeff Brumfield, with Steve Martin and "Detective" Marcus Finn in the other 15-A cart. They weren't there yet, so he took the opportunity to putt a few. He practiced putting from inside 10 feet. He wasn't concerned as much about the longer ones, just wanted to be comfortable over the shorter ones and feel the feedback of hearing them rattle at the bottom of the cup. After 15 – 20 putts, he wandered back to the cart.

"Detective" Marcus Finn was a retired Roanoke Police Detective. Everyone called him Detective or Detective Finn. Hardly anyone remembered his actual first name, Marcus. Few remembered Marcus Finn, Class of 1969, Patrick Henry High. Six feet two, All-state in the 100-

yard dash and at running back in football. Fast, lean and competitive. He had matriculated at UVA and gained 863 yards his Sophomore year. All-ACC Sophomore year running the 100 too. Suffered a nagging hamstring early in his Junior year and his output dropped to 578 yards on a 4-7 team. By his Senior year, with a new Head Coach, the emphasis shifted to a passing game. His touches dropped again so that he only gained 466 yards and his pro dreams faded away. Stayed in school and got his degree in Criminal Justice. Joined the Roanoke Police Department the year after college and worked his way up to Detective. After retiring, "Detective" stuck as a nickname. He was one of a handful of African Americans on the GRITS Tour. Played to an 8-handicap and could hit it a mile. He was not to be trifled with. The other GRITS members gave him a wide berth.

Steve Martin was an unofficial Official of the GRITS Tour. Irish red hair, easy disposition, a 7-handicap. The "Official" scorecard for the round was on the steering wheel in front of him. Seemed like a nice guy.

The range area, putting green and greenspace adjacent to the Clubhouse were ablaze with activity. The sunlight shone brightly on the colors of the day. It was "Alzheimer's Awareness Month", and Dorsey had worn purple as requested on the website. A handful of guys had read it too, so maybe twenty percent were in some shade of purple. The rest of the crowd favored the burgundy and burnt orange of Va. Tech, the blue and white of James Madison, with a very few sporting The University of Virginia navy and orange. Dorsey even noticed one shirt with the burgundy and white of Hampden-Sydney.

There were other allegiances expressed as well. His 24-handicap cart-mate Jeff Brumfield featured the navy and orange of Illinois. His hat was from the US Open at Erin Hills, and the bag had a medallion from the Open at Shinnecock. Brumfield's bag, clubs, and approach were polar opposites of Dorsey. He had a special bag with a rack that lined his clubs up numerically, facing out so that you could see each clubs' number. The clubs were shiny and wiped clean, gleaming in the sun. Dorsey figured the guy must be an Engineer of some type but couldn't be sure without asking. That could wait.

Color-coordination was very hit and miss among the group, as was tailoring in general. It was a fact that men didn't much like to shop and this group was no different. Dorsey had also known for some time that there probably weren't enough mirrors in America, or people wouldn't leave their homes dressed like they did.

As usual, among the overall group there were black knee braces, wristbands and other forms of support, including knee high support hose. On the practice putting green Dorsey noticed a number of those rubber fitted things on the end of putters that would allow the player to pick up his ball without bending over. Aches, pains, Tylenol and Advil were standard equipment on the GRITS Tour. On his way around the clubhouse, he had noticed one of the players pulling his clubs out of his SUV which was parked in a "Handicap" spot, the blue and white placard attached to the front mirror.

Proudfoot and Jeanette mumbled a few words of encouragement to the assembled crowd. Proudfoot admonished anyone with a net score in the 60's to hang around, because they didn't like having to chase them around to hand out their trophies, or worse, they didn't have a winner's picture for the online newsletter. Jeanette was resplendent head to toe in purple, including a purple ribbon to hold back her ponytail and purple socks to complete the outfit. She had set up a table to sell Raffle Tickets and the tickets were purple too. While everyone milled around, Dorsey went by the table and bought 20 Raffle Tickets for the day. Jeanette seemed like a genuinely good person. She had a nice hug for almost everyone who bought her tickets. Dorsey admired her pluckiness in hanging in there with a bunch of old men, outnumbered 120 to 1.

Once the muttering and hemming and hawing were complete, the carts were released to cross over each other, cut one another off and lumber toward their assigned tees in no particular order. Proudfoot had warned everyone to be in the carts, not standing around, because at prior events there had been some issues of cart vs. player where the player hadn't come out so hot, and it had influenced their round. And they were off.

Having been early as usual, Dorsey was driving. He had asked Brumfield if he preferred to drive before they started, but Jeff didn't take the bait. Since they were headed to #15, they snaked back down past the Clubhouse, down #18 fairway, across #17, past the 16th green on the left, to the 15th tee box. Everyone got out, milled around, generally shook hands, gloved up, and got ready to hit. Brumfield had groused continually so far about how the carts were lined up, how high the rough was, and so on until Dorsey had simply clammed up and not commented any further.

Brumfield stepped first to the tee, announcing he was ready, took a few cuts and swung away. Not a bad result either. A little short, but on the putting surface so not too bad. Dorsey hit third, thought he was taking his slow and smooth swing, but pushed it in the general direction he always did on this hole, right of the green, toward the sand trap. He was pretty sure he had found the trap and knew that would be trouble. He didn't pay attention as the others hit, just got in the cart and drove.

Once the carts had arrived greenside, Dorsey was happy to see that he had gotten a break and was short and left of the trap. He gathered his thoughts while Finn hit up from in front of the green. Dorsey then hit an Ok-to-decent chip that, though skulled a little, made it over the corner of the bunker and drifted to about 4 feet below the hole. A good result. Finn was away at this point, so Dorsey had time to collect himself and focus on saving Par. He lined up the uphill putt, tried to calm his nerves, hit a solid putt only to see it slide by to the left, maybe 6 inches from the hole.

And then disaster struck.

Rather than mark his ball Dorsey elected to tap it in. Instead of going around the hole and lining up the tap-in, he took the shortcut of reaching awkwardly across the hole and jabbing at the ball. He almost whiffed it. He moved the ball maybe an inch, then followed through with the tap-in. As the group left the green Martin, the primary score keeper, asked for their scores and glanced at Dorsey.

WHO HELD UP 4 FINGERS !

Dorsey knew this was wrong the moment he did it, but it was too late. As they continued toward the cart Martin, the official scorekeeper for the group, was walking backward and said to him "Dorsey, that was a 5. They don't allow gimmes out here."

Dorsey's heart stuck in his throat. He knew that. Why had he held up

4 fingers? He knew it was a 5! What had made him do that? He quickly followed up with Martin… "You are exactly right, I know better than that, it's a 5. I apologize, I realize what I did, it won't happen again." Martin made it even worse by sliding up to him very gently and saying "They're sticklers out here. I'm sorry man, but I have to put down the real score". He was so nice Dorsey couldn't stand himself. He tapped Martin on the shoulder and repeated himself. "You are right. It was a 5. I'm really sorry". Martin smiled back at him while the other two averted their eyes, but the damage was done.

Dorsey, who had spent the past few weeks wondering if Pharratt had cheated had just one-upped him. He not only did something semi-illegal, it was compounded by raising his 4 fingers when he knew it was wrong. What had gotten into him? How could he have done that? He was blown away at his own stupidity. And for the most part, his tournament ended right there.

He stepped to the 16th tee and blasted a low tailing drive down the right side of the fairway into the rough, almost behind a tree. He smacked his second shot past the tree, but across the fairway so that all three of the other guys had to spend time looking for it. Martin found it on the sidehill of a ditch about 40 yards short of the green. Dorsey gouged out a mediocre chip shot that was way short, 25 yards from the pin which had a cross hill lie with a huge left to right swing. He left that putt about ten feet short, missed the one for a 5 and trembled in one for the 6. Double bogey.

Number 17 is a 140-yard par 3, and Dorsey managed to pull his high fading 6-iron to the corner of the green furthest from the hole. He hit a miraculous lag putt to about nine inches, which he proceeded to jerk past the hole, not even close to going in. He did make his 6-inch tap-in for that Bogey. As they drove to the 18th tee Dorsey realized that in the first 3 holes he had thrown away 3 shots with ridiculous putting. One horrible lag putt on #16, and 3 putts under a foot that he had missed. Two 3-putts in the first two holes.

Dorsey achieved a tiny bit of redemption by hitting a good drive on the short Par 5 18th. He smoked a 3-wood for the second shot to the rough about 35 yards from the hole. Somehow, he managed to hit a very smooth pitch that rolled out to about 2 feet from the cup. He made the putt! Eureka. Birdie.

As the group drove past the Clubhouse, Dorsey let Brumfield take the cart and jogged upstairs to the snack bar. "Is it too early for you to sell me two Mountain Lites?" It was around 10 AM by this time. Dorsey collected the two beers, jogged down the stairs and over toward the tee-box. The other three were waiting for him, since he had the Birdie and by rights he should hit first. He stopped short and said to them "Guys, please, go ahead, hit, I need a minute to pull myself together". Dorsey hit last and his troubles reared up again.

He hit his high power-fade, only the ball didn't fade. Instead, the ball stayed in the air a long time before they all heard the "thwack" when it hit a tree to the left of the fairway. Everyone fanned out and ended up spending their time looking for Dorsey's ball. Then they watched as he chumped it about 50 yards, then watched again as he hit it to the absolute back of the green, and 3 putts later he had another 6. Three Double Bogeys in the first 5 holes.

On #2 Dorsey hit a slicing 3-wood that found the bunker to the right and below the green. Bogey. On #3 his low liner to the left got caught up in the rough, from which he proceeded to chump his second shot just over the creek. On the Par 3 #4 hole, he actually found the green, then left his putt 6 feet short. By some miracle he rattled that one in, his hands shaking like a leaf. The fun continued on the #1 handicap hole, number 5, when another high fade didn't fade. Punch out from under the tree, a wild slash to the back sidehill behind the green, weak chip and 2 putts, another double bogey 6.

On the par 5 #6, Dorsey uncorked a really big drive, just way left. Which shouldn't have been a problem, since it was pretty open over there. Except that his playing partners hadn't been watching and his ball couldn't be found. Dorsey found himself racing back to the tee and re-hitting before the group behind them could hit. He hit a good drive, great second shot, nice chip and made the putt for what should have been a Birdie but was actually a bogey since he had to re-hit. Little consolation that while he was running back and forth, and after he re-hit, they found his first ball lying serenely in the grass, past where they had been looking. Too late, he had already re-hit.

The day continued on like that. Timid chips, tense putts, high fades that didn't, bounces that went the wrong way. A stupid Double Bogey on #12, a yanked 6-iron from the middle of the fairway on #13 and a chumped second shot on #14. Double Bogey, Triple Bogey, Double Bogey. He ended the day with another 97, the same that he had shot at London Bridges. Only this time, for whatever reason, they only gave him 20 strokes, not 22, so it was a net 77.

His cart mate, Brumfield, who was a 24 handicap, shot an 85 / net 61. The guys in the other cart, were lower handicaps, which figured since Steve Martin had shot a 78 with a 7-handicap and Detective Finn had shot an 85 with 8 strokes, net 67. Dorsey was just about a stoke a hole worse than the rest of the foursome. He felt bad that they had had to stand around and watch him play. It was a wonder that they could record good scores with him playing like an idiot. He was fuming inside but shook hands, thanked them for their patience and tried to get the hell out of there.

Dorsey dumped his bag near the clubhouse door on a rack with about twenty others. He took the steps two at a time back up to the clubhouse bar and got himself another cold Mountain Lite. Jeanette and a handful of guys were down at the other side of the club room. Pharratt had her backed up against some folding chairs, gesturing with his hands in the air, apparently going through his round shot-by-shot. Jeanette was almost climbing into the chairs to try and create some space between them. Her eyes were wide open, her face was turned to the side and her hands were stretched out in front of her.

Dorsey didn't want to be rude, so he slid down there to at least speak. As he got closer, he was reintroduced to Carlotta Ferry, Jamie George and Fawn Ridgeline. Irene Proudfoot and Halle Hopper were standing nearby. He didn't want to make eye contact with anyone. He was disgusted with what he had done on the first hole and disgusted with how he had played. But he tried to be nice anyway and feigned interest by asking Ferry and Hopper how their rounds had gone. He didn't volunteer anything about his round. After shuffling his feet a few minutes, he mumbled something about needing to get home and turned to leave. Halfway through his pivot he remembered the Raffle Tickets in his pocket, fished them out and extended his hand toward Ferry. "Hey, Maynard, I'm leaving, take these, maybe you can win something."

Carlotta Ferry almost bit his head off. "He doesn't need any more damn Raffle Tickets!" she spat at him.

Dorsey physically jumped backwards and managed to shove the tickets into Hoppers' hand. Not understanding what was going on, he muttered "Have to get home" and slunk toward the door.

He went back down toward the Bar and ordered another Mountain Lite to try and cool his nerves. He sat and sipped for a minute, then decided that a restroom break before his drive home would probably be a good idea. He came back to the Bar and noticed that at the other end of the room Carlotta wasn't among the group. Good, he didn't have any interest in running into her again. Thinking that she must have gone to the restroom too, he chugged what was left of the beer and beat it down the back steps to grab his bag and head for the car.

He was met by Ferry at the bottom of the steps. Dorsey looked directly at him and asked him "What did I do to Carlotta?"

Ferry looked down at his feet then looked up weakly "Remember how I told you she accused me of having something going with Jeannette after she found all those Raffle Tickets in my pocket after London Bridges?"

Dorsey tilted his head and said "Yeah, but that was stupid right?"

Ferry came back with "Yeah it was stupid. And do you remember Martin asking me and Hopper to give her a ride to the park-and-ride from Draper Mountain after that Tournament?"

"Yeah"

"Well, Jeannette apparently had an extra set of shoes with her when she got in the car. And she left one of the pairs stuck up under the front seat when she got out. And Carlotta found them"

"Ouch" was all Dorsey could offer. Then "Didn't Hopper cover for you? It was all innocent right?".

Ferry looked strained and responded "Well, Carlotta has known Hopper for a long time. Let's just say she doesn't consider him the best character witness." Dorsey didn't know what to say so he just moved away and headed for his car.

On the way to the car, on the way home, for the rest of the day and for most of the next few weeks he couldn't shake the catastrophe that was his round. He may blank out how he had played but he wasn't likely to forget what he had done on the first hole anytime soon. He bounced back down the steps, slung his bag over his arm and kept his head down all the way to the car. He popped open the truck, threw the clubs in, kicked his shoes in, putt on his flip flops, poured out the remnants of the Bloody Mary, poured in the beer (a weak red-eye) and gunned it out of the lot. What an idiot.

Dorsey didn't mention any of this to Luisa. He steered away from the subject and skirted the whole thing. Inwardly he moped around, but outwardly, he just didn't want to talk about it. They had a quiet little night, and he didn't think she noticed what was going on with him and that was the way he hoped it stayed. He slept fitfully, tormented by how he could put the incident behind him and move on. His only hope was that time would heal it.

The next day, Wednesday, was pretty much a lost day. Puttering around in a fog chastising himself for what he had done. The sane part of his brain realized that the other three guys could care less, and that they certainly weren't even thinking about his gaffe. After all, Martin had corrected him. The proper score had been recorded. In that sense, he hadn't cheated. No harm, no foul. The moral letdown still stuck with Dorsey. He knew he was probably beating himself up beyond what the situation called for, but that didn't matter. He was bummed out.

Reasoning that the only thing to do was to get back on the horse, he was at Blue Bells at 8:30 Thursday morning. He got paired up with a twosome he didn't know, thank Goodness. Since they were sent out as a threesome, he got to ride by himself which was also good in allowing him to not have to chatter and interact much. He was in no mood to be convivial. He shot an almost effortless 86. It wasn't great, and of course could have been better, but he hoped it was the beginning of healing. The difference was that he played relaxed, just let it flow. Without the pressing and grinding of trying too hard, he was able to enjoy himself a little and hit some nice shots. His putting was never great, but at least for this round, it was tolerable.

The round did have a troubling feature. On the 3rd hole, Dorsey hit a nice drive and reached for his 6-iron. Which wasn't there. He shook all of the clubs around, poked at them to make sure it wasn't buried in there, but no 6-iron. He spent a lot of the rest of the round trying to reconstruct where he might have left it. He thought back over the final holes played in the Tournament and couldn't remember when he had last hit it. On #9 he had hit a 9-iron in, on #10 it was a 4-iron, on the par 3 11th he hit a Rescue Club, on the 12th it was definitely a 5-iron, on #13 it was an 8-iron and on #14 it was a Pitching Wedge. He couldn't work back any further and couldn't remember if he had walked with two clubs on any specific shot, and maybe left it when he walked away. Besides, the Tournament had been at Blue Bells only two days before. Surely someone had turned it in by now. No such luck. Neither Bryan or the kid in the clubhouse had seen it. They checked behind the counter, in the cart barn, with no sign of it. Dorsey went home empty handed. He was trying to be pleased that he had shaken off the horrors of the tournament round, but now found that another boneheaded thing to beat himself up about. His mood was still on the gloomy side when he got home about two o'clock.

His phone rang around three.

"Hello"

"Dorsey, this is Manny Proudfoot". Dorsey's heart once again lodged in his throat.

"Dorsey, we had a little incident at the Tournament on Tuesday and I wanted to talk to you about it".

Dorsey's mind raced as his pulse soared. "What's it about Manny?"

Fearing the worst, that he knew exactly what it was about. Were they going to kick him off the Tour? Publicly shame him? Really, was it worth this to put himself out there and invite this kind of crap?

"I'd rather not discuss it by phone, it's sort of a sensitive subject. Can you meet me at Blue Bells on Monday around 10?"

"I can meet you right now, Are you there? Or maybe tomorrow?"

Dorsey did not want this to go out any further than necessary.

Confronting whatever it was sooner rather than later was far and away his preference.

"No, not really, I'm headed to the Lake in a few minutes and will be down there all weekend. Let's do it Monday at 10 OK?"

Dorsey didn't have much choice. "Sure"

They hung up and it was left to Dorsey to mull and fume all weekend and wonder what this would lead to. He felt like a truant school boy and didn't need the aggravation. All weekend he worked up the worst scenarios including the one where he told Proudfoot to shove it and never went back to Blue Bells again. After all, two months ago, he had never set foot on the place. He would simply ride into the sunset. He really didn't need it. It was a long, long weekend and he had to do his best to fake his normal cheery self to try and keep Luisa from noticing and thereby ruining their weekend. Monday couldn't come soon enough.

# CHAPTER 6

## June 11
## The Meeting

**"I play golf with friends sometimes but there are never friendly games."**
Ben Hogan

Dorsey made it to Blue Bells about 10 minutes early on Monday. He went around the back to the Pro Shop as always and went in the back door. Bryan was at his usual spot, phone up to one ear while typing into the main computer.

Dorsey said "Proudfoot?" and Bryan jerked his head and mouthed "Upstairs". Upstairs, not down here in the Pro Shop office? Upstairs in the Corporate Offices? What tha?

Dorsey went through the interior door to the stairs and took them two at a time. He turned left toward the Corporate Office but slowed immediately. The office looked full. Dorsey could see Proudfoot sitting at the big desk and could make out Ridgeline leaning against a cabinet off to the side. As he got closer, Steve Martin turned in the doorway and faced him. No expression at all. Dorsey slid past him and into the office as Proudfoot looked up at him. Dorsey's emotions had started off last week embarrassed, chagrined, humbled and depressed. By this morning the emotions quickly turned the corner to pissed off and ready for a fight. He stood at the front of Proudfoots' desk and tried to keep his face blank.

"Oh Hey, Dorsey, there you are, howya doin?"

"Not bad, good morning Manny".

"So, how ya enjoyin the Tour?"

"It would be better if I were playing better"

"Yeah, we can all say that...."

Dorsey didn't respond, waiting for Proudfoot to get on with it. Were they really going to make something of this? Really? Was this that big a deal? He had already run through his arguments over the weekend. After all, the proper score had been recorded. No actual offense had occurred. He had felt bad enough long enough that he felt like he had already paid his penance. Bring it on. Dorsey had already decided he wasn't going to be but so contrite. After all, the punishment needed to fit the crime. He had already punished himself plenty. Waiting, he could feel his ears getting red and his face growing hot.

Proudfoot started in." We had a little incident at last weeks' Tournament that we wanted to talk to you about". It took Dorsey everything he had in him to not speak, but he was not going to be the one to break the silence. He looked at Steve Martin but couldn't read anything at all from him. Proudfoot picked it up after a pregnant moment. "We understand that you misplaced your 6-iron."

Dorsey choked out a "Yeah". He couldn't believe how tight his throat felt.

Proudfoot started up again… "Do you remember where?" then laughed. "Of course you don't remember where, or it wouldn't be lost. But do you remember the last time you hit it?"

This was a little unexpected since Dorsey was all ready to leap over the desk, swing from the hips and tell them all to go to Hell. He tried to breathe while staring at Proudfoot with a lump in his voice box. After he pulled himself together a little, he started in … "Actually, I've had the chance to think a lot about it. I don't know if you've ever lost a club, but it's a pain in the butt and I've thought back as far as I could and can't come up with anything. But I played here on Tuesday for the Tournament and then on Thursday to try and chase away the Demons. I was sure someone would have turned it in. I asked around the Clubhouse and no one could tell me anything. Then I thought back over the round and still couldn't come up with anything."

Proudfoot; "You seem nervous man, do you want to sit down a minute?"

Dorsey's head was all over the place, but he blurted out a "No". And sat down.

Proudfoot nodded and kept going; "Well, we don't want to put you

on the spot, but can you take us back through the last time you think
that you may have had it?"

Dorsey was puzzled and asked the question;" What's this about? I have
a replacement 6-Iron and the lost one will probably still turn up. What's
the deal?"

Proudfoot leaned in and gave Dorsey a fatherly look. "It would be
good if you could trust us a few minutes, we're all on the same team
here, but it would be helpful if you could go over it with us before we say
a lot more. Trust us for just a minute, Ok?"

Dorsey was glad to hear the part about everyone being on the same
team, relieved they weren't talking about his putting gaffe on #15, but pretty
confused, yes sir. He started in, looking at Steve Martin the whole time. He
worked backwards through his round. "Well we finished on #14 and I had
chumped a few shots on that one, so it was only a wedge into that green. On
#13 I had a perfect setup for an 8-iron that I pulled way left of the green.
On #12 I had a 5-iron that I skulled short of the green. Sometimes I take two
clubs to a shot if I think it will help me concentrate but since I was driving
the cart, I think I just pulled the 5-iron and looked up on it, so I skulled it.
On the Par 3 11th, I popped a Rescue Club way short, so that wasn't it. On
#10 it was a 4-iron from the middle of the fairway yanked along the path that
kicked down in the fringe left and pin high. On #9 I gouged an 8-iron short
from the rough, then a Pitching Wedge that hit the false front and rolled
back. On #8 I hit a good 4-iron onto the green before I 3-putt that one. On
#7 I skulled a 3- wood, hit a good 4-iron short and Pitching Wedge on. On
#6 I only had about 40 yards in and hit a good Pitching Wedge. Made the
putt for what should have been a Birdie, but it was actually a Bogey since
we weren't able to find my Drive and I had to re-hit. On #5 I hit the 6-iron.
Pulled it way left on the side of the green, hit a bad chip and 3-putt from
there. So, I think # 5 was the last time I hit the 6-iron."

Proudfoot and the other two stared at Dorsey dumfounded.
Proudfoot finally spoke "Well, I almost feel bad for you making you
re-live a round like that. I guess it could have gone better pretty easily.
That's amazing that you can recollect all of that. Sounds painful".

Dorsey looked Steve Martin in the eye and said in a measured voice
"It actually started out worse than that and I never got over it. It is a

round that is stuck in my brain."

Proudfoot glanced back and forth between Dorsey and Martin and let it go. Then Proudfoot went on." So, after the round, what happened?"

Dorsey leaned back a little, sensing that he worst of this could be over. Or so he thought. "What do you mean what happened? I got out of here as quick as I could and went home to get drunk and forget about my round. It's just that he whole thing start to finish was enough to make me think about quitting. At least for a day. And losing the 6-iron was just the icing. I did think about the whole day a lot. In addition to playing like a moron, losing the 6-iron made me remember everything."

"Good, I want you to remember more for us." Proudfoot had on an exceptionally friendly face this time. "Try and go back to when you left the course. Did you go straight to your car? Did you hang around? Did you leave your bag and go to the restroom? Try and remember everything you can."

Dorsey leaned forward with his elbows on his knees, staring at the floor between his legs trying to pull the memory back. "I took my bag off the cart by the pro shop and left it stacked on the rack with 12-15 others. I came up here to get a beer. I saw Maynard Ferry, Randy Ridgeline and George George in a group at the other end of the bar and I spoke to them. Ferry's wife was there, so was Ridgeline's, so was George's." He nodded slightly to Ridgeline in the corner of the room to acknowledge that he was talking about him, and knew he was sitting right there. "I walked down there and since I was leaving early, tried to give Ferry the Raffle Tickets that I had bought from Jeanette earlier. Carlotta Ferry almost tore my head off with that, I don't know why. She almost spit at me 'He doesn't need any more damn Raffle Tickets!'"

"It was kind of awkward with Ridgelines' and George's wives both there, and I didn't know what to make of it. The minute I said something, Carlotta Ferry, Jamie George and Fawn Ridgeline turned and huddled away from me and started in like they were hatching a plan to take over the world. Their heads were bobbing up and down and every few minutes one of them would turn around and glare at me. The whole thing creeped me out, so I was itching to get out of there. If you remember, you and Irene and Hopper and his wife Halle were standing just to the side of the Ferry group."

"I took my beer out on the porch since the atmosphere was so tense in there. I stood outside a few minutes and finished my beer. I went by the locker room up front, then came back to get a beer to go. I didn't see those guys again, so I just went out the back, down the steps, grabbed my bag and went around the building to the parking lot to my car. That's it."

Proudfoot, Ridgeline and Martin exchanged glances. Proudfoot piped up "Did you see Ferry or his wife or George leave? Did they leave together?"

Dorsey shook his head, still staring at the floor. "I don't know".

Proudfoot leaned back in his chair with a wrinkle in his brow. He looked back and forth between the other two and offered. "Well, Ok, I guess that's it. Thanks for coming in."

Dorsey lifted his head toward Proudfoot. "You guess what's it? What's this about?"

Proudfoot again looked back and forth between the other two, sighed and started in again. "Someone busted out a window in Jeanette's car. In broad daylight with a lot of people coming and going in the parking lot"

Dorsey was still puzzled. "What's this got to do with me?"

Proudfoot sighed again. "It looks like it easily could have been done with a golf club. And since your 6-iron is missing…"

Dorsey started fuming. "You don't think I did it ?!"

Proudfoot let his eyes drift side to side again. "No, not really. We just needed to hear your side to try and sort things out. "

"This is bullshit" Dorsey blurted.

At this point Ridgeline chimed in. "it's been noticed that you buy a lot of Raffle Tickets. You seem to be particularly friendly with Jeanette. We were just wondering if your golf club and your relationship with her might have something to do with her broken window."

Dorsey fought to hold back what he really wanted to say. "I do like her. I think she works hard and is a nice sweet person. I admire her doing what she does around all of these smelly men. I don't have a crush on her and I don't have a beef with her. I just try to support her. I think she deserves it."

Proudfoot gave him a calming voice. "Dorsey, you have to understand, we are just looking after Jeanette. We have to do what we can to figure out whatever."

Dorsey jumped back at him. "If it was me I wouldn't be stupid enough to have everyone looking for my 6-iron, would I ?"

Proudfoot leaned in again. "Good point. We already thought about that. We just wanted to know if you knew anything that we don't" Then after a pause, "That's it Dorsey. If you think of anything that could help us, please let us know, OK?"

Dorsey stood and glared at all three of them one by one, then shouldered through the door. Halfway down the hall he heard his name "Dorsey!"

It was Steve Martin; "Dorsey don't think anything of that, it's just a little crazy and we're trying to figure out if anyone intentionally targeted Jeanette. It's really not personal."

"To you maybe." Dorsey fired back. Then stopped himself. "Look, I thought you guys were calling me in to ream me out over the gimme putt I gave myself on our first hole. I've been sweating that all week and what just went on in there really rocked me."

Now Martin sounded conciliatory. "Dorsey, that's behind us. I didn't tell Proudfoot about that. I know it was a momentary thing. Any of us could have done that. The proper score was reported, and we went on with it. It's a non-event. But if someone is messing with Jeanette on purpose, we need to figure it out. If you think of anything else you may have seen or heard, call me or Proudfoot, Ok?"

Dorsey looked him in the eye "What's the deal with Ridgeline? Does he have some kind of beef with me?"

Martin tilted his head and replied "No, I don't think that's personal either. He's a retired Salem Detective. I think he likes to stick his nose in stuff when he can. He could be helpful. Maybe the thing with Jeanette's window was a coincidence. Maybe he'll find your 6-iron. I don't know. Just try and let this slide off of you. No one is on your case. Try to have a good week, see you at Hanging Tree."

"OK" Dorsey muttered meekly, then went on "Ok, so then I want to thank you for the way you handled my gaffe at the Tournament. You were cool. I appreciate it."

They both made kind eye contact and shared a firm handshake. Then Dorsey turned back down the stairs out into the parking lot. His confusion was short of rage, but also short of relief.

# CHAPTER **7**

## Hanging Tree Practice

**"Golf and women are a lot alike. You know you are not going to wind up with anything but grief, but you can't resist the impulse."**

Jackie Gleason

June 22

Dorsey had thought he would get shut out of practice for the June 25 Tourney at Hanging Tree. He was supposed to have company in town that would keep him from playing, but they had cancelled so he had the time. Even better, Marvin Pharrattt had called and asked him to join a foursome on Friday. Wow. This guy might really be for real. Maybe he was just a friendly guy who liked to play. Either way, Dorsey was happy to join the group.

Since they had a 9:43 tee time, Dorsey found himself at the course early. He explained to the guy at the register (George) that this was his practice round before next week's tourney. George asked if Dorsey remembered him. Dorsey just cocked his head and looked. The guy had huge forearms. George explained "I'm the guy that you pay at the Tournament. Don't you remember me asking if you were related to Jeff Whitlock? Me and Jeff worked together at the Highway Department." Dorsey mumbled that he hadn't been in town long, and a lot of it had been a blur, sorry I didn't remember you right off, blah, blah, blah. He continued to stare at the guy since he looked so weird. He definitely had a comic book character look about him with his squinty eye and bald head but Dorsey hadn't completely made up his mind yet about which character he was reminded of. He halfway expected George George to pull out a can of spinach at any moment.

George didn't let him go with that; "Guess yuh heerd about that stuff with Jeanette didn yuh?"

"Stuff with Jeanette?"

"Yeah, seems like some folks may not want her out here" George continued.

"Not want her out here? Where did you get that? Does anyone know if Jeanette's car was the target? Maybe someone wanted to take out the frustrations over their round and her car happened to get in the way."

George smiled a little smirk "There's them that don't think maybe she belongs out here peddling her Raffle Tickets and her chips and drinks. Seems to me that whatever money she's pocketin' could be goin' into the Tour. A lot of these guys don't have a lot of money. Anything she gets might be better spent elsewheres."

In his wildest dreams Dorsey had never considered these arguments. To him it seemed the poor girl worked long and hard with very little result for her Charity "Do you think a lot of the guys think like that?"

George leveled his gaze and looked at Dorsey through only one of his eyes "Some do. You buy a lot of them Raffle Tickets dontcha? And then give her the money back when you win?"

"I did that once. I think she works hard and deserves our support."

As Dorsey pulled away from the counter, George gave him another look "Didja every find your 6-iron?"

Dorsey's head snapped up; "How do you know about my 6-iron?"

"Only that theys some people at Blue Bells lookin for it."

"Like who?"

"Oh, Proudfoot, Ridgeline, folks like 'at. Theys actually spent some time poking around and askin' about it. You didn't find it huh?" A dark grin creased his lower face.

"Nope. But I'm not worried about it. I have a replacement that will work just fine. It will turn up eventually"

George grinned his greasy grin again. "We all hope so."

Dorsey backed out the door and made it out to where the starter was without getting a cart. He was trying to shake off the conversation he had just had and figured he would let Pharratt get the cart and sort out who rode with who. Maybe he would just putt a few to kill a little time. As he headed by the putting green, the starter, a sunburnt smiley-faced guy introduced himself as Barney Geary. Dorsey explained he was early and just killing time, which got Geary going. He explained he was retired and taught golf at Northlake High. As they made their introductions, a swarthy, athletic guy came up and they all started chatting. This guy introduced himself as Briscoe Sisson.

Once Dorsey had explained that he was playing on the Senior Tour, the conversation heated up quickly. Geary leaped right in "I'm a 4 Handicap and I played that damn tour for four years. I got tired of losing to guys with 26-handicaps. I would shoot a good score, maybe a 68 or so, net 64 and some dufus with a 26 handicap would shoot an 89 and take home the trophy. I got sick of it so I quit playin'"

Briscoe Sisson kicked in at this time "I'm a 6-handicap myself and I know exactly how Barney feels. I have to give up 10 strokes to guys that I play straight up a lot of times. The handicaps are questionable, they don't get adjusted often and the high handicappers have all the advantage."

Unfortunately Dorsey took the bait and threw in his two cents; "Well, I'm a 22 myself and even I think things could be organized better. We should be flighted better; net scores should count more and I think the Triple Bogey thing is too much. Maximum Double Bogey would make the tournaments move faster. Anybody over a 10 handicap shouldn't be competing with you guys and taking away what good golfers are doing."

At this Geary practically leaped across the cart-path and spoke his peace "Well, Manny Proudfoot is a 26-handicap and he likes his strokes. He needs the Triple Bogey thing because he makes a lot of them. As long as he's running the Tour, things ain't never gonna change!"

Dorsey felt he'd said enough, probably too much. These people were touchy about things that they felt strongly about. They felt strongly about a lot of things. Things like Politics, Religion, Females and Giving up Strokes. It was a minefield of opinions and Dorsey vowed again to try to keep his thoughts to himself.

Thankfully, Pharratt pulled up with the cart and made introductions

to Woody Crane and Ernest Bass. Bass was decked out in full West
Virginia University regalia from his hat to his shirt to his bag. He wore
dark sunglasses and carried his 245 pounds on a formerly athletic frame.
Woody Crane was about 6'3" and lean. He was tall enough that he bent
over at the waist to address the ball like a stork. And he hit it hard.
Dorsey watched him hit all through the round and couldn't figure out
where the power came from out of that body. He figured it was good
fundamentals, acquired early in life. With Bass it was a little easier to see.
He was strong and hard looking, if a little less polished. He hit the fire
out of a lot of shots too, it was just less predictable and less consistent to
know where it was going.

Dorsey hit the ball well, and all over the place. A pulled drive on #2
onto the #3 tee box. A pulled drive (too much club) on #3. A Par on
#4, but another pull into the junk on #5. To get through the round he
had to contend with a pack of out- of- bounds, under trees, and the
usual number of chumps and 3-putts. Pharratt couldn't hit it far, but
when everything was tallied up, he was right with Dorsey. Crane shot an
82 that could have been better, but he hadn't played Hanging Tree in
a while and got fooled on club selection a few times. Bass was up and
down but had some good holes for an 86. Dorsey stopped looking at the
scorecard but was pretty sure he had ended up right at 100, pretty much
the same as Pharratt.

He probably should have been more upset, but he wasn't. He had hit
the ball well and had somehow regained some of his distance. Hanging
Tree was a tighter course that Blue Bells. He knew he had left 10 strokes
out there. He had learned something from the round and had some
definite changes in club selection for some of the holes. If he could
keep it in the course, things could work out. This was the wildest he had
been in a while, with penalty strokes and lost balls that he hadn't had to
contend with all summer. Maybe, just maybe, he could put it all together
somehow.

He realized that he had one problem that he hadn't faced up to
before. In Florida it had been very loosey-goosey golf. Since the alcohol
content was high and they rarely played for money his standards had
gotten lax. Too many gimme putts and a Mulligan here and there could

convince you that your round maybe wasn't all that bad. In a brand new way, Dorsey was facing up to the fact that if you played them all down, counted all of the strokes and putt until you holed it, his golf game might actually stink. Golf might not be that much fun playing this way. He wasn't out here to beat himself up and be bummed out. He had just wanted to have some fun. With six Tournaments remaining, he told himself that he needed to either play better or face the fact that he just wasn't very good. Again he went home puzzled.

# CHAPTER **8**

## Hanging Tree

**"The woods are full of long hitters."** Harvey Penick

June 25 – 8: 10 AM
Par 72
5773 from the Gold Tees
Slope 68.4 / Rating 119
84 degrees, 72% Humidity, Little or no breeze – Hot and Muggy

Dorsey's group drew 4-A. The group was Dorsey, Dooley Hopper,
Deuce Acton and Wright Strange. He had fun playing with Hopper
before but didn't know the other two. He was riding with Wright Strange
who was the official scorekeeper for the foursome. He couldn't help
but wonder if Strange was a plant and Proudfoot had picked Dorsey to
ride with him so that Strange could keep an eye on him. He decided to
put his paranoia to the side, be the perfect playing partner, pay strict
attention to the rules, move the cart when appropriate and hold the
flagstick when he could. All you can do is all you can do.

Dorsey had arrived early again. He had a strategy gleaned from his
practice round and intended to stick to it. On the range he hit 3 clubs;
the 3-Wood, which he planned to use a lot from the tee and knew he
would need on some second shots. From the practice round, he felt his
6-iron could be his "go to" club, since it seemed that distances from 138
– 142 came up a lot.

He had pulled a Taylor Made 6-iron from an old set of clubs that were
in storage. When you lined it up and looked down on it, the look was
very close to the look of the Ping 6-iron that was missing. He didn't feel

100% confident in it yet, but he was getting there. It would have to do. He also took his 9-iron to the range, which he could use from 70 to 120 yards. He felt that by focusing on these clubs, keeping the ball out of the woods and getting to the green, it could be a decent day.

Proudfoot stood on the Hanging Tree balcony overlooking the putting green and went through his routine – putt them all, count them all, have a good day. Since it was still Alzheimer's Awareness Month, Jeanette had outdone herself in Purple for the day. She pretty much always wore Purple, but today she had gone all out. Sometimes the outfits were Purple mixed with white or black. Today was Purple Purple Purple. As always Dorsey admired her pluck and thought she was brave and sassy to show up like that. To him, she managed to make it look sweet and fresh. He had a hard time figuring out why anyone would take offense to her. But here in the Valley thinking was sometimes a little different. He hoped that over time he wouldn't get narrow like some of these people seemed.

As they moved out to 4-A Dorsey had a chance to take in Wright Strange. The guy looked like a hockey stick. Narrow and angular, thin but fibrous, strong and reedy. As Dorsey had waited in the cart before the round, he had taken in Stranges' clubs and bag. The bag was Callaway with a Callaway towel. a Callaway umbrella tucked into the bag pocket. The clubs were Callaway. Each club – not just the woods as with most golfers – but EACH CLUB had a red Callaway headcover. The covers for the woods were knit but the ones for the irons were some sort of vinyl (plastic?). The Putter cover was an elaborate combination of vinyl and knit. All in red and white. It made it easy to pick out Strange when he came striding up and settled into the cart. Red and white Callaway hat (with black trim). Red, white and black Callaway shirt. Red Sans-a-belt slacks. Black Callaway shoes. Dorsey knew he needn't bother to ask what brand of ball Strange would be playing.

They hardly talked at all as they wound down #1, up the hill past the #2 tee box, past the Par 3 #3, and pulled up adjacent to the #4 tee box. Dorsey felt like it wasn't a bad draw to start on #4 which was the second easiest hole on the course. It would be a little odd when they came around and had to finish on #1, #2 and #3, and Dorsey made a mental note to take a breath and reset himself when they did. He had had trouble with those 3 holes, particularly #2 and #3. And he had finished weakly in the Tournaments he had played so far. But for starters, he felt good about #4.

Wright Strange hit his Driver, which surprised Dorsey since it was a short hole. And he hit it hard. Unfortunately, he pulled it left over the big rock in the fairway and once it hit the hard stuff, Dorsey knew it was gone. Like a lot of the other GRITS guys Strange hadn't played Hanging Tree much, so he didn't know what he was up against. The course isn't that long on a lot of holes. Even on some of the Par 5's your best bet on a second shot was to lay up with a 5-iron or 6-iron rather than hit it harder and bring in trouble. Dorsey wasn't sure of the protocol, and since he didn't know Strange, was reluctant to give advice. He decided to keep his head down and keep to his own strategy.

Dorsey knew Strange's ball was almost surely out of bounds. Since Strange didn't seem to know that, they drove all of the way up, looked for the ball, then Strange had to peel back and re-hit his Drive He was fuming, hit Driver again and pushed it to the right, past Hopper's ball. It wound up in a scruffy area under the trees with little grass and it was lying 3. Dorsey steadied himself, stayed down and hit his own Pitching Wedge to about 15 feet, pin high. Nice. Strange had trouble with the patchy grass and scuffed his ball all the way to the back of the green. Since he was away, he putt first, got it within 4 feet and ultimately made that for his Double Bogey. Dorsey lined his Birdie putt up but tried not to grind over it too much. The ball slid by on the left but stayed next to the hole for a 3-inch tap in, which he took his time on. He didn't want to start with bad vibes as at Blue Bells, so he lined it up carefully before tapping it in. Cool. Dorsey 4, Hopper 4, Acton 5, Strange 6. A good start for Dorsey.

On #5 Dorsey knew there was a bad ravine down the left side and slightly overcompensated aiming to the right. He got a little lucky since he hit it a little fat so that it stopped short of the trees about 165 yards from the hole but with a clear view. The reason #5 was the number one handicap hole had a lot to do with the green. It was uphill all the way on the second shot, to a crowned green. And if you hit it above the hole, it was almost impossible to stop your putt coming back down the hill. Dorsey hit a sweet 4-iron that he caught flush. It was a high straight beautiful thing, but he knew it was long the moment he hit it. It was above the hole and even though he gauged the speed well on his downhill putt, he had to hold his breath thinking it might roll all the way off the front of the green. It didn't, but he had about 12 feet uphill left. He babied it and left himself 3 feet, but he stroked it firmly for his 5. Not bad. Bogey on the #1 handicap was always acceptable.

Dorsey had minded his own business in playing the hole and had walked a lot of it to keep it moving. After everyone's second shot he had grabbed his Putter, certain his shot was on, even though he knew it was long. He paid little attention as the others zig zagged across the fairway wending their way toward the green. He was too focused on his own downhill putt to keep track of the others. But after marking his ball for his final 3-footer a bad thing happened.

Strange had hit Driver again and apparently hit his tee shot too long into the deep stuff. He only advanced it about 30 yards when his club caught in the thick rough. The 90-yard approach was only a little too long but left him a sidehill 10-footer. When he hit the putt, he didn't hit it high enough and it slid by on the low side, about 3 inches below the hole. For no apparent reason (frustration?) Strange reached down and swatted the ball with his club AWAY from the hole giving himself the Gimme. You could tell just before he backhanded it that he realized what he was doing and tried to stop it, but he couldn't stop the club momentum and the ball rolled about 12 feet down the slope. Dorsey watched closely as Strange realized what he had done. The ball now lay about 13 feet away, not 3 inches. He lined up the putt too quickly and missed it. He tapped that one in for a 7, not the 5 he should have had. Dorsey then made his 3-footer and everyone turned and walked quietly to the cart. There wasn't any discussion since Strange knew what he had done. Dorsey could almost see the steam rising from his ears.

The next batch of holes were played in relative silence. After all, Strange was the official scorekeeper, and he had just done something really dumb. He was fuming, and all Dorsey wanted to do was stay away from him and concentrate on his own game. Hopper and Acton pretty much stayed to their side of the fairway too. Strange was an 8-handicap, and had thrown away 4 strokes in the first 2 holes. Dorsey had been there and knew it was up to the player to pull himself together. He tried to be supportive and call out good stuff when Strange hit good shots. A chump here, a fat one there, a few skulled wedges and a few missed putts, but overall things seemed to be moving along.

Number 6 was what should have been an easy Par 3. It didn't set up well for Dorsey's eye, so he managed to hit it short, chump a chip and 3-putt for a 5, his first Double. The Par 5 #7 was the number 11 handicap, 468 yards. Dorsey hit 3 good shots back to back and two decent putts. Par! He picked up another Double Bogey on #8, the number 3-handicap.

As Dorsey's group neared the #9 tee box at the precipice of the hill, they could see the group ahead just off to the right where the cart path curved before heading down the steep decent across the creek to the green. One of those players was out of his cart pounding what had to be a snake with what appeared to be a 7-iron. He didn't just hit it once or twice but swung the club violently 15 or 20 times. Apparently, the snake skin was tougher than the guy anticipated. Later after they had hit, his group had cruised slowly past the snake which was still writhing a little, not quite dead yet. Duece Acton pronounced it a blacksnake and suggested that someone should put it out of its misery though he wasn't going to be the one to do it. No one else in their group volunteered either. They all agreed that it was somewhat of a shame to kill a blacksnake, since they tended to chase off the copperheads that were known to inhabit Hanging Tree.

The snake incident rattled Dorsey a little bit but he did manage to Bogey #9. Strange had recovered and begun to play better. The primary issue that he had was that he hadn't played the course much and kept hitting too much club or leaving himself on the high side of greens which made putting very delicate. Hopper seemed to be playing well. Acton had a good short game and could really putt. Dorsey liked watching players like that and always hoped he could learn something from them.

The 10th hole is a 436-yard Par 5. You aim at a giant uphill slope where you are hitting crosswise just to get it on the fairway. The second shot is from an extreme slope and you can't really see where you are supposed to hit it. Dorsey had chumped his second shot on this hole several times before, mostly due to the extreme uphill stance. Today he managed to hit it smoothly to the top of the hill. Strange had hit his drive and found the fairway but chumped his club into the hillside as Dorsey had done so many times before.

Dorsey hit his 6-iron, which was too much club and he hit it well, into the fringe on the little mound behind the pin. Strange dumped his in the bunker. By the time they walked off it was Dorsey with a 6, Hopper with a 6, and Acton got his Par – the guy could really play. Strange had another Double Bogey. For him, it was a long frustrating precursor to the back nine. Dorsey wasn't unhappy with 6.

Number 11 yielded pars for Acton and Strange, Bogey for Hopper and a really stupid no-excuse Double for Dorsey. Number 12 was Dorsey's highlight for the day. Uphill Par 3, 167 yards. Dorsey stayed down on a Rescue club and swung smoothly. A light mist had started to fall so the sky was grey and he couldn't absolutely follow the flight, but he could tell he had hit it well. As the ball melded into the grey sky he just yelled "Go!". It was on a good line.

When they pulled up, there were two balls on the green. Dorsey had already grabbed his putter, he was sure he was one of them. As they moved toward the green, he and Acton glanced at each other. Nearing the ball furthest from the pin, Acton said "This one's me. You're the one at the cup." Dorsey's heart beat faster as he neared his ball and confirmed it was indeed his. The ball was less than a foot from the hole. He marked it and moved behind it surveying what he had left. Often with Birdie putts Dorsey preferred that they be at least 4-6 feet so that you didn't feel as bad if you missed it. With this one missing it would really be a bummer.

Dorsey took a deep breath, took nothing for granted, probably took too long over the putt and rolled it in for his Birdie 2. Eureka! On the way to the cart he told the others that he was proud of the shot but prouder of making the one-foot putt. He was. And glad he hadn't missed it. He knew that whatever went on for the rest of the day he would have this little nugget with him to keep his spirits up. He had made a great shot and finished it off with the putt. He wondered what he would win for the "closest to the pin."

Number 13 was a 489- yard Par 5 and the longest hole on the course. Dorsey was tempted to offer advice, but he didn't. He wasn't sure if it was "legal" to give other guys advice and just as important, wasn't sure if they wanted it. He had offered course advice during the Practice Round, but that was different. This was the Tournament and he wasn't sure what was allowed. He kept his mouth shut.

On #13 Strange hit his drive hard. For his second shot, he was about 240 yards out. He had a look around the corner and could see the right side of the green. He swung hard and pulled it just a bit. The ball was hit high and stayed in the air a long time. It looked like it had a chance to fade back to the green, but no such luck. After an eternity in the air they could all hear the crack as it came down short and left and in the trees. As Strange drove to the green, Dorsey could feel the heat coming off him. Dorsey and Acton did a cursory walk to help him look for his ball while Hopper hit up, but they knew it was futile. They did find the ball. But it was 12 feet down the hill in the leaves against a fallen limb. Strange took his unplayable, then shanked a chip that barely stayed on the hill. He had to chip again from the fringe and three putts later had an 8.

Dorsey was shaky on the pitch-shot, but it did make it to the green. Two putts later he had another dumb Double Bogey that was clearly self-induced. Hoppers chip had climbed the hill and he managed to get up and down for his Bogey. Acton was cool as a cucumber rolling in his Birdie. Strange could barely watch as the others finished up, clearly burning inside.

As they went to the 14th tee, things were quiet in Dorsey's cart. He knew how best to play the 14th but still wasn't comfortable offering advice. Strange stepped purposely to the tee with his Driver. He hit the ball hard, but it began to fade right halfway up the hill. It. It didn't make it all the way down to the water, but it came close.

Strange was away and chumped his shot up the hill so that it rolled halfway back down the fairway. It was on the extreme uphill slope. Since he hadn't lost his turn yet, he lunged at his third shot that appeared to be long, way past the pin.

Dorsey walked to the top of the hill onto the green and continued toward the back. There was one ball visible, but Dorsey wasn't sure if it was him or Strange. As he got closer, he saw the red Swoosh. Dorsey had gotten four cases of Red Nike PD long balls when he left the bank five years before. He liked them because they were distinctive, and he had never seen anyone else play them. He didn't have to mark them which made things simple. After Nike had announced they were going out of the equipment business he had found them marked down at a local Muni and bought out all they had. He figured he had at least a three to four-year supply and didn't have to worry about marking his ball. The red Swoosh was easy to spot.

They found Strange's ball 10 yards over the green. Strange's hockey stick features were on full display by this time, arms pumping, shoulders thrust forward, scowl on his face, not happy. Dorsey moved quietly to the side while Strange lined up his 4th shot. He skulled it. The ball skid all of the way down the green and kept going, probably 25 yards down the hill. It was still his turn. Strange stalked to his ball, though his shoulders were slumped more than before. He punched a lackadaisical chip up the hill to about 12 feet. Dorsey lagged his putt down the hill but was timid and left it 3 feet short. Dorsey was next and had to settle for a 4-inch tap in and a 5. Strange missed his 12-footer and tapped in for his 7, Triple Bogey. The cart was quiet again as they pulled past the clubhouse headed across the street to #16.

Jeanette had her card table set up in the cart collection area offering Raffle Tickets, water, chips, and crackers. Dorsey spoke up "Hey can we stop here a minute?" Strange curled up his lip to say something but let it go and pulled to the side. Jeanette offered Dorsey a big hug though he was mindful of the humidity and how sticky and smelly he must be. Jeanette didn't seem to pay it any mind. The other cart pulled up and Jeanette gave them a hug as well. Strange stayed near the cart fussing in his golf bag to get ready for the next set of holes.

Dorsey gave Jeanette $14 for 20 Raffle Tickets. Hopper gave her $7 for 10 and Acton gave her another $7. Dorsey was proud of these boys for their support of Jeanette. He got some chips and offered to buy something for Strange but was shaken off. Hopper and Acton bought some stuff, climbed back in their cart and away they went.

As they rounded the clubhouse Strange piped up "You sweet on her?"

Dorsey almost dropped the chips he was trying to open and looked at him "Why would you say that?"

"It's pretty well known that you buy her Raffle Tickets and give 'em back if you win."

Dorsey couldn't believe it "That happened once!"

Strange muttered back "Well, people just talk that's all. She is a widow. And a lot of guys ain't sure what she's doing out here anyway. You got a wife?"

Dorsey held up his left hand with the Platinum band on it. "I'm taken. And she's certainly not threatened by Jeanette. I've told her about Jeanette and she thinks it's kind of cool and gutsy for Jeanette to be out here in the hot sun with all of these smelly guys, trying to make the world a little better place. That's how I feel too."

"Huh." Was all that Strange had to offer. It was the first and longest conversation that they had had all day. Certainly the closest thing to a personal conversation. Once again Dorsey was left inwardly shaking his head trying to figure this group out.

Dorsey didn't like to keep his running score during a round and it was difficult when you started in the middle of a Nine. Mentally he knew he was playing well and better yet, scoring well. He was pretty sure he had at least three Pars and a couple of Bogeys. And no Triples. He tried to put this out of his mind but couldn't help a glance at the scorecard in front of Strange. He couldn't read it as they were bouncing toward the 15th tee, so he turned back to the business at hand.

Fifteen was another shortish Par 3, another downhill thing off a cliff. He hit the 6-iron well, it did the high fade he liked and settled to the far right side, 20 feet, pin high. Strange hit his long into the stuff off the back. Dorsey ran his lag putt across the green on the high side and was pleased to see it settle two feet directly below the cup. Strange had trouble with the wire grass and left it just on the fringe to the top of the

hole. His lag putt ran well past and he missed the uphill comebacker –
another Double for Strange.

Strange was having a bad day for an 8-handicap and Dorsey could
feel him getting ready to take it out on someone. They had #16, #17,
#18, #1, #2 and #3 left to play. Dorsey had a decent round going and
didn't want to get his mind off track.

On #16 Strange provided Dorsey a good chuckle. They had hit down
the hill to a clearing about 110 yards from the pin with an open look
at the flag. As Strange dropped Dorsey off at his ball he muttered "I
must have dropped my headcover back there" and wheeled the cart
back up the path. Dorsey watched as he rode in circles for a while then
turned the cart back toward Dorsey. Dorsey asked him, "Did you find the
headcover?" But Strange merely ducked his head and shook it side to
side.

As Dorsey walked past the cart to his ball, he noticed a flash of red
that seemed out of place. Moving around to Strange's side of the cart
he tapped an item that was tucked under Strange's armpit. It was the
headcover. It had been there the whole time. Strange was so tight by this
time that he couldn't even feel his arm pressed against his body. Dorsey
chuckled inwardly as he moved to his ball. But he kept it to himself.
Strange was having one of those days.

The rest of the round went quickly. For Dorsey it was Bogey on #16,
Par on #17 and a really good Par on #18. The atmosphere in the cart
was still tense so where he could he would take a few clubs and light out
toward his ball.While the others batted it back and forth he had time to
collect himself, focus on the shot ahead and execute as best he could.

When they made the crossover back to #1 Dorsey reminded himself
to mentally refocus for the three holes they had left to play. It almost
worked. He Bogeyed the Par 5 1st, Bogeyed the Par 4 2nd but then did
have a sloppy Double on the Par 3 3rd. All in all, he knew it had been
an improvement. One Triple, a handful of Pars and a bunch of Bogeys.
That was his game on a good day. It had been a good day.

Dorsey practically broke his neck trying to look at the Scorecard on
the way in since Strange was apparently in no hurry to add up what
he had done. When they pulled up next to the cart area, Strange took

the card off the steering wheel and bent over as he added them all up.
Dorsey had to wait for the verdict. Strange finally offered up the card
– Acton 78, Hopper 92, Dorsey 88 and Strange 95. Dorsey was tickled.
It wasn't that "all that hard work had paid off" because Dorsey didn't
practice. More to the point, he had kept his wits about him and played a
respectable round. Finally.

# CHAPTER 9

## Hanging Tree Results

**"Take two weeks off and then quit the game."**

Jimmy Demaret's advice to an unhappy duffer

2:30 PM
Hanging Tree Clubhouse Snack Bar

Dorsey didn't take any chances with his clubs this time. After shaking hands with the other three, he picked his bag off the cart and headed for the parking lot. He unloaded his pockets of golf balls, tees and ball markers and shoved them approximately where they belonged in the bag. He retrieved his phone, keys and sunglasses. He pulled his flip flops from the trunk and dropped them to the ground. He hoisted the clubs into the trunk, then pitched his shoes in behind them, and stepped into the flip flops. Very deliberately he shut the trunk and hit the clicker so that he could hear the horn sound confirming the car was locked.

As he turned and headed back to the Clubhouse he immediately ran into Pharratt. Dorsey blurted out "Howdya do man?". Admittedly he was excited to talk about his own round, not necessarily Pharratt's.

Pharratts' expression didn't change much, it never did. Just a twitch of his lower lip and "Oh, same ole same ole, a 99."

Dorsey wanted to share his good humor and came back with; "Well man, it's a tough course. 99 isn't a bad score."

Pharratt looked up and asked; "How about you?"

Dorsey was only too glad to respond. "Look I felt awful whining at you all through our practice round last week. Today I pulled out an 88. And I give you all the credit for listening to my moaning and helping me get out all the bad shots. I appreciate it."

Pharratt looked back, not knowing how to respond and offered "Good for you, good for you."

Dorsey made his way into the Clubhouse where a good crowd had gathered. He saw Dana Blades near the bar and made his way in that direction. They waited in line and Dorsey slid ahead so that he could buy Blades a Mountain Lite. While they were waiting Dorsey asked him "So… howd it go?"

Blades came back with, "74. That and 50 cents will get me nothing. It was a fun day, the course was in good shape, I have no complaints."

Dorsey winced. Since Blades was a 4-handicap that meant a net 70. Some high handicapper would certainly clip him. Dorsey paused in mid-thought realizing with 88 and 22 strokes, he would net out at 66 and beat him by 4. He didn't mention this, just handed Blades his beer, tapped him on the shoulder and offered "Good round man."

By this time the big spreadsheet with all the Gross and Net Scores was being tabulated. Randy Ridgeline, George George and Proudfoot were all huddled around it with Sharpies, reading from cards and relaying scores back and forth. Naturally Dorsey's eye searched for his name. He saw the Gross – 88 but next to it was the net – 68. Wait a minute 88 – 22 was 66, not 68. And then he remembered. As a Rookie on the Tour, Proudfoot put in a floor on what he could score. He knew it early on, so it wasn't a surprise. Even with 22 strokes the lowest score allowed would be a 68, at least until his handicap was fully established by playing the first 4 Tour events. Hanging Tree was the 4th. At this point Dorsey almost wished he had blown up again. It would have been better for the following events' handicap. Whatever. He would have to take consolation in the fact that he had a good day. A 68 wasn't going to finish in the money, not with all the strokes given to the field. Oh well, enjoy the personal satisfaction. Keep your whining to yourself.

Dorsey positioned himself off to the side with his Mountain Lite, watching as Proudfoot and his posse finished filling in the big spreadsheet for Flights 1, 2 and 3. As they finished the winners emerged and the non-winners drifted away. Dorsey was playing it cool so that he not seem too anxious about collecting his prize for Closest to the

Hole on #12. When Proudfoot picked up the markers for the various holes, Dorsey's ears perked up. When Proudfoot announced; "Closest to the pin on number 12 is Ray Bugman." Dorsey almost fell off the porch. Bugman stood up, collected the envelope with the free round at Hanging Tree inside and said to no one in particular "I live in Radford. I'm not likely to be back here soon. Does anyone want this?" Dorsey then had to watch as a guy across the table from Bugman said "Sure" and reached out for what should have been DORSEY'S free round!

Dorsey was dumbfounded and speechless. How could Bugman have hit it inside of Dorsey? His shot was only a foot out! Later Dorsey would kick himself for not marking "1 foot" or "12 inches" next to his name on the marker. Either Bugman had hit his to inside a foot or more likely, a later group had come along and in order to putt had moved the marker to the side and forgotten to put it back. By the time Bugman had hit his shot the marker could have been ten feet away. Maybe he was innocent. It was the only justification Dorsey could come up with as to why he hadn't won. No way Bugman had hit inside of him. There wasn't much to be done about it without looking like a jerk. Dorsey just shook his head and pitched his empty can into the trash.

Dorsey moved across the room to the outside porch. There he could spot a batch of wives including Irene Proudfoot and Halle Hopper. Fawn Ridgeline and Jamie George were grouped off to the side seriously bending the ear of Carlotta Ferry. He couldn't see the expression on Fawn's face, but he also couldn't miss the scowl on Carlotta's. She glared at him from across the porch and Dorsey pretended to wave at someone over her shoulder. With that, Carlotta stormed off the porch towards the parking lot. Dorsey stayed put. After a few minutes he turned completely around and took in the view of McAffee's Knob.

After feigning interest in the scenery, he turned back around, only to run directly into Steve Martin and Jeanette. Both of them were sporting bummed out, stern expressions. Jeannette appeared to have been crying, with her face all screwed up, ready to re-open the floodgates at any moment. "What's up guys?" Dorsey offered.

As Jeanette looked at the floor, Martin looked at Dorsey, apparently seeing him for the first time. "Jeanette's coin bag is gone."

"Gone?" was all Dorsey could think to say.

"Yeah, well actually it's her money bag. You know, one of those canvas bank bags. It had all of her money in it. It's Purple. And it's gone."

Dorsey looked at Jeanette, whose head was still facing the floor and asked "Gone from where? When is the last time you saw it?"

Since Jeanette's lower lip was quivering too much for her to speak Martin continued for her; "Gone from the card table downstairs. Gone when she walked the twenty feet to the ice machine down there after the Tournament. Gone after she had collected her money for the day and gone before she could walk up here with it."

"You didn't go to your car or tuck it somewhere or put it somewhere for safe keeping or anything like that?" Dorsey was trying to help.

"We've been over all that. It's gone." Said Martin.

"Well, it'll turn up, don't you think?" tried Dorsey.

"It needs to turn up in the next five minutes before Proudfoot announces the Raffle" Martin answered.

"Ouch." Said Dorsey "How much was in it?

Finally Jeanette was able to mutter; "Probably close to $200 with my drink and chips sales but definitely $120 or so in Raffle money. That's the usual amount."

Dorsey looked at them both and sighed to himself. As he reached for his back pocket he repeated back to Jeanette "So the Raffle winnings should be about $60 is that right?" She just shook her head up and down a few times but didn't get an answer out. Dorsey opened his wallet and looked at the two of them. He peeled out three $20 bills and handed them to Jeanette. As she started to protest, he held up his hand. "Let's just get through this Raffle today, OK? We'll worry about the rest of this later. I don't want to see you go down in flames. The bag and the money will likely show up. Just take this for now, try to stop crying, put on a brave face and let's move it along. OK?"

Jeanette leaned in for what looked like would be a serious embrace, but Dorsey stopped her. "No worries Jeanette. But folks already seem to think you and I have something going on. Let's keep this businesslike for now. Go do the Raffle and we'll figure out the details tomorrow or some other time."

Jeanette did her best to dry her eyes and compose herself before turning away from Dorsey and Martin. She pushed her shoulders back and moved toward Proudfoot at the Scorers' table. For some unknown reason, she had gotten in the habit of recording the numbers that were sold for any day, along with keeping the matching stubs in the bag. She didn't have the stubs, but she had the numbers. By the time Proudfoot was ready for the drawing, she had scribbled down some numbers and it was easy enough to fake drawing them out of her hat. "09573" was called with no takers. Then "09628" was a hit and Briscoe Sisson stepped forward to accept his $60. He stuck it in his pocket after a hug from Jeanette. Before the crowd could break up Proudfoot announced." You guys can read I hope. If you see you name up here and it looks like you won something, hang around and come pick it up. For the rest of you see you at Blackbird on July 30th. "

As the crowd melted away, Jeanette rejoined Dorsey and Martin. She was crying again, but not quite as hard. She went to hug Dorsey again, but he leaned back and held her off with one hand. Martin looked at Dorsey and said "That was quick thinking and a lifesaver. You didn't have to do that."

Dorsey smiled at them both "Ah, but I did have to do that. No one else was around to do it. And it needed to be done."

Martin and Jeanette just looked at Dorsey without saying more so he offered. "Jeanette you seem to be on a run of bad luck. I just hope it's really bad luck and not bad actors. Martin, we need to pay a little more attention to Jeanette and give her some kind of security support. Once with the windshield is bad luck. Twice with the money bag is worse luck. I really don't want to see strike three for Jeanette here. We should think about if we can help her change her luck, just in case it's someone, not bad luck."

Martin and Jeanette stared back at Dorsey blankly again as he headed down the steps toward his car. For at least the fourth time in his experience with GRITS he was leaving the course confused and with more questions than answers.

# CHAPTER 10

## Practice with Junior

**"Probably I'm a hell of a lot more famous for being the guy who hit the golf ball on the moon than the first guy in space."**

Apollo 14 Astronaut Alan Shepard

Great Falls

July 24

Beautiful day in the mid 80's, low humidity, good visibility

Junior Loaf was able to meet up with Dorsey for a practice round at Great Falls. The drive was just under an hour from Roanoke. Junior had made his way across the mountain to Floyd to meet up. They both got there around 10 on a warm morning that would get warmer. It was 10 degrees cooler than Roanoke, and the air up here felt thinner and the sun felt closer.

Great Falls is an old-style kind of place that you wish there were more of. Nice unimposing little clubhouse with snack bar. Sweet little swimming pool area about half filled with the high-pitched sounds of kids' play and splashes from cannonballs. There were two plastic slides into the pool. You could be pretty sure that a game of Marco Polo was about ready to break out at any minute.

Dorsey was in the mood for a light game, having become tuckered out from the competitive aspects of the GRITS. He was tired of " playin' 'em all down", not taking any Mulligans, and having to putt them all out. He felt like he needed an easy day in the country which was why it was fun that Junior had been able to join him. They paid their fee inside, found their way to a cart and pulled onto the first tee-box. Ahead

on the 1st green they could see a threesome of ladies, but they knew that
they wouldn't catch up with the ladies any time soon, or at all. The guy
at the desk had told them that these ladies played there at least three
times per week, that they all had their own carts, that they shot in the
80's and that Junior and Dorsey would be lucky to keep up with them.
Perfect. He also explained that there weren't any tee times scheduled
behind them, so take your time. Perfect on top of perfect.

Dorsey teed up first and hit a low burner to the left side of the
fairway. Junior hit his first one in the woods and reteed. His second ball
had a high arc but got a nice bounce and ended up just to the right and
behind Dorsey. They were off.

Dorsey barely kept score, but he didn't want to infect his game with a
lot of Mulligans and Gimmes either. He wanted a break from the GRITS
tour but also didn't want to get too far from the discipline of it. Junior
hadn't been playing a lot, so Dorsey encouraged a liberal amount of
Mulligans and generous Gimmes for him.

Mostly they just played along and caught up about stuff. Dorsey
explained as to how he and Luisa were doing just fine, thank you,
and that everything in his life was hunky-dory. Junior started talking
about the goings-on with the Mountain Valley Pipeline and how folks
up around Floyd were beside themselves after three years of fighting a
pipeline that no one wanted. He explained how some of the families
that he knew personally were dumbfounded that land which had
been in their families for generations could be invaded by a bunch of
exploitive outsiders that no one could identify. He got pretty worked up
talking about the use of Eminent Domain against private landowners
for Private Profit. The Blue Ridge Parkway is the Number One tourist
attraction in the United States and here we were carving it up like it
was nothing. It wasn't right, it wasn't American, and we should all be up
in arms about it. Dorsey didn't say a lot, he just nodded and listened.
Junior's points couldn't have been more apparent, and it was a sad state
of affairs.

Dorsey parred #1, the short Par 4 then Bogeyed the 2nd, the longish
Par 4. Never could seem to get his tee shot past that tree to have a clear
shot at the green. He Bogeyed #3, the Par 3, after leaving it short and

in the bunker. Junior went Bogey, Bogey, but Doubled the Par 3 since he had gotten pretty worked up by this time and had swung harder than he needed to on his Tee shot. As they turned toward #4 Junior had pretty much used up his anger at the Pipeline folks and was tired of talking about it. He had been immersed in this thing for months. He had known a number of the affected families since childhood, and in addition had several of those same families as clients. He just sort of ran out of gas about the pipeline and got a little quiet.

They both hit their drives on # 4 and as Junior slumped back in the cart he huffed at Dorsey "So how about you and the GRITS tour?"

Dorsey started composing his answer as he walked to his ball. He only had about 98 yards to the pin which should have been a nice two-thirds 9-Iron. He was organizing his thoughts instead of paying attention to the shot so that he got under it, hit it high and short, still about 7 yards short of the green. He was still thinking about where to start when he chumped his chip shot, left it short, then left his lag putt short and rolled the next one by before tapping in for his first Double Bogey of the round. Junior meanwhile had been able to ignore most of this floundering but still coming off of his Mountain Valley High, skulled his second shot but at least recovered for a 5.

Dorsey finally got out a sentence as they headed to the 5th tee. "There's a lot going on with the GRITS Tour. Maybe not life and death stuff, but plenty of odd stuff that I can't make sense of. I'm beginning to think that some of the parts that seem random and odd are connected somehow and that I'm missing the big picture. "

Junior encouraged him to continue "Like...?"

Dorsey did; "Well, starting with Proudfoot. He does a great job of putting this Tour together and we play a lot of nice courses that otherwise we wouldn't be on. Everyone agrees with that. He's got Ridgeline, George George and a couple of other flunkies around him that seem to do his bidding. Not everyone's a Proudfoot fan either. He rigs the handicaps so that the better players feel like they're shut out of a chance to win, and meanwhile he tends to place or show at every event. It really upsets the better golfers to lose to high handicappers time after time and I see their point."

"But you like the Tour?"

"I do. I joined to meet people and play pretty courses. That's working for me, so I shouldn't have any beefs. I'm a terrible golfer but even I'm competitive and would like to feel like I have a chance to win, and I don't know if I really do. I'm just trying to shut up, lower my expectations and enjoy the ride."

"Hmmm" was about all that Junior could offer. "OK, what else?"

"What else, what else?" Dorsey repeated as he thought what else. "Well, Ok, some of the players are just weird too. I had this guy Pharratt that I played with at London Bridges and I thought he cheated, then he was really nice to me and asked me to play a practice round with him, and now I think he may be creepy because of the way he acts with Jeanette."

Juniors eyebrow went up at this "Jeanette?"

Dorsey stared him down with "Yeah, Jeanette. She's this nice girl that shows up to sell Raffle Tickets and snacks and gives the proceeds to Alzheimer's. She's just nice and tries hard but I feel sorry for her being the only woman around all of these men out there. She's got a lot of spunk."

Junior felt compelled to ask; "You sweet on her?"

Dorsey practically leaped across the cart at him "No man, you're just as bad as the rest of these guys! I've only got eyes for Luisa. There is no way on this earth I am ever going to do anything to mess up life with Luisa. In fact, I told Luisa all about her and what's going on with Jeanette and the Tour. I just feel a soft spot for this girl and now I'm getting the impression that Pharratt may be creeping her out."

"Ok, Ok, take it easy. Don't get defensive. I know you're solid with Luisa. I'm just trying to get the straight scoop, that's all." Junior felt defensive himself now.

Dorsey continued. "It's not just Pharratt. It seems that some of the players' wives aren't too crazy about Jeanette's presence on the GRITS Tour either. Maynard Ferry's wife Carlotta has whipped some of the other player's wives into a dither about Jeanette too. George George actually went off on me how he doesn't think she should be out there because she's diverting money from the Tour! The mindsets of some of these people completely baffle me. It looks to be like a storm is building that could be bad news for Jeanette. Look, she's had her car window broken and somebody stole her Alzheimer's money bag, just at the last two events. It doesn't look good for her and I'm wondering if I'm the only one who's seeing a trend here,"

Now it was Junior's turn to ponder the events. "Wow, do you think you're the only one connecting the dots?"

"I don't know man, and I don't know if they're dots or Ink Blots. Maybe I'm hallucinating. Maybe it's just me."

They rode on in silence and Dorsey didn't see a Par for a while. Like the round at London Bridges, he got to see the course yet didn't play it very well. They got a six pack of Mountain Lite at the turn and things started to look up. By the middle of the back nine they were in a better mood and their round reflected it. Since they had each unburdened themselves of their major worries, the round flowed.

Without an acknowledgement from either of them the golf got better and the competition heated up. On #12 and #13 they traded Bogeys. On #14 Dorsey uncorked a big drive and followed it up with a smooth (substitute Taylor Made) 6-iron that took a big hop in front of the green and rolled 12 feet from the Blue Pin. He missed the Birdie putt but was pleased with an easy tap-in Par. Junior's hole was played a little more routinely. With a decent drive, 2nd shot on the front fringe, a good lag putt but missed the 4-footer and had to settle for Bogey.

Number 15 was 141 yards, a downhill Par 3. Dorsey pushed his 6-iron to the right and thankfully just above the bunker, Pin High. Junior's 7-iron was a little short, but on the dance floor. He watched as Dorsey hit an indifferent pitch to about 8 feet. Junior had to lean into his putt to get it up the hill and was pleased to see it break right and stop 18 inches below the hole. Dorsey took a long time lining up his putt but rolled it smooth and heard the gratifying sound of it falling into the cup. Junior felt the heat as he bent over his 18- incher but rolled it in as well. Dorsey up by 1 in the unannounced competition.

The 16th was a short Par 4 and both made un-stressful Pars. Dorsey retained the hill for his drive on the 427-yard uphill Par 5 17th. He tried to kill his drive and mostly succeeded in pushing it right with a high slice into the thick stuff halfway up the hill. Junior took a more conservative cut and was rewarded with a straight ball short of Dorsey but in the fairway. On his second shot he made the top of the hill leaving himself only 125 or so to the Pin. Dorsey lashed at his ball in the weeds and was only able to advance it 75 yards or so, though it was in the fairway. His third shot was blind up the hill and he caught it good but pulled it. He wasn't sure what he was left with. As they crested the hill Junior was enthused to see he had nothing but fairway between him and the green and he hit a smooth 8-iron down the hill to about 25 feet right of the Pin. Dorsey was more left than he had thought and had an awkward angle across a trap with the green running away from him. Taking care not to dump it in the trap he hit it too hard and it scooted all of the way across the green. Pin high but still 30 feet away. He took his time on the putt but yanked it a little and it curled beneath the hole to 3 feet. Junior was cool as he lagged his putt to the Pin and finished with his Par 5. Dorsey made the 3-footer for a 6 but the "match" that hadn't been discussed at all was tied.

Number 17 was a dogleg left long, long Par 5 to an elevated green. Dorsey hit a good drive around the corner that Junior matched. Junior hit an indifferent fairway wood that drifted into the thick stuff while Dorsey uncorked a smooth 3-wood that ended up 147 from the Pin. Junior couldn't muscle his third shot onto the green, but it was in the front fringe. Dorsey stayed down on his uphill 6-iron and it found the front, but a long way from the hole. Junior made a nice chip to about 7 feet. Dorsey hit a very weak lag, missed the remaining 8-footer before Dorsey missed his putt as well. They both tapped in for Bogeys. Match still tied.

The 18th is a 328-yard Par 4, the 14-handicap hole. Junior had taken honors and laced his best drive of the day down the middle. Dorsey managed an OK drive, but it was short of Junior's. He only had 117 yards to the hole but came up a little on his 8-Iron and thinned it to the back of the green, but it stayed on. Junior only had 98 yards to the Pin and hit a smooth 9-Iron that never left the flag. It was high and bounced once before rolling to within 6 feet of the Pin. Dorsey did his best on a long lag putt but it slid by 3 feet to the low side of the Pin. Junior stayed cool on his putt and made their first Birdie of the day to win the match. Dorsey had played the last 5 holes at one over Par and Junior had done it in even Par.

Neither one made any effort to total the scorecard since it had been a beautiful day and they had been able to set their cares aside. Totaling the score would have been beside the point. When they parted in the parking lot to head their different directions they had a nice fist bump and patted each other on the back, wishing a safe drive. All the way home Dorsey couldn't help but wonder. Was he making things up or was there really something going on with the GRITS Tour that he couldn't quite get his mind around?

# CHAPTER 11

## Blackbird

**"Golf is a good walk Spoiled"** Many attribute the quote to Mark Twain, notably author John Feinstein who wrote a definitive book on Golf that carried that title. With research it can be determined that the origin of the quote is murkier, as with many, many things surrounding Golf.

**"Without betting, golf is nothing more than a long walk with three other liars."** Titanic Thompson - "The Man Who Bet on Everything"

July 30 – Monday
Blackbird Country Club
Par 72
5665 yards from Gold Tees
Slope 66.7 / Rating 72.2
64 degrees. Steady rain. Winds gusting to 15 mph

Early in the morning, multiple times before getting in the car Dorsey had checked his email, and the Weather Channel. The forecast hadn't been good. He had driven the 53 miles to the course alone and it had taken over an hour what with the trucks on I-81, and winding through the stoplights downtown to get to the course. He was sure that they would cancel, or at least back the tournament up an hour, maybe start at 11 or 12. Pulling into a parking space and stepping out of the car, two golfers in rain gear and ponchos walked toward his car. "What's the report?" he asked weakly.

"We're playing." Was the reply.

He got his bag out of the back, put on his black shoes, which he felt wouldn't get quite as ruined as his white and tan ones, and shuffled toward the clubhouse. He stacked his clubs on the rack outside and went in to pay. George George was at a little card table on the back deck, took his money without a word and made a check mark next to his name. "Hole number 7" was all he said, without even looking up. Dorsey could picture him with a corn cob pipe and a sailor hat.

Dorsey shuffled away and tried to get his bearings. In a way this wasn't bad news. One key reason he had come at all is that the schedule indicated a rain date that he couldn't make, he would be traveling with Luisa. It was now or never as far as playing Blackbird. Oddly he also felt that the conditions were the same for everyone and if he could man up and play through it, he would be pleased with himself. If he kept his head on straight and his expectations in line, maybe he could even score Ok.

The week before the tournament Dorsey had Howard Eugene in town, a buddy from Florida. He had driven down from Michigan to check out Dorsey's new situation, and particularly satisfy his curiosity about Luisa. Howard and Dorsey had gotten in a round at Blue Bells and one at Hanging Tree. The fairways had been drenched, it was cart paths only and they had to play between rain clouds, but they did manage to get in full rounds at each place. They had played the Gold Senior tees and Dorsey had played well. Rolling them over and taking a few Gimmes he had recorded an 80 and a 79! He knew these weren't real scores because he had taken two Mulligans at Hanging Tree and one at Blue Bells. Even so, the scores amounted to an 84 and an 81. Dorsey was encouraged.

Wright Strange had called for a practice round at Blackbird on Friday after Howard left. Dorsey was skeptical of playing three times in one week and of jinxing how well he was playing. There was no good reason not to make the drive and at least see the course. He didn't know Strange that well but since he was still the new kid in town, he was always open to anyone with a friendly invitation. Strange had even offered to drive. He didn't play as well as he had at the familiar courses but at the end of the day the card showed a 92. He felt like he had his game under control and had shaken off the tentativeness and jitters and was ready to play. Except for the rain…

As he waited with the others Dorsey took in the surroundings.
Blackbird was a step up from the courses that GRITS had played so far.
It wasn't just a guys' enclave, with a minimal snack bar and not much
else. It was a Country Club in the original parlance of the word. Built in
1956, with the architecture of the day but updated and added onto over
time. Outside was a nice throwback pool area with its own snack bar,
diving board and lifeguard on duty. On a sunny day you could almost
pick out the Prom Queen from the group of skinny teenagers clustered
around.

In addition to the more typical guys' snack bar there was a restaurant
with white table cloths and nice views of the putting green and
mountain ridges beyond. Waiters in black and white were clearing the
breakfast tables and resetting for lunch. Off the "Men's Grill" was a
card room tucked between the Grill and the locker room. Adjacent to
the Dining Room was another open room for meetings, receptions and
the like. In the outer hallway Dorsey noticed that the Kiwanis met every
Wednesday for lunch and the Chamber met monthly as well. It was a
sweet place, a reminder of kinder, gentler times.

Circling back to the porch, Dorsey ran into Marvin Pharratt and they
exchanged pleasantries. He saw Steve Martin across the room and they
nodded at each other. He got a Mountain Lite and went to sit under the
covered deck and take in the proceedings. Most guys were grumbling as
to how crazy they were to try this, with varying degrees of optimism or
not. There was an array of ponchos, windbreakers, multiple caps stacked
on top of each other, any creative means that might keep the water out.
They all knew that their efforts were in vain, they were going to get wet.
Wet to the bone. Mostly they just made sure their laces were tight and
put on their game faces as best they could.

Proudfoot took over the "Mr. Microphone" and congratulated those
in attendance for being men about the whole thing. He noted that there
were a significant number of no-shows, so that he and Ridgeline were
adjusting foursomes to make the field as compact as possible. The next
day when Dorsey reviewed the scores and attendance, he would count
40 no-shows out of the 120-man field with 7 more "WD's" (withdrawals)

as the round went on. Yes, absolutely it would be cart paths only. Rangers would be out constantly and if the weather lifted and the course drained, they would open select holes as they could. For the foreseeable future, cart paths only.

Proudfoot introduced Jeanette and gave her some props for showing up as well. He pointed to an open-sided wooden Gazebo near the first tee box and told everyone that's where she would be stationed, please support good ole Jeanette, etc. Dorsey glanced down toward the gazebo and immediately felt bad for Jeanette. It was one thing for the golfers to slog through the rain and mud but another thing for her. She would basically be standing still in the rain all day without even the ability to get in and out of a cart, shake off the rain or whatever. She would be a bird in a very wet cage. Oh well, she was a big girl. She could make her choices too.

Ridgeline announced that against his wishes they were going to be allowed to play "Paradise Rules". After a few seconds of silence, he was greeted with "What's Paradise Rules?" from 20 or more voices, so he had to explain. Paradise Rules meant you could lift, clean and place – anywhere – fairways, rough, traps, whatever. If a bunker had standing water, you could move the ball out of the bunker away from the flag and place it there. He explained it as though he had a dirty rag in his mouth and was disgusted that he was being so lenient. Dorsey thought it was a small accommodation for playing in a monsoon. After a few more minutes of muddling around, they were off.

There hadn't been any chitchat between Dorsey's foursome before the round. No one had been in the carts until the last minute. No one had hit balls or rolled putts, putting off the inevitable as long as possible. Casey Frey was driving the cart with Dorsey. The other cart for #7 consisted of Jeff Brumfield and Chandler Hoffman. He had never met Frey, had played with Brumfield once, and had heard of Hoffman. Hoffman was part of the clique of good golfers that hung around the GRITS tour and Briscoe Sisson had mentioned his name a couple of times.

At the first tee his group came together and had a powwow led by Brumfield. He lobbied for everyone to try and make sense of the

"Paradise Rules". Don't cheat but move the ball where you had to in order to get a decent swing without you or the ball being in standing water. He reiterated that everyone should be able to move the ball backward out of the bunkers since they were likely full of water. Dorsey chimed in that, on the rare chance that the ball could be placed in the bunker and it left a better shot than moving it out, they could hit from there. Everyone agreed yes, yes, makes sense as they picked clubs and got ready to hit.

Dorsey had already put rain gloves on both hands. His whole athletic career had been plagued by small hands. He had never gotten any complaints about the supposed correlation between that and other parts of his prowess, but athletically the small hands had been an issue more than once. He could whip a football 35-40 yards as long as it was dry. Basketball wasn't bad as he never could palm a ball anyway so passing and shooting were more a matter of leverage than grip. But golf had been a particular challenge because he absolutely struggled with slick grips. He had oversized grips on his clubs anyway due to the small hands and oncoming arthritis. He basically used a baseball grip on his clubs. Even with this apprehension, he wasn't inclined to make excuses. He viewed the day as a challenge and decided to try and have fun with it. It was 65-70 degrees, so he wasn't going to get pneumonia. He was actually sweating under the layers of golf shirts, rain jackets and ponchos that he kept exchanging as the round went on, looking for the driest of the wet ones.

Number 7 is a downhill Par 3, 136 yards. Dorsey pulled his replacement 6-iron and got ready to hit. Looking down at the Taylor Made, it looked a lot like his lost Ping. The shaft was similar, the head was similar, and it had a new thick grip on it. It mostly felt and looked like the Ping. There was a tiny amount of doubt about it still in the back of his mind, but overall, it was working out.

Brumfield hit first and hit a pretty good ball that cut through the rain and splashed to a stop short and right, but on the green. Hoffman hit next and hit a pure shot that cut through the weather and finished slightly below and ten feet right of the pin. His first good shot of the day, with many to follow.

Dorsey hit next and stayed down on the ball pretty well. He actually swung a little too easy, so the ball drifted high and right just below the back trap to the right of the green but pretty much pin high. Frey did not hit a good shot at all. His ball was also high and never had a chance. It found trees to the right and rear of the green that Dorsey hadn't even noticed before. Those trees really shouldn't have been in play at all. He had to drop from the drop zone short and left of the green, chumped that one, left a long lag putt short as well. He ended up holding the flag with his ball in his pocket and a 6 on the card. Dorsey hit a decent chip that curled 6 feet below the hole partly because of the moisture on the green. He stayed with it, got a two-putt and his Bogey. It was an OK start. Brumfield made a nice lag putt and a nice 4-footer for Par. Hoffman's Birdie putt was good all the way and he had a nice start to his day. For their opening hole it was Birdie, Par, Bogey and "Other".

The short Par 4 #8 was only playing 304 yards. Dorsey hit a low drive that skidded forward 40 yards after it hit the first puddle. He had 106 yards to the green, took an extra club and got it on. Hoffman hit a beautiful drive as if it was a nice sunny day and had another look at Birdie, which he missed. Brumfield played it pretty straight up and got himself another Par. Frey continued his struggles and Dorsey actually lost touch with him for a while. Walking to his ball, back to the cart, walking to his ball, back to the cart. He reached the green where the others stood trying to not pay attention.

Frey hit up, then marked his ball as Dorsey finally had honors to line up his Birdie putt. He didn't think there was much chance of making it but did hit a forceful lag through the puddles and was able to tap-in for his par. Frey putt up after that for what he declared to be a 6. So, for the group, Par, Par, Par, 6. Dorsey wasn't feeling half bad about the way things were going. To this point he had been able to keep his hands on the clubs, hadn't tried to overswing or expect too much. He was almost having fun. Number 9 played out pretty well, a careless Bogey, but not bad. There was another Bogey on #10, but after all, he wasn't expecting but so much.

On #11 the unraveling began. Dorsey got under his 6-iron and hit it high right and short just behind the bunker. With "Paradise Rules" he could lift clean and place so no worries. Except he lost focus in his backswing and dumped it in the bunker. With the Paradise Rules, he put it back to where it was the first time and punched it onto the green about 15 feet below the hole. Missed the putt, so he ended up with a dumb Double Bogey.

On #12 he thought he was keeping his head down and swinging easy but pulled his drive into the trees 60 yards ahead of the tee box. This wasn't actually where the damage was done. He hit down on his shot from under the trees and only advanced it another 50 yards. He was still 230 from the hole. He hit a decent 3-wood, a lackadaisical chip shot and two putts later had the second Double in a row. Even so, the wheels hadn't fully come off yet.

For the next 7 holes Dorsey had the worst run of chumps, misshits, bad swings and shanks that he could ever remember. He couldn't hold the clubs to save his life. He switched from the rain gloves since they were saturated and back to a regular glove. After several more successive shanks he went back to the rain gloves. The others in the foursome pretty much stopped talking to him which was fine because generally he was in different parts of the hole than they were. It got really tiring walking all the way back to the cart to re-club after shank after shank. He started just hitting whatever was in his hand, which was often a 4 or 5 Iron, which are tricky clubs to hit once you get inside of 100 yards.

Things reached the height of absurdity when Dorsey realized that there was a pool of water in the bottom of his bag. Apparently, there weren't any drain holes which made sense since no one would have designed the bag anticipating it filing up with that much water. Surely no one would try to play in those conditions. Dorsey tried sticking the club end into the bag first which would leave the grips on the high side. Then he had to fight to get every club out and since the numbers on the clubs were at the bottom of the bag, he had to pull them randomly until he found the one he wanted. He might have laughed if he didn't feel like he was closer to crying.

For the next seven holes he only 3-out on three of them. On the other holes he simply picked up early and tried to hold the pin for the rest of the group. From what he could tell Hoffman wasn't phased by what he was doing and for the most part Brumfield, even though he seemed to be walking a lot, was able to stick to his game too. Dorsey passed him or caught up with him a couple of times as he cut back and forth across fairways (on foot) as he tried to will himself back into the round.

Dorsey thought about quitting but didn't know how to go about it. They were too far from the clubhouse most of the time to pull off his bag and walk. He told himself that he needed to fight through it and see if he couldn't find a way to play his way out of it. It was ugly. On the series of holes #14 – #18, Dorsey was a combined 15 over par. The prior week he had played these same holes at 1 over.

After a while it did get better. For whatever reason he played #1 - #6 a little better, only Triple Bogeying one of them. He didn't have any more Pars, but he didn't pick up either. To say it was a moral victory would have been a stretch, but he did finish.

Brumfield had the official card and pulled over after the 6th green to have them attest to their scores. Hoffman had shot a 76. Brumfield shot an 87. Frey shot a 102. Dorsey signed for a 106. It was the highest score that he could ever remember attesting to. It was a shot-a-hole worse than his target. But he had finished. When they got to the clubhouse Dorsey shook hands with the others but didn't have a lot to say. Frey was his newfound friend since he had found someone who played worse than he did. Turns out Frey was a 32 handicap, so he shot right on his number. Dorsey was 14 over his handicap and 16 over his target. For some reason he wasn't that bummed out. After all, he had gotten to play, he had finished and maybe this score would help with his handicap in rounds to come. Keep on the sunny side of life.

Before heading to the parking lot, he bumped into Wright Strange who had a seriously downcast look on his face. "What's up?" Dorsey asked.

"Well, I almost quit but didn't but maybe wish I had. I couldn't hit the ball anywhere and kept taking monster divots trying to push it down the fairway. I shot a 102, which maybe wasn't all that bad, but Proudfoot actually assessed me a 2-stroke penalty for signing up late, so it's a 104."

"What?" Dorsey asked.

Strange grimaced and said; "Yeah, I was here on time, but I went to the range to hit some balls and forgot about paying. By the time I remembered we were about to pull out, so Proudfoot assessed me 2 strokes. He says the rules are emphatic that the money must be in by 8:45. Nothing I can do about it. Miserable day."

Dorsey just looked back at Strange, having nothing to add. He thought about letting Strange know that he had still beaten Dorsey. Misery loves company. Dorsey wasn't in the mood to talk about his score.

After putting his clubs in his car Dorsey found a Mountain Lite and sat in a corner by himself watching the proceedings. Seventy-three of the original 120 golfers had finished their rounds. Pharratt had Withdrawn on his 5th hole. Of the 73 scores that were posted, Dorsey came in at 69th on the gross and last in the net with an 84. On the ride home, he would have to ponder if he really was this bad and if he really wanted to keep playing. After all, what was in it for him? Maybe competitive golf had passed him by and he should just hang it up. Who needs it?

He had bought ten Raffle Tickets from Jeanette with seven wet crumpled dollars that were floating in his pocket. When his number was called Jeanette had to walk all the way across the room to bring him his money. He stood up determined to not show the defeat that was burning inside him. As she walked toward him, he could see Carlotta Ferry glowering at him over Jeanette's shoulder. As Jeanette handed him the $37 in winnings Dorsey made every effort to meet Carlotta's glare with his own eye contact as he handed the money back to Jeanette with a flourish. He was pleased to see Carlotta turn to Fawn Ridgeline and Jamie George with disgust on her face. The three of them huddled immediately then turned to stare at Dorsey. They would have made the Witches of Eastwick proud.

Once he had given the money back to Jeanette, Dorsey made for the door, shaking a few hands and offering a few congratulations. On the way he felt a sharp elbow in the ribs and turned to see George George, who offered a very fake "Sorry" as if he hadn't meant to go out of his way to poke Dorsey from behind. Jamie George was peeking over her husband's shoulder, trying to see if she could assess the damage to Dorsey. Dorsey walked on, trying to not give them the satisfaction of seeing him wince in pain.

Dorsey passed by Jeanette on his way to the door and found her cornered by Marvin Pharratt. Apparently after withdrawing three hours before he had hung around for some inexplicable reason. At this point he was leaned over Jeanette with his hand on the wall over her shoulder pinning her in position. Dorsey could tell from the look on her face that she wasn't buying what Pharratt was selling. He gave a nod to Jeanette who slipped Pharratt's grasp and turned to Dorsey.

Dorsey looked at Jeanette with sympathy and quizzed her; "Rough day I guess?".

She smiled back and said; "You didn't have to give me that money back."

Dorsey just answered "Well, $37 is a pretty pitiful offering for you having to sit out there in the rain all day. Whose idea was it to put you in that Gazebo?"

Jeanette hesitated but answered. "Ridgeline thought it would be a good spot. I'm starting to sense that somehow, I've gotten on his wrong side. I can't quite figure it out."

At that moment, for the second time in five minutes Dorsey felt a sharp jab in his back. He turned just in time to see Pharratt, head down and arms pumping, heading through the door to outside. Dorsey wheeled around but it was too late, Pharratt was across the porch and out into the rain. He hadn't even gotten a fake apology this time. He looked at Jeanette with a "what tha?" look.

Jeanette half-smiled back "I think that was about me. He keeps asking me out and wanting to get closer and it ain't going his way. I think you could be collateral damage for being nice to me."

Dorsey shook his head slowly "A number of people around here seem to misconstrue being nice for more than it is."

Dorsey looked at Jeanette carefully and offered "Please be careful. There seems to be some bad intentions swirling around you. I don't understand it either, but I don't want anyone to mess with you so be careful." Dorsey tried to move things to a lighter perspective and interjected "Well, see you at your Tournament on the 12th."

Jeanette had set up an Alzheimer's Scramble (Captains Choice /

Best Ball) for August 12 at Hanging Tree. Dorsey had a lot of experience with Scrambles in Florida. It was becoming more apparent that his game wasn't up to Match Play. In a Scramble format he could still be helpful by pulling off some individual shots. The problem came down to the fact that he couldn't execute two or three in a row, much less eighty or so to put together a decent round. He could help a team by hitting a good one every few swings and contribute that way. Much less pressure.

Jeanette looked back at Dorsey with a grateful smile. "I really appreciate the ones of you that seem to be behind me. What I'm trying to do is lonely enough without thinking people are rooting against me."

Dorsey paused for just a moment and returned her look "I'll be there. Let me know if you think of anything that I might do to help you." Jeanette didn't say any more, just looked at him blankly as he walked across the parking lot to his car and pulled away.

# Chapter 12

## "Swing it to End It"

**"If you really want to get better at golf, go back and take it up at a much earlier age"**
Thomas Mulligan

Hanging Tree Golf Club
August 12 - Sunday
5th Annual "Swing it to End it"


1:30 Shotgun Start – Captain's Choice - nice afternoon, mid-70's
Hole Sponsors – Beer Sponsors – Putting Contest – Raffle Tickets
$ 65 per person - $ 260 per foursome


In the almost two weeks leading up to Jeanette's Tournament there had been a barrage of emails to the GRITS members. The Tourney wasn't limited to GRITS members but obviously they would be the primary audience and hopefully bring their non-GRITS friends along too. The Tournament would have a couple of pros and cons. For Dorsey, first and foremost, a Captain's Choice / Scramble was a big plus. On a course that he had had a successful round on recently. On a Sunday afternoon which was a little gentler than having to get up early. The con for Jeanette was that she didn't know how many of these guys wanted to play a Scramble. They were usually intense about playing their own ball. Sunday afternoon was likely on balance a deterrent since family duties would call out to many of the players. And an afternoon round could bring thunderstorms into play. Hanging Tree was familiar to everyone, so that was neutral. Dorsey also thought that $65 was probably a little rich for this group, so that was a con as well.

Jeanette had apparently been able to rally some financial support, so it looked like hole sponsors, beer sponsors, food sponsors and prize sponsors were coming to the plate. Good for her. Likely because it was the 5th year, this all got a little easier over time. And the fact that she was just a good egg.

Dorsey did an internal calculation and figured that Jeanette was probably looking for fifteen foursomes, or sixty golfers, half of what GRITS was able to do. GRITS had a lot of advantages of tenure, pricing, mid-week, etc. If Hanging Tree had cut Jeanette the same deal on greens fees as they did GRITS, that meant she was making $35 per head or just over $2000. Throw in the sponsorships, Raffles, Putting Contest and deduct some expenses for trophies and whatever and she hopefully stood to net $5000. Dorsey also calculated that she had to offer Hanging Tree a guarantee up front so let's say forty golfers' and netting $30 per on the entry fee or $1200. Good for her, it seemed to be getting a buzz and he had been excited to play.

Saturday afternoon before the Tournament Dorsey had been bummed to get an email, apparently from Jeanette that was short and sweet "Due to circumstances beyond our control tomorrow's Tournament has been cancelled." The email came out around 3 o'clock Saturday. It had the usual Purple Bunting Jeanette used and the usual banner and format of the GRITS website. Only when he picked up his voice mail Sunday morning did he realize something was amiss.

The voice mail featured Jeanette's voice, shaky and strained. "I'm calling everyone who signed up for the Alzheimer's Tournament tomorrow to let them know that the email you received was a hoax. We do not know who sent it and the Tournament will be played as originally planned." Her voice shook, and the message was short and to the point. She hung up quickly, presumably because she had a lot of calls to make.

By the time Dorsey received the voice mail, he and Luisa had made new plans to head up to Chateau Morrisette for the afternoon, drink a little wine and enjoy some Bluegrass music. The tone and timing of Jeanette's message convinced him that something bad really was afoot and he begged off with Luisa to head for the Tournament after all. His face and tone of voice quickly convinced her that he was rattled by the whole thing and that he was better off heading for Hanging Tree to see what was going on. He told her that it was entirely possible that the Tournament was going off as planned, and to look for him by 6:30 or 7:00.

When Dorsey pulled into the Hanging Tree parking lot, he could see further evidence that something was wrong. By the number of cars in the lot, it looked a lot more like a Monday or Tuesday afternoon than it should for a Sunday Tournament less than an hour before tee time. There were probably less than fifteen cars in the parking lot. He parked, changed into his shoes, grabbed his bag and headed for the Clubhouse. As he got closer he could see a lot of carts lined up with very few bags to go on them. There wasn't a lot of activity.

Making it into the Clubhouse Dorsey ran directly into Proudfoot and Jeanette. Her eyes were red, and her face was drawn into a downward slide. He didn't have to ask anything before Proudfoot started in; "It was a hoax. Somebody got into the GRITS site, swiped all the email addresses, used some clever fonts and page faces and sent out the bogus cancellation. Jeanette has tried calling everyone, but it hasn't been all that successful. She left a lot of voice mails, but even with the ones she reached they had made other plans after the email yesterday."

Dorsey swung his gaze to Jeanette who returned it with the most pleading, beaten look he could imagine. "So where does that leave us?"

Proudfoot spoke up again "Well, the show must go on. We need to feed the ones who showed up. We need to dance with the ones who brung us." Cliché after cliché rolled out of him, but Dorsey had already gotten the point.

"So how many people have shown up?" he asked.

"You make 11." Proudfoot responded.

"Ouch." Was all Dorsey could offer.

Proudfoot continued "A lot of the hole sponsors have hung in there. The Putting contest will be for about $20, not the $100 we hoped for. The beer sponsor is pissed because he has cases of beer on ice and it will be a pain for him to deal with, not to mention less visibility than he hoped for. He wants some of his money back plus reimbursement for the ice."

By this time Dorsey had clearly gotten the picture and Jeanette had sat down on one of the empty chairs in the snack bar.

"Who has shown up?" Dorsey asked.

"You, me, Steve Martin, Briscoe Sisson, Chandler Hoffman and a few of his buddies. Not many more. Some guys I don't really know from Salem. Looks like everybody can get some kind of trophy. Jeanette already bought 'em. We'll just have to figure out enough categories to make it feel like something."

Dorsey turned his attention to Jeanette "Any clues? Any ideas as to how you would like to move ahead?"

Her answer came as a choked-off voice behind a balled-up tissue "Manny's right. For me it's pretty much a total loss. By the time I refund some sponsors and haggle with Hanging Tree over what I owe them for blocking off the course all day, I will definitely be in the hole. The show needs to go on as best we can."

An idea struck Dorsey, "Where is Ridgeline? Where is George George?" He swung his gaze to Proudfoot then back to Jeanette "Where is Pharratt? Where are Maynard Ferry, Dooley Hopper and the rest of our regulars? What's going on?"

All Jeanette could offer was "I called them all. I didn't get any return calls. I can't explain it."

Dorsey looked blankly back and forth between the two of them as Steve Martin walked up. Dorsey looked at him and posed the question again "Any ideas?"

Martin looked back at Dorsey, shrugged his shoulders "I'll help Manny pair up whoever shows up and we'll have a Tournament. We'll honor the ones who showed up and get this behind us. I suggest that the group of us get together tomorrow and pick up the pieces. It's Sunday, I don't see accomplishing much else today."

The Tournament went off with a Shotgun start as planned at 1 PM. Except it was more like a cap pistol than a Shotgun. Fifteen golfers were paired. Three Foursomes, One Threesome. The Threesome could take turns hitting the extra shot their group deserved as if they had a fourth guy. Whoopee.

Dorsey played with Hoffman, Sisson and Martin. He was the "D" player in the group, but he had a good day. Though his heart wasn't in it, he was able to set aside the reality of what had happened and had fun playing with this group. After all, he hadn't done anything to cause what happened and for today, there wasn't much to be done about it.

Based on the strength of his group, they shot 16 under for a 56. Hoffman was so on it was ridiculous. Sisson rose to the occasion and had a good time trying to keep up with him. Martin played his steady round and made a couple of putts that counted, including a long one for Eagle on #18. They eagled two more of the Par 5s. They even used some of Dorsey's shots. It was his tee shot on #9 that ended up about 6 feet below the hole. Martin rolled that one in. Dorsey made a sidewinding 24-footer on #10 for an Eagle and his tee shot on #17 took a big hop in front of the green and rolled to about 8 feet. Sisson drilled the putt. Dorsey tried to enjoy the Scramble format and tried to enjoy being on a stacked team, but it was a hollow victory. His team teed off from #1 and finished 45 minutes ahead of the next team. When you only take 56 strokes, you can move around a golf course pretty quickly.

Jeanette was in the clubhouse when they came back around, off to one side huddled against a back wall. Dorsey couldn't really think of anything to tell her that he thought would make her feel better. She was an admirable person who was trying to do something right and for her troubles, she was being drug through the mud. The whole deal with the Tournament cancellation was clearly a plot by someone who was twisted and wanted to pick on her because they could. It made the other smaller, more subtle clues leading up to this seem a lot more calculated and ominous than they had first appeared.

Dorsey and Martin tried to console Jeanette and offer ideas about how to appease her sponsors, Could the day could be saved somehow? How might they go on without Jeanette digging deeply into her personal pocket to make things whole again? They didn't come up with much but agreed between the three of them and Proudfoot to convene the next day at Blue Bells and see what they could do..

They made a sad little parade as they came around the corner from the cart area carrying their clubs and Jeannette's leftover hole-sponsor signs and unawarded trophies. Jeanette was leading the group out to their respective cars and Dorsey saw her knees buckle before he saw the reason why. When he looked up he could see her VW with all the windows bashed out. Shards of glass were everywhere in the vicinity. Just as he was making sense of that he saw his own car, also off kilter. His tires were flat.

Incredulous, they all stopped and stared at the scene. Jeanette's finances had just gone into a steeper nosedive. On top of replacing and recouping the funds lost in the Tournament, she now had the additional burden of replacing the windows, working out a rental car, haggling with the insurance company and on and on. For Dorsey it was the realization that whoever had their sights on Jeanette had him in the crosshairs as well.

It took almost two hours to call a wrecker for Jeanette, AAA for Dorsey and get them all underway and headed home. The Hanging Tree staff had called 911, so the police were there asking questions and making notes. Dorsey was able to reach Luisa to let her know he would be a little later than earlier projected. It was getting dark when the hubbub in the parking lot broke up. Detective Finn hadn't signed up for the tournament, but he came by for the aftermath. Steve Martin offered to take Jeanette home. Proudfoot had slipped away a little earlier.

Dorsey was dropped off by the AAA driver at 8:45, with his Audi up on the back of the truck and swirling yellow lights reflecting in the front windows of the house. It took until almost midnight to explain what he knew to Luisa. He went over it a number of times while she mostly stayed silent. More than once she left the room for more wine and a cooling off walk. As Dorsey told the story it seemed equally as preposterous to him as it must to her. She didn't seem judgmental, in fact seemed quite empathetic toward Jeanette. He wasn't quite sure how she felt about his role in the series of events but knew it would help if he could enlist her in solving the riddle. A female perspective as well as another woman for Jeanette to lean on would definitely be a plus. They got to bed late and he slept little. He could only hope that in the light of a new day, things might make more sense.

# Chapter 13

## "Swing it to End It" Debrief

**"The score a player reports on any hole should always be regarded as his opening offer."**
Thomas Mulligan

Monday August 13
2:30 PM Blue Bells Snack Bar

Proudfoot had scheduled the meeting for 2:30 at the Blue Bells snack bar to not interfere with his normal Monday morning 8:00 AM tee time. He had standing tee times between 8:00 – 8:20 Mondays through Thursdays with a rotating cast of twenty or so players, with normally twelve to eighteen showing up. Some of these guys were not on the GRITS Tour, as they were older and not interested in the competitive aspect. They just wanted to play golf to get out of the house. Mulligans, Gimmes and rolling it over were more easily accommodated within this group.

Proudfoot had settled at one end of the snack bar with Ridgeline and George George seated at the same table. They were part of the morning foursomes and part of the GRITS regime, so Dorsey conceded that this made sense. In attendance were Steve Martin and of course Jeanette. "Detective" Finn was there seated next to a guy in a tie, who identified himself as Don Francisco, part of the Valley Sheriffs' Community Outreach Unit.

Dorsey's ears did perk up when Ridgeline spoke first. Once a cop, always a cop. "So, who wants to start? Jeanette, how about you? Any clues? Any theories? Can you picture who might have done this, and specifically, do you think it has anything to do with GRITS?" Ridgeline was going to run this show? Hmmm.

Jeanette was looking pretty ragged this afternoon, not nearly as put together as her normal self. "Well, after a sleepless night of thinking, I believe that there are a lot of suspects". She looked squarely at the two officers "Am I supposed to be talking about what I think with you two or are we sure that everyone here needs to know my suspicions?" When she said this, she looked directly at George George.

Finn spoke up; "Well, that's somewhat up to you. This is not really a crime yet, since we haven't identified motives or suspects or anything like that. Right now, it is vandalism which could rise to the level of a felony based on the dollar amount and based on if it's determined that this is definitely directed toward you. It's your choice what you want to say. On the other hand, these gentlemen are here, indicating that they are interested in finding facts, so in that sense, the more the merrier. They more hands working on it, the faster we may move. If you are uncomfortable, you can leave out things that you want to. You are not under investigation and you are not under oath. You can consider yourself a bystander if that makes it easier."

Jeanette stared at her hands a moment and continued, looking again at George George; "In thinking back over the past few weeks, it seems a lot of people out here don't want me around. George, you have been vocal about the idea that I am sapping funds from the tour." George moved to speak but thought better of it and simply stared back at her, so she continued. "Some of the wives have been pretty much openly hostile to me. Marvin Pharratt and a few others have flirted with me so hard I have had to practically hit them with something to keep them off me. So, yeah, I've been going over everything that has happened to me over the past few months and I have a lot of theories, but not anything I can call anyone out on."

Finn took this in and leaned in to focus, "Well, let's start from the beginning. With your windshield from the Blue Bells Tourney. Any ideas on that?"

"No, just that it was mean", Was all Jeanette could offer.

Finn shook his head up a down a few times and looked at Proudfoot. "The email list is on the website, right? Anyone could copy that?"

"Sure" came out of Proudfoot's mouth.

Ridgeline jumped in at this point. "I've had a chance to look at the email that came out. Pretty simple stuff to copy our list, our format, our logos. Unusual maybe for people our age, but anyone with a little tech savvy could do that. It was sent from a Valley Library computer at the Grandin Road branch on Saturday. Even that is a little sketchy. You can set up email for later delivery, so it could have been staged Friday, Saturday, or earlier. It's a Public Library. They do log in who is using computers but faking ID's with them wouldn't take a lot either. As a matter of fact, one interesting tidbit was that we found Tom French, your deceased spouse, logged in to one of their computers last week." He sat back and shot his smuggest look in Jeanette's direction.

Jeanette just gasped and stammered. "Someone is really cruel."

Finn leaned into the group and tried to steer in another direction. "Dorsey, what's your perspective on this? And your car? Do you think you were targeted? Why did they only deflate your tires, and not knock your windows out? Any ideas?"

Dorsey settled forward in his chair and tried to be calm. The questions sounded a little like an accusation, but he didn't want to get worked up if the Detective was just doing his job. Answering as calmly as he could; "I don't know, I don't know, and I don't know." Everyone stared at him a minute. Then he went on; "I think some folks think that I'm friendlier with Jeanette than is the norm around here. I think that maybe they were trying to send me a message without doing too much damage. I've noticed some of the things that Jeanette mentioned, and I think that may have drawn attention to me."

"Like what?" Finn asked.

"Like George George sniping at Jeanette in public. Like Marvin Pharratt maybe being jealous of me since Jeanette seems to prefer my company. Like Carlotta Ferry and some of her crowd wanting to clear Jeanette out of GRITS entirely. Just stuff like that."

This time George George wasn't able to restrain himself. "Why, you interfering hacker! You're new to this tour and I'm not so sure you know what you're talking about at all. We've run this thing for sixteen years without needing your opinion! I doubt we need it now. As for Jeanette,

I think she's a fine lady and we've tried our best to support her little cause."

Jeanette went after him on this; "Her little cause! Alzheimer's is not MY LITTLE CAUSE! It's a deadly disease that kills millions of people. We are all candidates for it. It killed my husband and I'm only doing what I can to do something good."

Proudfoot lifted both his arms and waved for attention. "OK, let's not let things deteriorate. We all have a common goal of figuring out what has gone on here. If nothing else, for the good of the GRITS, it would be in our best interest to sort this out. George, please try and respect that Jeanette has had some bad stuff happen to her. If this tour is going to continue we need to nip this kind of stuff in the bud sooner as opposed to later."

The meeting did manage to begin to be calmer as it loped toward a finish. Nothing was resolved beyond everyone agreeing to try and come up with answers and think about whodunnit. After another hour or so of head scratching and posing questions to the air they broke it up and everyone wandered back to their lives. Again, Steve Martin was chaperoning Jeanette. Dorsey got into Luisa's X5 and headed home. He hoped his tires would be fixed by the time he got there. He longed for a time he could drive away from Blue Bells without questions, doubt or confusion swirling in his brain.

# CHAPTER **14**

## Luisa and The Country Crock

"The most exquisitely satisfying act in the world of golf is that of throwing a club. The full backswing, the delayed wrist action, the flowing follow-through, followed by that unique whirring sound, reminiscent only of a passing flock of starlings, are without parallel in sport."

Henry Longhurst

Wednesday, August 15
Noon – Country Crock Cafe

Dorsey had called Steve Martin early Wednesday morning. The Monday meeting had accomplished little and left him that much more unsettled. He suggested that Dorsey, Martin and Jeanette get together and talk a little more confidentially, with a lot smaller crowd. Martin agreed and explained that Jeanette was meeting with Detective Finn at 10:00. Noon at the Country Crock should work. If anything changed he would let Dorsey know, otherwise see ya there.

Dorsey's car had been returned by AAA the afternoon before and otherwise there appeared to be nothing out of place. He had once again had a long session with Luisa retracing the conversations at the Blue Bell afternoon meeting. He had filled her in about the Detective and the Community Outreach Officer. They discussed Jeanette's listing of potential suspects. Going over what he perceived of the positions of Proudfoot, Ridgeline and George, and referencing Carlotta Ferry and Marvin Pharratt. Saying it all out loud sounded somewhere between a real plot and a silly farce. He knew there was something there, but he couldn't identify it just yet. Luisa had remained calm, filled the wine glasses and interjected little. What questions she did ask were ones he had no answers to. After a few frustrating hours rehashing the afternoon meeting, they called it a night.

As Dorsey located his keys and sunglasses getting ready to leave at 11:30 Luisa stepped from their bedroom. Hair combed, nice summer dress, her lipstick and sunglasses in one hand, cell phone in the other. Dorsey looked at her quizzically and she spoke up; "I'm going with you." Dorsey knew better than to try and talk her out of something once she had made up her mind. It was clear that she had. They walked quietly down the stairs to the basement garage, got in his Audi, pulled out and drove away. Not much was said on their way to Country Crock. Dorsey had a healthy regard for feminine insights in general and Luisa's especially. He hoped that Martin and Jeanette wouldn't be put off by Luisa as a surprise package but knew if they gave her the benefit of a doubt, things would go fine.

Martin and Jeanette were already seated at a booth when they came in. Jeanette looked up suspiciously eyeing Luisa. Martin at first just cocked his head but then stood up and offered Luisa a handshake. Dorsey couldn't read Jeanette's mind as they all settled in and Luisa spoke first. Looking directly at Jeanette she led off; "I'm Dorsey's significant other. I am not part of GRITS. I haven't been to any events. As far as that group goes I am anonymous. Dorsey has explained what has been going on with you. I'm thinking that you could use a woman near you that you can count on."

Anyone that knew Luisa knew that when she indicated she could be counted on for something, she could be. Jeanette seemed to appraise Luisa's opening statement, along with the empathy on her face, and the strength and humility in her eyes. Dorsey could tell that in this moment Jeanette made her decision. She just gave a quiet nod and; "Thanks, I appreciate it."

Dorsey broke the moment, turning the scene over to Jeanette; "Well, what do we know that we didn't know before?"

Jeanette gathered herself and plunged in. "Well, they haven't found the weapon of glass destruction" That helped. Everyone chuckled and seemed to relax just a little. "Everything we're going to talk about today has to be just between us. I need to trust somebody and you three just got elected. I firmly believe someone is out to harm me and am very concerned it could escalate from here. I can't trust but a few people. You three are it."

After a pause Jeanette went on; "On Monday I laid out my personal suspect list and that hasn't changed. Finn shared some details today and encouraged me to keep them close because they may be things that only the one who is doing this would know. Knowledge is power." She hesitated a moment and looked directly into Dorsey's eyes "Did you ever find your 6-iron?"

Her question jolted Dorsey back in his chair "No. Does Finn have me as a suspect?"

Martin chimed in quickly. "Well, as luck would have it, you have an alibi. At Blue Bells when the window was busted out, you were in a foursome with me. At Hanging Tree when they were all busted out, you were in a foursome with me. Just for the record my interest in this whole thing goes back to the fact that I was Jeanette's husband Tom's best friend. My vouching for you should shut up anybody that wants to single you out. On the other hand, the fact that it could be your 6-iron may actually give us some leverage in an odd sort of way."

Dorsey came back at Martin "What do you mean "could be my 6-iron?" Where is it? I can tell you in a minute if it's mine for sure. What do you mean by 'leverage'?"

Martin answered. "It could be your club because none of us has seen it. As for leverage every little tidbit we know but don't let out could be a chip we can use if we need it. For example, this meeting should never be known about among anyone else. The fact that Luisa is now in our inner circle needs to be kept quiet. The fact that no one knows who she is could help us down the line. If this is really going to turn into a cloak-and-dagger thing then we have to keep a lid on what we know and what we want others to think we know."

"What else did you get from Finn?" was all Dorsey said next, turning to Jeanette.

Directing the conversation to her made her head pop up from the thoughts that she was working on at that moment. "Finn says that busting out windows may not be as easy as it looks. Car windows are pretty resistant to someone busting into them. The golf club likely didn't do it. To shatter the windows quickly and quietly would more likely be done with some sort of air-gun or Taser that carried a projectile charge, or even a small pistol. Having your 6-iron missing could be just a diversion. Similar in a way with your tires being deflated. To do it with a screwdriver or something would be a joke. It would take too long and increase the risk of being seen. More likely it would be some sort of pneumatic hand-held device that would pop the stems out quickly and quietly."

"What does that mean?" asked Dorsey

Jeanette answered slowly, weighing her words carefully "It means it was likely done by someone who knew some stuff about this stuff. Someone like a cop maybe."

That statement landed like a thud on the table as they all came to the next thought together. Ridgeline.

Martin spoke next; "Ok, let's not try and solve this right off the bat. Some things that haven't seemed like a thread to this point may be. Some things that may seem obvious now may be premature. Jeannette let's explore some other ideas, OK?"

Jeanette was more than up to the task, "Ok, working out from the center there's George George. He seems to think that I'm taking away from the Tournament. He's been vocal about recruiting others to think that me and Alzheimer's are sapping energy and money that could be going back into the Tour. It doesn't matter if I don't get where he's coming from and it doesn't matter who is right. He is inside the castle and if he says it, some of the old guard are going to believe it. Does he hate me enough to whack out my windows? I don't know. I do know that some of these guys have a lot invested in GRITS and like it the way they've been running it. Any deviation from the norm threatens their little nest. GRITS may not reward them financially, but it does boost their dormant little male egos. Their egos may have not had a stroke in a while. Maybe, just maybe. Am I going too far?"

Martin reassured her "No, not necessarily. We have to look for motive. Male egos often create motive. Go on."

Jeanette gulped and went on. "Then there's the women. Carlotta
Ferry seems to hate me. She seems to have infected some of the other
wives too. I used to be friends with Irene Proudfoot. Tom and I went on
vacation with Jamie and George George. Halle Hopper babysat our kids
years ago. Fawn Ridgeline hasn't spoken to me in weeks. I'm not saying
that we were close with the Ridgelines, but Tom and Roger coached
our boys in soccer together. I don't know what changed but I seem to
be on the outside looking in with that group and I don't know exactly
why. It does scare me because I can feel the frost coming off of them.
They don't make eye contact and they turn the other way when they see
me. I realize that I could be a threat now that I'm single. It's common
knowledge that I got some insurance money. It's like they want to stand
guard between me and their husbands. It's all a little strange. I still miss
Tom, and since we're sworn to secrecy among this group, none of those
men do a thing for me. Not that I'm looking. I'm not. Tom was the only
guy for me and I'm sure as hell not ready to look for someone else. If I
were, it wouldn't be anyone on the GRITS Tour. Not anyone I've seen
anyway". At this point she looked back and forth between Martin and
Dorsey. "Not anyone that ain't taken at least." With this she reached out
and squeezed Luisa's hand. "Your guy is safe with me. Looks to me like
he's a lucky guy."

As uneasy as this exchange made him, Dorsey was pretty sure that he
was glad he had heard it. Luisa wasn't exactly the least jealous woman he
had ever met, but she was reasonable. He sensed that since Jeanette had
addressed the issue head on, Luisa was on board. He hoped so. He had
no designs on Jeanette and had no interest in any way ruffling Luisa's
tail feathers. In addition to not wanting her to go off on something
not material to the subject, he felt Luisa was smart enough and clever
enough to contribute to the effort as things unfolded. Luisa seemed to
take Jeanette's statement at face value and so did Dorsey. He knew for
his part that he wasn't straying anywhere. Having Jeanette say something
out loud may have helped. Luisa nodded, and they returned to the issue
at hand.

Jeanette went back to the subject. "So that's it for the women. I
don't know how seriously we take them but as we know, women can be

capable of anything, especially in a pack. Oh, I skipped over Ridgeline and George George. Or did I? Anyway, I don't trust Ridgeline to run whatever this is. An Investigation? So, OK, he's a retired cop. Retired from the Salem Police. But what does that mean? He's been retired over ten years. I'm sure there have been major tech advances since he quit. Does he still have any contacts on the inside? Or is he just a suspicious person who drifted into that career forty years ago and now he thinks he's Columbo? I think he may just be assuaging his own ego. Maybe he loves all of the cloak-and-dagger? Finn didn't seem to have an opinion of him one way or the other. Seemed to think he may be harmless. I don't know. He just seems to want to point fingers and see if he can be a hero. Columbo or Clouseau? I'm not sure which one he is and I'm not sure he can keep a secret. Knowledge is power in the world of gossip. Any little thing that he gets his mitts on can be spread like wildfire. He may have a conflict between his wife and her coven. I don't see him in the inner circle. We need to keep it close at hand."

Dorsey was impressed at how Jeanette was laying things out, and how she seemed to have a grasp of potential threats. He glanced at Martin who was nodding up and down and to Luisa who was simply taking in Jeanette's analysis. He couldn't read much on her face, but he didn't see eye rolls or skepticism either. He looked back at Jeanette and nodded, as did Martin and Luisa.

Jeanette continued; "OK, so that leaves little people like Pharratt and whoever else we don't even know is out there. Who knows?" She took a much-deserved breath before she continued "For my money maybe I should just shut it down and evaporate. I'm pulling less than $100 per tournament for my cause and meanwhile it looks like I'm risking my neck. What exactly is the point?"

Dorsey, Martin and Luisa looked back and forth to each other. None of them had a good answer either. Dorsey chimed in "What is your relationship with Proudfoot?"

Jeanette took another breath and got back to it "Manny and Tom were close. Manny has always been kind to me. It was his idea to bring me in after Tom died and add the Alzheimer's cause to GRITS. He has made accommodations for me and for the most part big-brothered me.

One thing that occurs to me is that even though Proudfoot, Ridgeline and George look like a unified front, don't forget this is a volunteer organization. They could be pulling a few dollars out for themselves but probably not much. Maybe some free rounds of golf. It's more likely that they're getting their jollies being on the inside, being able to strut a little because they are seen to wield tiny bits of power. That also means Proudfoot doesn't really have any control over them either. It's not like they're getting a paycheck or he's controlling their pensions. Each of these guys is in it for whatever reason they're in it. And any group has its' cliques. After sixteen years we would be naïve to think that little sects haven't been formed, favors haven't been done. As petty as this sounds, for some of these guys it is their lives. If they don't have GRITS all they have is their wives, TV and occasional grandkid visits. GRITS is the one thing that they can look forward to. They have been running it as they see fit and it gives them something back in the bargain."

Dorsey almost asked Jeanette if she had a degree in Psychology. Her synopsis covered a lot of bases. He didn't ask because he was afraid it would come out wrong or sound condescending. He changed course "So what's next?"

Jeanette came back with "Well, Finn suggested we meet once a week. His guys are going over my car to see if there was anything we might learn. He checked with Hanging Tree but they don't have parking lot video or anything like that. To this point no one has volunteered that they saw anything. Proudfoot has agreed to send out a blurb through the website asking for information. Anyone who might know anything can respond to Proudfoot or Finn and the site will mention an anonymous option through Crime Stoppers if people are afraid of blowback. We'll just have to see if anyone comes forward or we think of anything creative."

Martin took up the conversation at this point "I've encouraged Jeanette not to quit. I'm hoping that we have a group of men that will help form a silent protective barrier around her. We have to believe that we have a lot of guys who want to do the right thing. We have the Hidden Hills Tournament next week, on August 20. Jeanette will be riding with me to the club and we will be looking for volunteers to stay close beside her just in case. I'm not concerned in the least that anyone will try anything with me. I've known most of these guys for over sixteen years and I just can't see them attacking me. That doesn't mean they are done with Jeanette. We'll have to try and keep an umbrella over her."

Hearing this Jeanette dropped her head on her chin; "I hate this. I believe strongly in what I'm doing and I'm doing it for Toms' memory. I think I owe him more that giving up based on a few busted windows."

At this point Luisa spoke for the first time "I want to help. These people don't know who I am. Maybe I can blend in with the woodwork somehow and help keep an eye out. Maybe if I hide in plain sight I could be part of the umbrella." They all looked at her at once wondering where she was coming from. "I have some friends that are members at Hidden Hills. Let me think about it. I don't have to tell them what I'm up to. Maybe I can have lunch, join in a Bridge game. I don't know. I promise I won't expose this group or what I'm doing." She looked back at Jeanette "I'm asking for your permission and your trust to let me try and help you." Jeanette only nodded but her expression said thank you.

The group muddled through the rest of the lunch that they had ordered, pretty much leaving the topic where it was. They were all distracted but at the same time burned out from thinking about it all, at least for the moment. They broke up with Dorsey and Luisa heading to his car and Martin and Jeanette heading to Martin's car. Dorsey and Luisa only talked about what had now become "The Investigation" a little on the way home. When they got home, Luisa retired to her studio and Dorsey took Anya for a long walk. The night passed quietly, a few wines and one of Luisa's homemade (healthy) pizzas on the porch.

# CHAPTER 15

## Hidden Hills

"**Although golf was originally restricted to wealthy, overweight Protestants, today it's open to anyone who owns hideous clothing.**"

Dave Barry

Monday, August 20

Hidden Hills

Par 71

5365 from the Gold Tees

Slope 68.1 Rating 120

Crisp morning conditions beginning at 68 degrees, moving to 78 by noontime. Little or no wind.

Hidden Hills was yet another step up the ladder for the GRITS Tour. Nestled against the folds of Sugarloaf Mountain, Hidden Hills is a rolling, first class, well-groomed, fun layout. It is beautiful even by Valley standards. It boasts a majestic two-story brick clubhouse with banquet facilities, a snack bar for golf, a white-table-cloth dining area, ballrooms, Men's and Women's locker rooms, Indoor tennis and a "Wine Shoppe." "SHOPPE." Dorsey loved that.

In addition to the golf Hidden Hills also features tennis with eight outdoor clay courts and four Indoor courts. The place is nice. Very Private, very well done. Named two years in a row as Platinum winner for best country club by Valley magazine. Bravo.

The morning dawned as nice and crisp as a fall day, reminiscent of football and multi-colored leaves, though it was still August. Dorsey felt a little guilty putting his shoes on in the parking lot, so he sat in the front seat to tie his laces, as he didn't want to appear out of place. He had taken extra care to wear a little better red shirt, black shorts with black socks and shoes. A more formal look, but it also made him feel more ready to play.

As Dorsey came around from the parking lot he was greeted by the standard site of his GRITS peers swinging, swaggering and working themselves loose. The atmosphere was more guarded than some of the other sites, almost reverent. It was nice for Dorsey to feel part of it, no longer intimidated and overall playing well. The "Wreck in the Rain" of Blackbird had receded into the background and there had been some good rounds, including the practice round last week here at Hidden Hills with Wright Strange. Strange drove Dorsey a little crazy with his fixation of constantly taking his head covers off and on, leaving them, dropping them, running over them and constantly fussing with them. They had become good buddies once they figured out who they knew in common and established relative pedigrees of money, social status and busted relationships. They were both here for the golf, not very good, but avid. It was working out nicely.

He introduced himself to his foursome in the carts labeled "5-A" and set about getting loose himself. He wasn't in the mood for the range and decided that the putting green might make for time better spent anyway. After the way he had been playing the past few weeks, and in the practice round, he felt like he was hitting the ball well. Putting was most everyone's bugaboo and it certainly was his.

Dorsey's foursome included Buddy Clampett, a wrinkled 24 handicap who wore glasses and an owlish squint. In his cart was Earle Van Dyke, a lean and lanky 7-handicap who wore his clothes well and had probably never had a pot belly in his life. Dorsey's cart mate, Billy Flynn, had beaten him to the punch by arriving earlier than Dorsey, and putting his bag on the non-driving side. Dorsey not only had to drive but the official scorecard was attached to the steering wheel. He tried to shrug it off, rationalizing that the extra work might take his mind off his own game and offer a diversion.

Proudfoot walked around the cart area with his cordless Mr. Microphone and told everyone that there would be a delay. Hidden

Hills only had 50 carts and with 120 golfers signed up. There would have to be some walkers, be considerate, let them hitch a ride, and so on. The delay was for Hidden Hills to finish up mowing on several of the tee boxes and make everything ship-shape. The Hidden Hills pro, a sawed off 30-something took the mic and did his bit about using the 90-degree rule, staying off tee boxes and generally behaving yourselves. Dorsey understood that at heart he was only trying to protect his club, there had been some overnight rain. The guy didn't have a lot of finesse and his remarks came out as talking down to a bunch of Senior citizens that by and large knew golf etiquette. He said the right words, they just came out a little acidic.

Based on the virtual rainout at Blackbird, Proudfoot hadn't been able to get a decent team picture. He had decreed an extension of "Alzheimer's month" and the Purple had come out in force. Dorsey reckoned that probably 100 of the 120 in attendance were in some shade of purple, or at least a passable blue. It was quite a sight given the Senior physiques crammed into these colors. Dorsey was glad it was slightly overcast at the start.

He tapped Flynn's shoulder and pointed to one golfer. The guy had on an orange shirt, orange hat and white golf shoes with orange laces. Dorsey asked Flynn "Do you think he didn't get the memo or maybe he's color blind?"

Flynn surveyed the guy Dorsey was pointing out and chuckled "That's Trey Woods. He was the golf coach at Patrick Henry for 30 years. Their colors are Purple. He must have 20 Purple shirts. I don't know what got into him today"

Starting on 5-A wasn't a bad thing to Dorsey. Yes, it was a tough hole, a Par 5 uphill and long. It slanted left to right so that all four drives ended up in the right rough, but in play. Dorsey could not believe how much his hands had shaken hitting the first shot. He hit third, after Clampett and Van Dyke. He could barely put the ball on the tee his hand was shaking so bad. The group for 5-B was standing around watching and he could feel his heart racing. It was ridiculous. He managed to get a shot airborne, having it flutter to the right rough, but he had caught it well and he could see it sitting up. Whew.

Flynn hit his long and straight. It still found the rough, but seventy-five yards ahead of Dorsey. Everybody spread out and found their balls. Clampett was twenty yards behind Dorsey and chumped his ahead. Dorsey stood over his ball, halfway submerged in the grass and felt his heart racing again. This was not what he was looking for. He caught the shot clean and hit it hard and straight. Miraculously it perched on the left side of the fairway impossibly clinging to the slope. He took a breath as the others found their shots and hit ahead.

Dorsey stood over his third shot, 118 to the pin. His heart was still racing and he could not believe it. This was so stupid! He bent over the ball which was well below his feet. He pushed his hands forward to get the "forward push" Sisson had told him to get. He knew that with the ball this far below his feet, it was likely to go left. He hit it clean and it screamed high and left. He had hit it well but had no idea how much room was up there where he had hit it. He felt like the distance was good but had no idea what he may have found when it came down. He practically abandoned Flynn, which was OK, because Flynn was off walking with a towel and three clubs in his hand. Dorsey gave a cursory look at the other cart and tapped the accelerator pretending to be polite while waiting for them to hit. When he finally had clearance, he sped up to the far left of the green and exhaled outwardly when he saw his ball, above the pin, in the rough but alive.

Dorsey waited for the others to come up, not at all paying attention to what they were doing. He kept his head down, made clean contact and watched as his ball skipped past the pin, headed downhill but mercifully stopping on the fringe 20 feet below the pin. He tried to breathe as he walked past the others, attempting to be respectful as they putted back down the same hill. Clampett and Flynn both left their putts short, with tough downhill putts still to follow.

Dorsey lined up his putt when the time came and promised himself he wouldn't leave it short. He drilled the putt on the exact right line and it hit the cup full on. Thankfully, it only popped ten inches from the cup. With his hands still shaking, he managed to grunt the putt in for his 6. He was happy with the result and curious as to what in the world was going on with his emotions. He knew he had to calm down. He had hit good shots and in doing so, made himself miserable.

Since he was scorekeeper, Dorsey had to pay attention as they all called out their scores. Dorsey 6, Clampett 7, Van Dyke 6 and Flynn 5. Not a bad start for him and Flynn had made a nice downhill slider for his Par.

Number 6 was a very short hole. Dorsey's tee shot exploded off the club heading straight for a thicket of trees on the right side of the fairway about 120 yards off the tee.. That ball was never seen again. Dorsey took one in, two out and dropped his third shot. He was still 180 out but abandoned all caution and sent his ball screaming toward the trees to the left and above the green. The only notice he got of it was when he heard it slam into a tree near the out of bounds marker. The ball was buried in some thick rough and he was only able to chop it out twenty yards (4). Still high above the green he hit a shot that rolled and rolled to the back of the green (5) then missed the thirty-footer (6), took his 7 and picked up. He was disgusted with a Triple Bogey on one of the easiest holes on the course. Flynn 4, Clampett 4, Dorsey 7, Van Dyke 7. When Dorsey looked at Van Dyke curiously Van Dyke replied, "Three shanks back there, I had to pick up too".

Number 7 was a simple Par 3. Dorsey hit a nice tee shot above the hole 20 feet away. He punched at his putt with no authority. It stopped 2 feet short above the hole, so he naturally missed that one. He made the comebacker, but it was a 4. Clampett had gotten a 4 from below the trap and Flynn had just missed a Birdie putt and tapped in for his 3. Van Dyke hit into the front left bunker and took two to get out. Another Double Bogey for him and he was fuming. The guy obviously had more game than he was showing and was having a tough day.

On Number 8 Dorsey hit a decent drive but pulled his second shot way left of the green. Even though he did get his pitch over the bunker, it was weak and left him with another downhill putt. He missed that one too and got himself another Bogey. Van Dyke did find the bunker and blasted out almost over the green and three-putt from there. He had smoke coming from his ears by this time. Dorsey 5 Van Dyke 6 Clampett 5 and Flynn 4.

Dorsey hit a high beautiful drive on #9 followed up by a sweet 6-Iron just above the hole. Miracle of miracles he managed to two-putt for his first Par of the day. Clampett Parred and Flynn Parred. Van Dyke had pulled his drive from the elevated tee and hooked it just below a willow tree. After fumbling around in the woods for a while, he finally blasted out of a greenside bunker and had himself another Triple Bogey. He was red in the face and practically quivering. After all, the guy was a 7 handicap and in the first five holes had two Triples and Two Double Bogeys.

At Hidden Hills the clubhouse perches up on a hill and you drive down a winding path to the tee boxes for #1 and #10 and then veer off to whichever one you are playing. They are side by side about 10 yards away. There are no monument markers at Hidden Hills since I guess they figure that the members know where they are going and don't need them. The GRITS group could have used them as numbers 1, 10, 12, and 17 were a little tricky to find if you didn't know where you were going.

As Dorsey's group waited on the 10th tee box for the group ahead to move out, the group turned around and came back at them. As they got there, they giggled and said they had teed off from the wrong box and should have been on #1. They thought it was funny until Flynn spoke up "Well, that's a 2-stroke penalty for each of you for teeing off from the wrong tee." The group didn't respond and nothing more was said until they had pulled away. Flynn turned to Dorsey and said "I'm serious. I'd like to see their cards when they're done to see if they each added in those 2 strokes." Dorsey was pretty sure that Flynn meant to report it to Proudfoot after the round. Ouch.

Dorsey's drive was hit hard but floated high and right between the #1 and #10 fairways. By the time Dorsey was lining up his pitch, Clampett and Van Dyke were looking for a ball in a waste area not near anything. The next thing Dorsey knew Van Dyke was peeling his bag off the cart and shaking hands with everyone. He looked at each of them and said he just couldn't take playing like this, that the shanks were too much for him. He started walking to the clubhouse.

Dorsey was a little distracted and bladed his pitch over the green. He worried that it might be gone but found it in the thick grass and punched it onto the green. He lagged a putt to eighteen inches and marked it but when the time came, he only tapped it six inches and had to tap it again for it to go in. Clampett had made it up and down in 5 and Flynn had too. As they called out their scores and Dorsey called out his 7.

Flynn said "7?".

Dorsey, remembering the same situation at Blue Bells told him "Yeah, I double-hit the 18- incher."

Flynn looked at him and said "Well, I'm not so sure anyone saw that." Trying to be supportive.

Dorsey calmly replied, "it is what it is". He later wondered if this was a test. After all, Flynn had not seemed in the mood to cut the group who teed off from the wrong tee any slack. Why Dorsey?

The day went on like that. Dorsey probably missed ten putts from a total of fifteen feet. He chumped shots in the grass, ran them past the flag and generally through away one a hole. He had some moments, like the Birdie on the tough Par 5 12th. And he mostly never really got in big trouble, just continued to throw them away. On the Par 3 15th he slapped his tee shot right, which then hit the cart path and was gone. Another 7. One saving grace was that Flynn was fun and on the first pass by the clubhouse he had bought Dorsey a beer. When they came around again after 18 Dorsey bought a six-pack. They laughed and giggled and had a good time.

Flynn actually suggested Dorsey get some lessons. Dorsey told him "Don't think less of me, but I'm fine with my game the way it is. You are suggesting more commitment and practice. I'm telling you that's not gonna happen." After that Flynn seemed to understand. On #9 Dorsey threw in one last comment that he felt like there were an "infinite number of combinations for him to shoot a 95."

When they tallied them up after putting out on #4, Dorsey proved prophetic. Dorsey 95, Clampett an even 100 and Flynn 80. Clampett seemed content with his score and Dorsey wasn't at all upset. Flynn was the low man by 15 strokes and he was beside himself with how he had played. Golf is like that. Dorsey knew better rounds were in there and he also knew he had hit some good shots. He was optimistic that at

one of these events he was going to put together a decent score. In the
meantime, he had fun, largely because he enjoyed Flynn and Hidden
Hills was so pretty.

What no one had known was that Dorsey had a plant, really a group
of plants, in the clubhouse. At the end of the Dining Room was a Private
Room suitable for small meetings, family gatherings or lunch for eight
to ten people. It sat all the way past the entrance, past the full bar, past
the Dining Room. It had a beautiful view of the mountain range and
putting green. Today it also had a perfect view of the small Gazebo
where Jeanette had set up her shop and a view of the grills being set up
by George George where he planned to cook his burgers and hot dogs
later.

As it turned out, George wouldn't be cooking them today, just
hanging around and glad-handing. The Club had taken one look at the
coolers of burgers and dogs that George was lugging in and decided that
they had their own standards to maintain. Thank you very much, but
Hidden Hills would provide the grills, the setups, the meat and the chefs
to prepare the burgers. They had acquiesced to the $5 burger fee but
had been insistent that they would control the quality of the output.

George started to throw a hissy fit about what he would do with all
the food he had brought, and all the trouble he had gone to, but he had
met a stone wall of resistance.  The club stepping in was a win-win for
Proudfoot and GRITS, so the show went on.

The GRITS group made their normal 9 AM shotgun start and was
heading for their 9-hole mark when Luisa and her posse settled into
their table at 11:15. Bunny Hazeltine's other best friend was Alexas
Haney, a member of Hidden Hills. Well, Alexas was a little more than a
member. She had served out various stretches on the Board at Hidden
Hills and been credited with championing the Junior Golf programs,
specifically the Girl's program. These programs had received her intense
focus over the years and were the models for Country Clubs throughout
Southwest Virginia.

Most High School Golf Teams have six to eight members, typically
the privileged sons of prominent locals, who had the connections and
the bucks to support their kids' greens fees and get them onto the

better courses. Hidden Hills High School, down the road from the Club, had twenty-nine members on their golf team. Alexas had poked and prodded the High School and the Club into a unique alliance that assured anyone with an interest a chance to play. Kids got hands-on instruction from a team of school coaches and from the team of pros at the Club. There were no fees.

One key was that kids were not allowed to play full holes until they could Par nine holes, starting from 150 yards from the green. Short games had to be in sync before playing the full course. In this manner, kids grew into the big course only after learning fundamentals of the short game. Girls and Boys played on the same team, since there was no official Girls Team. Over the past few years, a few Girls had made the playing team, and had played events. Three of them had won college scholarships despite not having a girls' team to play on.

Kids received the best instruction, liberal playing time and were provided with exceptional competition through both hosted tournaments and targeted travel opportunities. It was the norm that at least one of "Alexas' Kids" would get themselves a top-flight golf scholarship every year. The scholarships weren't just to college golf factories. They included Ivy League opportunities that would carry them forward into the better lives that they had been groomed for. The Junior Golf Program and Alexas were keys to membership demand at Hidden Hills. If your kid had an aptitude for golf, Alexas could help them on their way. She was very connected. Also, on July 25 she had won her third Valley Women's Golf Association City-County Championship. She had been playing for 30 years and for herself was disappointed that there weren't more. This one had been sweet, marking one in each Decade since her college days.

Alexas' golf exploits were only marginally top of mind for Luisa and Bunny. They acknowledged, admired and cheered on her efforts. Neither of them were athletes. They were proud to know that their friend was a golf presence in the Valley, but their bonds centered more around their shared experience as former Soccer Moms and the travails of life and family. One common thread had kept them together for years, so the Pinot Grigio was poured shortly after they sat down. As they perused the menu that they pretty much had memorized, they nonchalantly glanced out over the vista in front of them trying to pick out patterns of inconsistency. They planned to stretch lunch out a while today and enjoy the mission before them.

When Dorsey's group had come by the clubhouse (twice) he had not made any signal nor contact with Luisa. The idea was to keep her undercover and see what she could see. The three women were still there as the golfers finished and made their way toward the clubhouse. The women had perked up when Pharratt had come skittering around from the cart return area and had perched himself on the edge of the Gazebo. His upper lip quivered, and his tiny hands pawed at the air as he tried to engage Jeanette in conversation. She leaned away from him and was able to keep him at bay until Steve Martin got between them to shoo him away. It didn't appear any harm had been done and he was nowhere to be found after that.

Proudfoot and his crew had set up their tally boards under a veranda just off the Dining room where Luisa, Bunny and Alexas nursed their Pinot Grigio. The three women had stretched out the drinks to not get ahead of themselves. They had scheduled Ralf, their on-call Uber driver to pick them up later just in case the alcohol got to be too much fun. For now, they were fine, up to that time a little bored but as everyone came in they sat up to pay attention.

Hidden Hills suffered from the same set of issues felt by Country Clubs everywhere. Falling membership, rising cost of maintenance. Even with a first-rate club and great offerings, it was becoming increasingly harder to attract new members. Millennials weren't interested in a game they considered too slow. Even tennis has a niche following. Dorsey had encountered a number of GRITS players that "used to be a member of Hidden Hills". When the kids left home, the fees were hard to justify. When you became a snowbird or succumbed to the decline of your game, you lost interest. Hidden Hills had gone all out for GRITS in the hope that a first-rate presentation might lure back a few members and help turn things around

The GRITS wives were out in full force, thanks to gracious and well distributed invitations. If Hidden Hills was going to put on the dog, they

knew that the wives had a say in how household money was spent, so
they wanted them there. Same way you sell Insurance or Time Shares.
Dorsey got to meet Susan Flynn and Lisa Hoffman for the first time
as well as a few of the other wives. They made a nice-looking group,
dressed very brunchy, very clubby.

In the group were the usual female crowd of Irene Proudfoot
and Halle Hopper. Fawn Ridgeline, Jamie George and of course the
ubiquitous Carlotta Ferry stood off to the side in their little group. The
first two were nice enough, Dorsey had taken a liking to Halle Hopper
particularly. Carlotta Ferry gave him her usual turned-up-lip smirk and
looked past him when they had a chance to speak, which they didn't.
To Dorsey's eye she had outdone the orange thing for the day. He
alternately couldn't look directly at her but at the same time couldn't
look away either. Her face was the most brilliant shade of orange he had
ever seen on a real person. She was either about to blow a gasket or had
confused today for Halloween, he couldn't tell. Her constant chomp
on her chewing gum was with her today as well. Her jaw moved like a
piston. He moved on from this group as quickly as manners allowed.

Proudfoot made his announcements and Jeannette did her 50-50.
The winners stepped forward for their trophy pictures while George
George and Randy Ridgeline stood off to the side pretending to tend
to the grill but actually not doing anything. Players patiently filed by
for their burgers since they were more appetizing being prepared and
garnished by the club than what GRITS usually dished out.

As everyone began to file out, Luisa sat up straight and did a double-
take. Alexas noticed and asked her what was up. Luisa just replied,
"I don't know but I think I just saw something that didn't compute
although I can't tell you what I actually saw."

Alexas responded, "Uh, try me."

Luisa slowly shook her head and answered, "That cart kid out there
just handed Jeanette a Styrofoam to-go container that could be a burger.
I think a minute ago I saw that cart kid arguing with that guy who looks
like Popeye. I may have seen the cart kid cook the burger he gave
Jeanette himself instead of having the chef cook it. I don't really know
if I saw all of that because it seems like a slow movie reel where I saw

different frames and I'm trying to put them all together. I'm not sure what I saw or if I saw anything."

In a flash Luisa was on her feet and headed for the parking lot. She caught up with Jeanette who was just unlocking her car door. "Jeanette, wait up!". Jeanette turned and stopped as she opened the door, the container still in her hand. Luisa closed the distance to Jeanette and said, "What have you got there?"

Jeanette looked at the white Styrofoam in her hand and said; "it's a burger for Brucie."

Luisa looked confused and asked; "Brucie?"

Jeanette laughed and said "My dog. I'm a Springsteen fan from way back. That kid back there told me they had extras and he cooked it for Brucie. Don't you think that's sweet?"

Luisa stared back at her; "It's not for you?"

Jeanette answered; "God no, I'm vegan. I don't eat that stuff."

Luisa had no comeback for that, so she just began to shuffle off; "Ok, cool, look we didn't see anything weird today. Your tires still have air in them and your windows are all intact. I guess all is well. Be safe and let us know if you know anything we don't."

Jeanette smiled back and responded; "Look, I appreciate the attention. Maybe I just had a run of bad luck. Maybe someone wanted to mess with me and got over themselves. I'll let you know if I see anything, but I think I'm ok. Thanks for the concern."

They parted, and Luisa rejoined Bunny and Alexas for one more Pinot and a final nibble on their crudité plate. Ralf picked them up as scheduled and they all headed home on time. Luisa had an odd feeling in the back of her brain and couldn't figure out why. She had this chopped-up movie reel winding and rewinding and she couldn't put it together.

She and Dorsey talked out his day and she got to hear about his bad round and his good time. He told her all about Billy Flynn and how much fun they had. She told him about lunch with the girls and how they hadn't really seen anything amiss. She explained what she had seen but couldn't identify why it had even stuck with her. They made it an early night, but Luisa didn't sleep so well.

# Chapter 16

## Brucie

**"I'm not an intellectual person. I don't get headaches from concentration. I get them from Double Bogeys."** Tom Weiskopf

August 21

Dorsey answered his phone around noon on Tuesday after the GRITS Tournament at Hidden Hills. It was Steve Martin. "Dorsey, can you talk?"

Dorsey shot back "Sure."

Martin was almost breathless. "Jeanette thinks her dog Brucie was poisoned by someone at Hidden Hills yesterday."

"At Hidden Hills? Was the dog at Hidden Hills?"

"No but somebody sent Jeanette home with a burger that she's pretty sure was loaded with something. The dog ate it last night and started foaming at the mouth and throwing up."

"Who gave her the burger?"

"That's just it. Some cart kid. But we don't think it came from the cart kid. We think someone put him up to it. The dog almost died."

It was taking Dorsey a moment to absorb all of this. "What do we know?"

"Not much. Jeanette says the kid came up to her as she was leaving with the Styrofoam box with "Brucie" written on top with a Sharpie. Says the kid was polite as all hell, told her it was an extra for her, gave it to her and that was it. She just thought he was being nice." Martin was still more or less out of breath.

Dorsey's wheels were spinning, trying to figure out what might be next; "Steve, I may have a way to gain us a little insight here. Is the dog alive? Is Jeanette OK?"

Martin said quietly; "Yeah, both are alright I guess. Jeanette's a little shook up as you might imagine, but she thinks the dog will live."

"How would anyone even know she has a dog?" came from Dorsey.

"She and Tom used to pose with the dog for Holiday cards. He's a big beautiful Saint Bernard. They used to put red bows or beer cans around its neck and pose for the pictures. Anyone who has been around GRITS long enough would know the dog and know its name. The dog is semi-famous around the Tour."

Dorsey chewed on this for a few beats before responding; "OK, I may be able to work something out. Let me get back to you." Martin didn't know about Luisa's little card party at Hidden Hills the day before.

Martin expressed his puzzlement, "Like what? We really don't know anything else."

"I heard you Steve. I have a theory. Just let me work through it and get back to you." With that they mumbled goodbyes and hung up.

Dorsey walked across the house and told Luisa about the call. Within a few seconds of his explaining what he knew to her, she was on the phone to Alexas. Within a half hour of that, Alexas had called her back and the two of them were on their way to Hidden Hills.


Tim Carpenter was caddying for his father and his father's business partner. The players were walking, and the caddies were carrying their bags. Though all of these guys knew Alexas, they hadn't expected to see her crossing the 5th fairway with another woman in the cart. Alexas apologized for the interruption and asked if she could talk to Tim for a minute. His father scowled at her but Alexas returned his look with a look of her own and Tim Sr broke eye contact first. The women gave up their cart and strapped the bags on it so that Tim Sr wouldn't have to carry the bag. They explained that they would catch up in just a moment and led Tim Jr. to a shady spot between the 5th and 13th fairways.

Young Tim was almost shaking by the time Alexas started in "Tim, you're not in trouble, but we need your help."

"Uh, OK" he croaked.

Alexas gave him a nice, firm look and went on "Yesterday, after that tournament, did you give a woman a to-go burger in a Styrofoam container?"

"Yes." He croaked even lower.

"You cooked the burger. Why?"

By this time young Tim was visibly shaking and definitely couldn't make eye contact. "Because this guy gave me ten bucks and a burger and asked me to do it. He said he was sweet on the lady but didn't want her to know it came from him, that he would tell her later but didn't want to make a scene right there in front of everybody." He finished but kept looking at his feet.

Alexas studied him closely. Tim was probably their third best junior golfer, a good student and had been raised properly. His father was a little bit of a case, but his Mom was a super person. "What guy? Do you know him? Can you tell me anything about him?"

"He looked like that guy in those old cartoons, you know, 'Popeye'."

# CHAPTER **17**

## Digesting the Burger

**"I played so bad, I got a get-well card from the IRS."**     Johnny Miller

Wednesday August 23 4 PM

Jeanette had called a meeting at her house in Raleigh Court. It was
a cute, one-floor-living, two-bedroom, one-bath within walking distance
of trendy Grandin Village. Very desirable, rare to find, yet within
reach from a price standpoint. Brick, sitting perched up at the top of
Greenwood Lane with an alley for parking and an entrance in the back.
There is a fenced-in yard with a wood deck off the kitchen. Quality
living.

The 4 PM timeframe made it a business meeting, so no Happy
Hour, at least not yet. Since it was Jeanette's idea, it was her guest list.
Dorsey, Luisa, Alexas, Steve Martin and Detective Finn. They all fit into
Jeanette's Living Area / Den scattered around on Wing Chairs with
Brucie sprawled at Jeanette's feet just next to the couch. The dog didn't
appear to have suffered any long-term consequences from his encounter
with the bad burger. To Dorsey's eye, Brucie did look particularly wary
and made it clear that he was the only one who would get in proximity
of Jeanette on this day. Jeanette opened the conversation "Well, I'm
just looking for ideas. Brucie here almost bit the dust and maybe I am
in worse danger than I may have thought. This thing seems to keep
escalating and I don't know who or why, so I don't know how to stop it.
I'm beyond scared and well into pissed off, so I'm not in the mood to
back away either. What do you guys think?"

Alexas was first to speak "Well, my little cart kid Tim Carpenter pointed his finger directly at George George. There doesn't seem to be much confusion on his part. Described his amazing likeness to Popeye, what he had on that day and what was said. Seems to be pretty cut and dried to me." Everyone looked at Detective Finn.

Finn chimed in; "Maybe. Maybe not. There is a whole lot that goes into an accusation like this. For starters, Animal Cruelty can be a Class 6 Felony. That carries a minimum of One Year and up to Five in prison. Tack on poisoning and it gets worse. Let's say somebody thinks it was intended for Jeanette. Let's say somebody says he and his wife were both in on it. That's Conspiracy. What starts out looking like a bad act against a dog can go all the way to serious jail time, maybe for both of them if she's in on it, and the end of life as they know it. I need to ask this group to give me some slack, let me do my thing and let it play out a little. I promise you that this is serious to me and I don't intend to look the other way. If you want it done right I need to ask for your support. Let's keep what we think to this group and let's try and keep our heads." When he stopped speaking no one else jumped in. They just let his words fall around them and took in their weight.

"Ok, so have you talked to George George?"; It was Alexas.

"No, not yet. I needed to see if Brucie was going to be Ok. If he hadn't made it, it could have actually affected the severity of what we're looking at. I wanted to meet with Jeanette and with you guys, to encourage you to let me do my work. I need to talk to this Tim Carpenter myself, which I will do ASAP. He shouldn't be too hard to find. After that I'll likely talk to George next. Even in that, I need to be careful. I'm not ready to accuse him of anything. Jeanette were you able to save any of the burger?"

Jeanette looked bewildered and replied; "Lucky for us I saved half of it for him for the next day. I have it for you. I wasn't sure if I should be following Brucie around with a scoop for the next few days."

Finn answered; "The sample should do it. I hate to say it this way, but since Brucie lived and Police resources are notoriously thin, I'm not sure I could free up lab time to analyze dog poop anyway." As Finn talked he had wandered into the kitchen and had started looking out the window to the back yard. "Jeanette, did Brucie go outside the same night that he ate the burger?"

Jeanette looked up blankly; "Uh, Yeah, he's a dog. That's what they do. That's what the yard's for. Why the question?"

Finn turned and looked around at them all;. "Because those mushrooms that I see popping up back there can be poisonous to dogs. There are over 15 types of mushrooms that could do serious damage to Brucie."

Jeanette looked up; "Fifteen types?" Like what?

"Well, like 'Death Cap', 'Angel of Death', 'False Parasol' a bunch of Hallucinogenic Toadstools and some others that might not kill him but could make him plenty sick. I think while I'm at it I'll gather some of these out back here and test them too. We could have more than one cause that could have made Brucie sick. Maybe there's not a crime at all."

# CHAPTER **18**

## Summer Doldrums

**"The rest of the field"**

> Roger Maltbie, on what he'd have to shoot to win

September 6

Summer in the Valley is vacation time. Sure, the weather can be hot, with temperatures in the low 90's. In the Valley it's a bowl and can tend to hold heat in. Up in Floyd or over toward the Peaks it is generally 10 degrees cooler and there can be a breeze. No matter, most folks in the Valley head out to Nags Head, Myrtle, Wilmington, Pawleys, Hilton Head, Kiawah and the like.

Dorsey felt the irony in all of this. For the past thirty-plus years he had lived within two blocks of the beach and had rarely gotten sand in his shoes. He compared this to driving around daily gawking at the mountains, wondering if Valley natives were jaded on them or if they still saw the beauty that he saw. He supposed they did. After all, he had still driven by the beach, and walked by the beach. He just hadn't gotten ON the beach much.

It turned out that Finn was still on the beat and he kept following up. No one was sure if there was a crime here, but it was close enough to keep an eye on. Finn and Jeanette met a time or two and compared notes. Luisa and Dorsey made treks around the region, to Richmond and even as far as Chincoteague for a painting confab. Granted, it was sort of a slow time. The Jeanette support group met at her bungalow on Greenwood for Happy Hour. Finn, Jeanette, Dorsey, Luisa, Alexas and Steve Martin.

Finn had talked to Tim Carpenter and had clarified that "Popeye" was George George. George George in turn protested his innocence and said that the burger was a gesture of good faith, that no good deed went unpunished, etc., etc. He had stumbled a little by referencing the fact that his wife Jamie George had prepared the burger and retrieved it from a cooler in their car; "Maybe the damn burger just got hot in the car!" was the straw George grasped at. This storyline went on to reference that they had been prepared to do the cooking themselves before the Club intervened. Of course they had excess burgers. Why let it all go bad when they had been sure the poochie would be grateful for the gift? So this questioning didn't get too far.

Then Finn turned to a new, deeper line of inquiry. It seemed that Randy Ridgeline had developed a keen interest in all of these goings-on. He had called Finn on multiple occasions and requested coffee, lunch or other sit-downs to talk about "this Jeanette thing.' For the moment Finn was chalking it up to the fact that Ridgeline was just a bored, nosy old Cop with nothing better to do than stir a pot that didn't have a lot of ingredients to begin with. His persistence made him notable. When no one else seemed to feel that there was a crime, Ridgeline seemed intent on personally solving it. None of them could make much of this, not really understanding where Ridgeline was coming from or where he thought this was going.

Jeanette commented that Pharratt had ramped up his pestering. He had taken to calling at least once, maybe twice a day asking to meet for coffee, go to lunch, have a drink. She had been creative with her answers thinking that maybe he would just tire out. He hadn't seemed to back off and in fact had seemed to push a little harder lately. She wasn't afraid of him exactly, but she did wish he would get it and move his focus elsewhere.

Near the end of the conversation Luisa produced a bag that she had brought in with her and pulled out a white plastic device, sleek and about 10 inches tall. She explained that it was a "Nest" and she wanted to offer it to Jeanette. Luisa felt that since things had moved closer to Jeanette's house what with the poisoning of Brucie and given this new shadow Pharratt was bringing in, it couldn't hurt. It was a simple device, unobtrusive, that Luisa sat on a side table next to the couch, facing the front door and front window. It had 180-degree range, so it also took in the kitchen door. You simply tuned it to your existing Wifi and downloaded the app to your smartphone. It was motion-sensitive and could even be tuned to account for Brucie, so he wouldn't set it off. If anyone entered the house and moved through that room, your cellphone would be pinged. Better yet, you would have a recording of what it saw. The video could be accessed through the cellphone or online. If you were in a particularly spunky mood, you could even speak through it and scare the beejeebus out of whoever had set it off. Jeanette at first thought that it was a little over the top, then watched patiently as Luisa set it up and showed her how it worked. What harm could it do?

# CHAPTER 19

## Junior comes aboard

**"Golf is more fun than walking naked into a strange place, but
  not much."**
                                                    Buddy Hackett

Great Falls
 Sept 13 - Thursday

With a big lapse of time before the September 19 GRITS Tourney,
Dorsey persuaded Junior to meet him for a round at Great Falls.
Beautiful weather, almost crisp on the drive up, tee off temp at 62
degrees, expected high of 74. They teed off at 9:30 with only a twosome
two holes ahead and no one waiting behind or on the putting green.
Dorsey made Junior drive the cart.

As they played the first few holes, they didn't talk about anything
much. Junior told Dorsey about being at the Floyd Country Store
the prior Friday night and how alive downtown had been with all the
pickin' and grinnin' from assorted groups that formed and reformed
throughout the evening. Inside the Country Store Gillian and Dave
had played, a rare treat in a "pop-up" concert that they had staged, only
announcing it on Thursday afternoon. They were between gigs and
looking to refine a few songs they had recently added to the show. Even
with little notice the show sold out in hours.

Dorsey told Junior that he and Luisa had also made it to Floyd over
the weekend. They had gone to the Chateau Morrissette Beach Music
Festival at the grounds next to the winery on Sunday. Pretty day, tents
and umbrellas. He shared how they had driven up the Parkway going
and coming, enjoying the ride instead of worrying about how quickly

they made it.

Their round went along at a Bogey Golfer pace with a handful of Bogeys and a Par or so thrown in. They finished up the front side with a 46 for Junior and 45 for Dorsey. Still room to each break 90 if they could just play slightly better on the back nine. At least that's what Dorsey was thinking. He couldn't tell if the score had registered with Junior or not. Dorsey decided that for his part he would bear down and see if he could shoot a 43 or better. Let Junior worry about himself.

Number 10 at Great Falls if a 447-yard Par 5 from the Gold Tees. The tee shot is blind in that you hit it over a long rolling downhill where you can't see the landing zone. The 2nd shot is also blind, again downhill, which obscures the nasty little bunker about thirty yards short of the hole in the middle of the fairway. Since it is downhill, if you hit a good drive and get a good roll, you can clear the bunker and if you hit it straight, find yourself on the green or at least just short in front. Dorsey did all of that and found the front fringe of the green. With the front middle Pin placement, he only had about 25 feet for an Eagle, which he missed, but he left himself an uphill 2-footer, which he made. Good start. Junior meantime had fumbled around, and not realizing that a game was on, had made a mindless Bogey. Dorsey was up 2 on the back and 3 overall.

Number 11 is only 312 yards, uphill all the way. Flying the second shot to the green takes the right club and a little courage. Left goes off the green and down the hill, long is in the bunker and right is another bunker. Dorsey hit a good drive, good 8-iron, but it rolled back away from the Pin. His lag was good but not good enough, missed the Par putt, tap-in Bogey 5. Junior started to perk up with his second shot, noticing that Dorsey was playing harder now. He hit his second shot a little too good, into the bunker in the back. Decent sand shot, missed putt, tap-in 5. Dorsey still up 2 on the back, 3 overall. He was giving himself a chance.

Once Junior caught wind that Dorsey was focusing, he put his head down and started to play in earnest. They both Parred the Par 3 12th, Dorsey with a nice chip from long left and Junior from a 30-foot 2-putt. The #13 Par 5 is a long twisting thing downhill to the bottom in front of a pond where you hope for a level lie. Even though it's only 401 from the Gold tees, going for the green on the second shot is almost always out of the question. Even with a good tee shot you are looking at 170-180 yards from a downhill lie across water to a green running left and angling away from you. Dorsey hit a 3-wood, 9-iron to try and find the flat at the bottom. Junior pulled a Driver into the trees on the left but had a clean look at the flat part of the fairway, punching a 9-iron himself to within about 6 feet of Dorsey's ball.

Dorsey smiled to himself as Junior drove the cart to their balls "Closest to the Pin for $5?" he asked. Now it was getting fun. Junior nodded and pulled his club since he was away. Dorsey usually hit more club than other golfers, so he didn't bother asking Dorsey what he was hitting. They were both 106 or so to the front of the green, estimating 121 to the back pin. Junior hit a 9-iron well, but it wasn't enough club. On the green, 15 feet short. Dorsey pulled out an 8-iron, kept his head down and swung easy. Too easy. The flight was high and short in the front bunker. He splashed out to 15 feet short and missed the putt to end up with a Bogey 6. Junior lagged his Birdie close, but it slid by. He tapped in for his Par. Dorsey had woken Junior up. He knew that they were playing for something. Junior had won the Closest to the Pin, Dorsey was 2 up overall, 1 up on the back. Dorsey tried to dig in.

Fourteen passed with two Hacker Bogeys. Fifteen was a 128-yard Par 3 across water with traps in the back Though it was only 128 yards, the water and the traps meant you needed to have your distance right too. Not only that, but a ledge ran right to left so hitting it short made for a difficult uphill putt over the ledge and of course long brought the traps into play. Dorsey thought too hard over his shot, bailed out and hit a high short thing that ended up pin high, but on the far, far right side of the green in the fringe. Not a good shot. Junior kept his cool, but hit it short, below the ridge. The lag putt took the hill and peeled away to the left and 10 feet below the pin. He short-armed the next one and tapped in for a Bogey 4. Dorsey hit a weak lag, a weak 2nd putt and missed the 4-footer for Bogey, recording a Double-Bogey 5. Great. Now he was even on the back and only one up on the Match. Plus, he was down the $5 for Closest to the Pin on #13.

Sixteen went Junior 5, Dorsey 6 (back-to-back Doubles), putting Junior 1 up on the back, even for the match. Dorsey pulled his act back together to Par the Par 4 17th but Junior parred it too, so no change in the overall. The Eighteenth is only 289 yards, Par 4, downhill toward a big pond guarding the green. Hitting Driver means bringing the pond into play. Dorsey hit a nice, high, relaxed 3-wood to the flat part of the fairway at the bottom of the hill, 115 to the hole. Junior hit his 3-wood as well, again within a few feet of Dorsey. As they drove the cart up, Dorsey couldn't help himself; "$5 Closest to the Pin?".

Junior just grinned back and said "I'm in." Dorsey was away by a few feet, chose his 9-iron, He thought he kept his head down but skulled his shot to the top right rear of the green, into that trap.

Junior couldn't keep the smirk off his face as he hit his pitching wedge. He was a little cocky and a little premature as his shot skimmed the reeds by the pond and stuck in the thick stuff short of the green. He hacked it out to 12 feet below the pin and took his time driving the cart around while Dorsey fumed. Dorsey took the long walk across the green to the trap, and hit an indifferent sand shot halfway to the hole. He hit an indifferent lag putt another half way to the hole, then missed the 5-footer to end up with a 6. Dorsey watched all of that patiently, hit his lag to 18 inches and tapped in for his Bogey.

With his run of three Double Bogeys in the last 4 holes, Dorsey had shot himself out of the round, out of shooting below 90 and out of two $5 bets. The final was Junior 89, Dorsey 90 and Dorsey owed Junior 10 bucks. They parked the cart, stowed their clubs in their respective cars, changed shoes leaning on their trunks and moseyed to the snack bar. Dorsey bought them two Pabst each and moved out to the veranda and plopped down next to Junior. "Aargh." Was all he could say.

They talked and commiserated for a few minutes, Dorsey trying to be congratulatory, Junior trying not to gloat. Once again at least one golfer (Dorsey) knew he was leaving the course having left some shots out there.

It was around 12:30 and the sun was high. The temperature had made it to 74 but there weren't any clouds in the sky. Junior leaned back sipping on his Pabst and questioned Dorsey "So, what's up with the

GRITS Tour?"

Dorsey took a minute to respond before starting in "Well, let's see, I think I left off with you with Jeanette's car windows knocked out and my tires flattened. I'm not sure that you are up on the attempted murder of her dog. Or maybe on her. But probably on the dog."

Junior looked up at this with a severe look on his face. Junior was a dog lover from way back, having had a string of dogs from college, through his single days and up to the present. After a few minutes, he nodded for Dorsey to go on.

Dorsey filled him in on George George, on Jamie George, on Luisa and Alexas' stealth operation, on Detective Finn and even on Marvin Pharratt's continued stalking efforts.

Junior was quiet through the story and when Dorsey finished just said. "Whew". They looked back and forth a moment before Junior took up the dialogue. "And you like this girl Jeanette and you don't think she's a nut case?"

"Nope. She just seems to be a nice good egg trying to do something to make the world a better place. I showed you her Alzheimer's website. She's pretty and spunky and trying very hard. Someone is trying to bring her down. The last time you and I talked was the first time I had said all of this out loud and even I felt it sounded sketchy. But now, to say that something is not happening would be like denying Climate Change. Somethings happening."

"And the next tournament is here in about 10 days? What is being done to make sure this girl lives through it?"

"Well", Dorsey began slowly, "Luisa has joined the posse and I think Alexas may come with her. We're trying to keep them incognito so that they can observe without being outed. Luisa did see the exchange of the bad burger at Hidden Hills, so their presence has already had an effect. Steve Martin will likely drive Jeanette but I'm not sure what else we might do. Detective Finn keeps reminding us that it's entirely possible that no crime has been committed, so the cops are not really involved. Not to mention he's retired anyway. He can only do so much."

Junior took all of this in and spoke his thoughts slowly "Well, maybe I'll just come along that day and do a little watching out myself. It's no problem for me to hang out here, this is like a second home for me anyway. And maybe after you chumps get done hacking the place up, I'll even get in a round myself. You think that this girl is worthy and needs some friends, right?"

"Yes I do." Dorsey said flatly. "I don't know what you might do or see but I think things are kind of critical and we need to keep an eye out for her."

Junior stood to leave, having tipped out his second Pabst. "Thanks for the beer and the entertainment. I'll be here."

They both meandered to their cars and made their separate treks home.

# CHAPTER 20

## Great Falls

**"Nothing dissects a man in public quite like golf."**     Brent Musberger

September 19
Par 72
5278 from Gold Tees
Ratings 64.5 / Slope 120
Great Falls, in Floyd, is generally 10 degrees cooler than the Valley.
Conditions for 9 AM Tee time 58 degrees. Estimated at 72 by noon.
Little or no wind. Perfect day for golf

The days were getting shorter. Everyone woke in the dark and left just as the sun shed its' first light on Bent Mountain. The forty-five minutes up Route 221 was a winding path so no one was able to make better time than the next guy. Cars started coming into the parking lot before 7:00 AM. First was the staff, turning on lights and starting up coffee. The GRITS volunteers – Proudfoot, George, Ridgeline and a few others showed up shortly thereafter. It took 25 minutes or so to line up carts pointed in the proper directions so that later they could easily fan out to their designated holes. Preprinted cart signs were sorted and stuck in the plexiglass holders so that the carts would have the proper names on them. All of this was done by 8:00. Four Great Falls staff carts had earlier moved out on each nine, with two staff in each cart. One cart would reset the pins to their pre-determined spots while the other carried weed eaters and rakes to touch up the tee boxes and rake the traps. They had gotten started at daybreak, so that by 8:15 their work was done too.

Marvin Pharratt was the first one on the putting green. He made no pretense of helping or volunteering anything. The staff wasn't even ready to open the range yet, so he putt across the dew and made tracks walking forth and back, shoving three balls around by himself. Dorsey and Junior had agreed to meet early too. Junior had been designated to pick up two egg, cheese and sausage sandwiches from the diner in Floyd. Junior was waiting at 7:45 when Dorsey pulled into the lot. Dorsey walked inside to where Junior was, with a slight wave to Pharratt as he passed him. "He's an oddball" was all Dorsey said to Junior as he sat down across from him.

"So, you're going to hang out here all day?" Dorsey said to Junior before his first bite.

"Nope, I plan to be in and out. After the group goes out, I don't see much reason to be here for a while. I've got an appointment at a farm nearby, so I'm going to go do that, then try and make it back before everybody comes in. When is Luisa coming up?" Junior asked through his first bite.

Dorsey paused while he finished his bite "Not until probably noon or so. Like you, she doesn't see much reason to be here all day. We're setting Jeanette up right there outside on the Veranda under the umbrella. She'll be able to do her thing all day when carts come by and the staff here will be right behind her. Only so much we can do without hiring an armed guard or something."

"Just ask her not to eat anything offered by anyone. In fact, I hope she brings her own lunch." Junior glanced sideways at Dorsey and Dorsey realized he wasn't kidding. Good point, Dorsey would mention it to Jeanette. They needed her help to control the environment.

Jeanette and Steve Martin slid into the parking lot around 8:15. Martin helped her carry her stuff to the card table set up on the Veranda. It had been decided that Jeanette need not venture out onto the course, at least not unless Martin or Dorsey were riding with her. Since they were playing, she was counseled to stay put by the Pro Shop, keep her back to a wall, not take snacks from strangers and smile, smile, smile.

Marvin Pharratt had been pestering Jeanette since she arrived. He practically sprinted from the putting green to Martin's car when they drove in, trying to carry her bags, set up her table, tell her how nice she looked and on and on. Once she had gotten reasonably set-up he didn't let up. "Jeanette, do you ever go to the Community Inn? Do you know about the Bloody Mary's at the Brambleton Inn on Sundays? Do you want to go to the Coffee Pot sometime for music?" Pharatt was relentless.

Jeanette finally snapped at him "Marvin, if you don't leave me be, I don't know what I'm going to do. C'mon man, I need some air to breathe!" With that, Pharratt had slunk away, head down, hands in pocket and muttering. He retreated to his assigned cart until the proceedings began.

Proudfoot lined them all up at 8:45, the Great Falls Pro did his thing, and Jeanette stood up to a round of applause. News about her had traveled through the Tour and someone yelled out; "How's Brucie?" Jeanette looked away for a moment, gathered herself and shouted back with her best smile "He's fine and he loves you all vey much!" The crowd seemed to accept that, and Jeanette moved off to the side by her card table. Proudfoot gave the word and sixty carts rolled off over the hills of Great Falls. The Great Falls GRITS Tourney had begun.

Dorsey found himself riding with Tony Sparano, who turned out to be an affable Asian ex-doctor. Around their 4th hole Dorsey was informed that not only was Sparano a 19 handicap, he was 79 years old, though he looked as though he could easily have been 20 years younger. They had hit it off immediately as it turned out that Sparano was also a very encouraging guy to ride with. Driving the other cart was Horace Brimley, also a 19 handicapper who mostly peered out from under his "VT" hat and occasionally muttered something through his brushy white mustache. He didn't seem like a bad guy nor a bad golfer, he just mostly kept to himself. As the round went on, he would prove to be a little explosive after a bad shot. So were a lot of guys. As luck would have it, Maynard Ferry was riding in the cart with Brimley. By this time in the season, even with 120 golfers, it was inevitable that Dorsey began to get some repeats in his foursomes. Dorsey kept a low profile early on, just shook Ferry's hand and rode along quietly. He had a bunch of questions about Ferry and his wife Carlotta. He decided that there would be opportunities as the round went on, so he tried to focus on his game. By this point in the season, Dorsey was a lot more relaxed about the GRITS environment and felt like it was about time to have a good round.

Their group was "13-B" which would not have been Dorsey's first choice by any means. The twisting downhill Par 5 made for a tough Driving hole for Dorsey, then most likely a layup to the bottom of the hill, then a good short Iron to the green. Plus, they had to wait on "13-A" which meant pacing around trying not to think the worst as he waited his turn. After a period of pacing he hit third in his group and caught a 3-wood at the bottom of the club. It barely got over 10 feet as it cleared the hill in front of them and was sliced. Since it stayed low, it rolled out nicely and he was left with 185 to clear the pond, and 224 to the center of the green. Not taking the bait, Dorsey laid up with a gentle pitch, leaving himself 112 to the center. It was a front flag, but he was only going for the middle, not the flag. Since he was still nervous, he came up on this one too, but it cleared the pond, hit the upslope at the green, popped up and rolled to the back fringe. Dorsey was elated. He was on with a chance to Par.

The others had been scattered around coming down the hill. Sparano had a wild wind-up swing, but he made good contact. Brimley punched his shots down the middle pretty consistently. Ferry's back seemed to have improved from their first meeting at London Bridges. No one had been able to go at the green in two and all had about the same shots at the green. Ferry was first and hit too much club, into the fringe at the back but at least not in the trap. Sparano and Brimley both hit under-control pitches to the middle of the green, in good shape.

Dorsey paced his walk to the back of the green trying to get his breathing under control while waiting for Ferry to hit. Ferry skulled his chip and it rolled gaily past the pin and down into the bunker. They all had to wait as he walked the long way around, settled himself and hit a so-so sand shot twenty feet past the pin. The front of the green was a false-front which meant from Dorsey's angle it ran away from him and down to the front trap. Ferry had found this out the hard way. Dorsey babied the first putt, babied the second one but was able to tap in for a Bogey. It was a three-putt, sure, but he was still happy with himself. No major damage. Sparano and Brimley both hit solid putts and tapped in for Par. Ferry lagged his short and three-putt, ending up with a 7. He walked off fuming.

Fourteen was a short Par 4 over a hill and then down. Three Pars and a Bogey from Ferry after a nice drive and chumping his second shot. Fifteen was a 121-yard Par 3 that Ferry dumped in the water while the other three all hit the green. Another three Pars and a Bogey. Though his back appeared in shape, he had not yet found his game. Sixteen was another easy Par 4, only 307 yards. Again 3 Pars and Ferry's Bogey. He was not having a good day, while Dorsey was on fire! Seventeen was a little more of a challenge and Dorsey leaned back at impact and floated his drive past the tree to the left in the fairway, but into the thick stuff on the right. He didn't have a good lie and could only punch it to the front of the trap, 15 yards short of the hole. Sparano faltered and found the trap on the right front. Brimley skulled his second shot 40 yards short. Ferry hit a good drive and a little too good second shot. After short-arming his pitch, Dorsey clenched up on a putt but managed to make a 5-footer for Bogey. Sparano could only make 5 out of the trap and Brimley's pitch was long so that he had a 20-footer coming back and he too made a 5-footer for Bogey. Ferry pitched to the green, but short, and hit his putt 3 feet past. He missed the comebacker and muttered "6" as they all walked off the green. Three Bogeys and a Double.

Number 18 was the one down the hill to the flat spot in front of the pond. Dorsey's drive was short and his 2nd shot was long and to the back. There was no way to stop his putt coming down the slope, so he had to putt back up and make a three-footer to save Bogey again. Still, all in all, it was a good start for him. Sparano played it textbook, hitting his 2nd shot to ten feet below the hole and making his Par. Brimley hit his second to above the hole and like Dorsey could only watch as it went by the cup to settle below the hole. Ferry dumped his second in the water and had to drop. He hit his next one to the back trap and meekly pitched it out. Then like Dorsey and Brimley he got to watch his ball roll downhill past the cup to 15 feet below. That was a 7 and his hole was over, Triple Bogey being the max allowed. Not a happy camper. Dorsey was pleased with himself, though knew better than to think it out loud

(The Golf Gods were always listening). In the first 6 holes he had 3 Pars and no Double Bogeys, No Triples. He was 3 over after 6. Hang on, hang on, hang on.

As they came across the lot toward the clubhouse toward #1, Dorsey spied Luisa with her easel set up facing up #18. It was the "signature hole" for Great Falls and she was going to see if she could supply them some notecards or better yet, some signed prints to sell in the golf shop. It wouldn't be much money, but it was a way to offset expenses and provide tax-free trips. If she just made enough to do that it was a win-win. Luisa looked like a sweet picture herself with her easel set up in front of her and a big sunbonnet on her head. He almost missed seeing Alexas on the driving range to his left. She had a bucket of balls spread out around her and was taking her time, focusing on pitch shots. Alexas looked nice too in long legged golf shorts and a yellow polo. She had a white visor on and a nice tan. Dorsey thought that having two attractive women mixed in with the GRITS crowd was a welcome relief. He did not try to make eye contact or acknowledge either of them, they were still "under cover". Nearing the clubhouse veranda Dorsey noticed that Junior had apparently introduced himself to Jeanette. Dorsey had explained to Jeanette who Junior was and that he was one of the good guys. It was an interesting sight as it seemed as they were sociable without being in contact. Junior was at the end of her table, partly turned away from Jeanette, maybe 8 feet apart. Their body language appeared intimate and distant at the same time.

Dorsey made his way over to speak to Jeanette as did Sparano and Brimley. They each picked up some crackers or chips. Dorsey tossed a $10 bill into her jar and took a Gatorade from the cooler. There was no charge for any of her snacks and Dorsey was sure that she made much more money this way than setting a price. He was pretty sure that many of the guys were like him, gladly overpaying just to show their support. He asked how her day was going. Without looking at Junior her eyes wandered his way and she spoke "Well, I must say this is one of the more interesting days I've had in a while. Maybe it's this mountain air and beautiful sunshine but I feel lightheaded like I haven't felt in some time. Almost makes me want to burst into song." Junior never had to do much to make an impression on women. His genuine shy nature and killer blue eyes made them all want to look after him. Or take him home. Or something.

Ferry had made a pretty big show of not getting anywhere near Jeanette. He had walked all the way around the back of the cart barn and down the hill to the first tee by himself. He stood waiting in the shade when the rest of the group drove up. Since they had to wait for the foursome ahead anyway, Dorsey took the opportunity to slide over beside Ferry "Hey man, what's up? So you had a couple of rough holes. We have a long way to go. Try to keep yourself in the game, it will come back."

Ferry kept looking at his shoes and grumbled "I wish it were just my game. Thanks to you Carlotta thinks I'm having an affair with Jeanette and will not give up on it." With this, he did look out from under his visor at Dorsey.

Dorsey was rocked back, he hadn't expected this. At all. After a moment he managed a reply "Thanks to me? What did I do?"

"Well you started the whole dang thing with them Raffle Tickets at London Bridges. Then you ducked out at Draper Mountain and Carlotta found Jeanette's shoes in my car. I had to sleep with one eye open for two weeks after that one." He was pretty much snarling by this time, so Dorsey stepped away.

It took Dorsey a few seconds to register what had just been said and apparently he needed even more time to process. He almost whiffed his tee shot completely, skulling it only 75 yards where it stayed in the rough. He punched a Rescue Club out onto the fairway, but he still had 135 yards to the green. He skulled the Taylor Made 6-Iron to the back trap, took two to get out and ended up with his first Triple Bogey of the day, a 7. Ferry had really thrown him with his comments. Ferry meanwhile played the hole almost as bad as Dorsey and got himself another Double Bogey. Somehow Sparano and Brimley managed to block out the scene going on around them and got Pars. Good for them.

With all of this in mind Dorsey was in no way prepared for #2, the number One handicap Par 4. He managed to finish the hole with a Double Bogey, but the wheels had pretty much come off. He recovered a little bit by parring the Par 3 Third hole, but his game was all but gone. They had to wait for the group ahead to clear the green, so Dorsey tried again to see if he could patch it up with Ferry. He didn't have anything against the guy; "Maynard, man, can I help somehow? You don't have anything going on with Jeanette, do you?"

Ferry's head spun around. He was seething at Dorsey; "No you can't be no help! Fawn Ridgeline and Jamie George are stirring this thing into a huge mess. I have never so much as hardly ever smiled at Jeanette, but according to them we're goin' hot and heavy. My advice to you is to keep away from me, keep away from Carlotta, watch out for them other women and tell your little buddy Jeanette to watch out for herself too."

Dorsey didn't have any snappy comeback for Ferry and didn't have any interest in pursuing the topic. He had gotten Ferry's message and moved off to the back of the tee box. He stayed away from Ferry for the rest of the round.

Dorsey pushed the ball around the rest of the course with the usual suspects of Bogeys and Double Bogeys. Even after having a good start, once it was all written down it came to a 94. Pretty much typical of how he had scored on the GRITS Tour, but today he felt like he had been sabotaged. Ferry never got it together either. He shot a 103 which was an outrageous score for someone who was really pretty good. Sparano shot an 84 and ended up winning his Flight. Brimley stumbled to an 89 after what looked like it was going to be a good day. Sparano was feeling pretty good about his round, shooting only five over his age. No one else was in much of a mood as they put their clubs away.

Dorsey immediately headed for the clubhouse and ordered two Mountain Lites. He found Junior sitting with Steve Martin under the scorer's tent. Luisa and Alexas were sitting at a checkered-table-cloth four-top just inside with a clear view of the goings-on. The next thing Dorsey knew there was a commotion at the other end of the veranda with what sounded like women shouting and the crowd swaying back and forth. Dorsey couldn't see who was at the center of it. By the time he did, his heart sank.

Carlotta Ferry was standing over Jeanette, who was seated in her chair, leaning back with looks of fear and horror on her face. Carlotta was in full bloom of Orange Face with her blood vessels seeming about to pop. Her hair was standing straight up, and her arms were flailing over her head. Her gum chewing had been momentarily suspended, with her jaw gripped tight. "And if I EVER see you within 20 feet of him again, I'll tear your hair out myself!" was what she said before stopping, out of breath, with spittle escaping her lips. She lowered her arms to place them firmly on her hips, legs spread wide, potentially about to strike. Poor Jeanette's face was bright red as well and Dorsey thought she looked like she might have been hit or slapped. Her golf shirt was wrenched to the side and bunched under her chin. She was clearly afraid.

At that moment Marvin Pharratt jumped between the two women. "Leave her alone! She ain't done nothin' to you! Now go on out of here and let this woman be!" If it wasn't such a scary moment it might have been hilarious. Pharratt came up just about to Carlotta's chin. She might have had him by thirty pounds or more. He bowed up like a rooster and stood his ground. No one at the scene could even draw a breath as little Marvin Pharratt saved the day.

Somehow what he did put a pin in Carlotta's balloon and she backed away and hissed "Maynard! C'mon dammitt! We're getting outta here!" She didn't look back and halfway to her Dodge Maynard materialized by her side. He hustled to unlock her door and held it open for her, then he flopped into the passenger seat. She spun gravel backing up and going the other way. A trail of dust followed them all the way down the drive and out onto route 221, presumably headed for Roanoke.

As Dorsey watched all of this unfold, he realized no one in the crowd of almost one-hundred people had said a word. Marvin Pharratt had not moved from the spot where he had confronted Carlotta. People moved in on Pharratt and began congratulating him for his heroic action. Jeanette was slumped limply in her chair staring at the ground. As she came around, she stood and patted Marvin on the shoulder. She dipped her head a couple of times and slid past him inside toward the Ladies Locker Room. No one noticed that after a few moments Luisa and Alexas followed behind her.

There were the other usual group of women still standing in a huddle

outside on the Veranda. Jamie George, Fawn Ridgeline and a few others
that Dorsey didn't know huddled and began to mutter in low whispers.
He did hear a few comments; "She had it comin'", "You cain't push
Carlotta.", "She better leave my husband alone too!", and "Why is that
Bitch out heres anyway?" Dorsey couldn't make head or tails of the type
of mentality that would create such mindsets about Jeanette. He really
didn't get where all this was coming from.

After a few minutes Proudfoot was able to restore some order by
compiling his scores, handing out his trophies and taking his pictures.
The crowd dispersed with no further mention of the cat fight they had
seen. Dorsey made his way inside to sit at the checkerboard four-top with
Junior and Steve Martin. Junior and Martin boxed up all of Jeanette's
paraphernalia and put it in Martin's car. Dorsey finished his second
Mountain Lite and figured that would have to be enough. With the day
he had it made better sense to get himself home before he partook of
any more medicinal alcohol. After a time, Jeanette, Luisa and Alexas
came out and Jeanette nodded to the guys. Martin took Jeanette by the
arm and led her to his car. Luisa and Alexas climbed into Luisa's X5 and
pulled away.

Dorsey tapped Junior on the shoulder and fist bumped him without
saying anything more than "I'll catch up with you later." And once again,
the drive away from a GRITS event left him more confused than when
he had arrived. More questions than answers.

# CHAPTER **21**

## Slap Analysis

**"You can conquer basketball. But you can't conquer golf."**
          NCAA and NBA Basketball Hall of Famer Michael Jordan

September 27 – Thursday 5:50 PM
Jeanette's Bungalow, Raleigh Court

Jenette had called the meeting and Dorsey and Luisa had picked
up Alexas at her house on the way. They were early, and Dorsey was
surprised to see Junior already there. Number One, he didn't know
Junior was coming and Number Two, that meant that Jeanette must
have invited him. When Dorsey, Luisa and Alexas came through the
front door and Dorsey saw Junior, he glanced to Luisa with a raised
eyebrow, but she had looked away and did not give him anything to go
on. Everyone there said their pleasantries and Jeanette offered drinks.
It was Happy Hour after all. Luisa had an A-Z Pinot Gris, as did Alexas.
Dorsey had Meridian Chardonnay, his drink of choice. It appeared that
Jeanette was having a "Get Bent" IPA and Junior was sipping on a Pabst.
After a few minutes of "Hi Howdy's" Detective Finn and Steve Marin
found their way in as well.

They all found seats around the room, with Luisa and Dorsey sharing
an oversized stuffed chair, Alexas looking all proper in a wooden chair.
Junior was sitting halfway out of the room in a kitchen chair turned
backwards. His chin was resting on his hands on the back of the chair.
Martin ended up on the Love Seat with Jeanette. Brucie was sprawled
at her feet. Finn was pacing with a clipboard in one hand. Martin
had accepted an IPA but Finn was true to the cop code and deferred.

Finn started in. Dorsey wasn't aware that this was Finns' meeting but apparently he had been busy since the earlier meeting at Jeanette's house, now over a month ago.

Finn started with acknowledging that he had interviewed Tim Carpenter, the golf cart kid and George George, who Carpenter had fingered for passing him the bad burger. Before he gave details, he explained that he was able to get the scrap of burger that Jeanette had saved analyzed. It was a bad burger. Not that it had strychnine or rat poison in it, but it was moldy, old and not fit to eat. It was possible that the burger had been left outside or in a car or somehow allowed to decompose in the heat. The problem was that this wasn't as clear cut as finding a chemical compound or foreign agent in the meat. It was just not a good thing to eat. Maybe poor housekeeping, maybe an oversight, but still in a grey area of finding a cause and tracing it to harmful intention. Maybe somebody just wasn't too smart about handling meat.

Tim Carpenter had pointed out George George as the one that passed the burger to him with instructions to grill it and present it to Jeanette.  George George implicated his wife Jamie as the one who had given him the burger in the first place. Finn had talked to Jamie who professed to be a dog lover and therefore mortified that such a thing could have happened from the good deed she was trying to do. Her acting wasn't very convincing, but she did have a story and she stuck to it. Finn reminded the group that after all, Brucie had pulled through and proving this grey area stuff wasn't going to be that easy. Was there really a crime?

Everyone around the room listened politely, with Jeanette leading the group in exaggerated eye rolls. Luisa was fuming. Alexas was working herself up pretty good and Dorsey was just dumbfounded. As they stirred in their seats, Finn raised his hand with "Wait, let's keep things moving forward here. Let's not get bogged down in this part just yet."

With that he moved on to the happenings at Great Falls and the Carlotta-Jeanette altercation. "OK, so I wasn't there. What happened?" For a moment they all looked at Jeanette who responded with "I wish I knew. One minute I'm selling Raffle Tickets and Potato Chips and the next minute this woman is all over me. I don't know that I was anywhere near her husband and she just came at me out of the Blue."

Finn took this in and looked around the room "Did any of you see anything?" No one spoke, most just looked down at their hands, and everyone shook their heads from right to left and back again. Finn moved his focus across the group with "Well, that's not gonna help much." With that, the looking down and head shaking continued on.

Jeanette piped up; "Well, the Bitch hit me! Ain't that somethin'? I mean whether I'm doin' her husband or not, isn't that a crime? She can't just come up and start slapping me and pulling hair, can she?"

Finn looked back to the group "Did any of you identify anyone who saw anything?"

More looking at the floorboards and more head shaking.

"Well, I'm not sure what we have here either. First, it's out of my jurisdiction. Second, you didn't file a report or anything at the time did you? At the moment we can't put our hands on anyone who saw anything. "

The staring down and shaking heads commenced again.

"Jeanette, I guess you could file a complaint with the Floyd County Sheriff. Without witnesses, without photos of bruises or a report, or an Emergency Room admission, I don't think we have much. We could try and interview everybody that we think might have been there when it happened, but again, Number One, out of my jurisdiction and Two, we have bupkus for evidence, a report, nothing, nothing, nothing. I don't see how it can go anywhere."

Jeanette chimed in "What about Pharratt? My White Knight. Did you talk to him?"

Finn: "As a matter of fact I did. He said that he had tried multiple times to reach you to get together and talk about what had happened and how he might help. You never seemed to get around to returning his calls, so his feelings got bent out of shape. He explained to me how hurt he was that after coming to your rescue you didn't want to give him the time of day. Seems his reasoning is that maybe if you were little more grateful when folks tried to cover your backside, maybe his memory would be better. Uh – his words not mine."

This produced Jeanette's biggest eye roll of the day so far.

"And we have another precinct that I've been hearing from. Seems Randy Ridgeline's wife Fawn has been filling up his ear about how she and her group of pals think that Jeanette might have been the aggressor here. Fawn and Jamie George think that if Jeanette weren't so provocative and flirty, then all this might not be happening to her. Again, her words not mine."

Jeanette's eyes did a major roll as she sprung to her feet. "Flirty! Why there's not a man among that crowd that I would flirt with if my life depended on it! Bunch a fat, jowly, smelly old men. She must be dreaming that I would ever have anything to do with that pompous washed up Cop she calls a husband! What are these women smoking to be thinking like that? No woman with any self-respect or a good set of eyeballs would have anything to do with that bunch of droopy old men. This just beats all!" She seemed to be tearing up with frustration, so she just sat down and massaged a wadded-up Kleenex for a minute while the others stared at the carpet some more.

Finn didn't say anything for a moment, silently offering a silence for anyone to fill if they had something to say. But they didn't. Their case with George George was dead in the water. Their case with Carlotta Ferry wasn't any better. Randy Ridgeline and George George, two key components of the GRITS Tour were apparently lined up firmly against them. And as a group they had done little or nothing to keep Jeanette from harm.

Finn excused himself and Steve Martin followed closely behind. Dorsey and Luisa and Alexas got their stuff together and filed out the door with their shoulders slumped. Dorsey cut a look at Junior, but Junior never looked up from leaning on his kitchen chair. His chin was still resting on his hands. As they got to the car he asked Luisa "Is there something going on with Jeanette and Junior?" She only shrugged and slid into the passenger seat without saying anything. Dorsey pulled away from the Bungalow wondering why so much seemed to add up to so little.

# CHAPTER 22

## New River

**"Hold up a 1 Iron and walk. Even God can't hit a 1 Iron."**
Lee Trevino – On how to deal with Lightning

October 8 - Monday
New River Course – Turkey Trot County
Par 72
From Gold Senior Tees 5903 – Longest Course on GRITS Tour
USGA Rating 69.5   Slope 128
At tee time cool mountain air 52 degrees high of 72 at midday. Breezy

The New River Course was beautiful. And LONG. And a long drive from the Valley. The longest course and the furthest away. Dorsey had managed a Practice Round with Wright Strange, Strange at the wheel for the drive from the Valley, almost an hour and a half to get there. The Course played long. It was wet in a lot of spots even though the weather was OK. Cloud cover, in the 60's. Little wind. The Course played through a "Holler" bordered on one side by mountains and on the other side by the River. For effect a train would roll through the Holler sometimes pulling coal down to Norfolk or wherever. The train would play a long soulful note which seemed out of Hollywood since there were no crossings to pull the horn for. It was a beautiful setting.

Many did not care for the design of the New River Course. It had been redone recently by a husband and wife team out of Florida that apparently had no love lost for average golfers. It seems a rich alumnus from the local University had paid for them to tough it up and modernize and had then donated it to the University. The University

Golf Team had a decided home field advantage because it was tougher than almost anything anywhere. The designers had favored elevated greens, liberal bunkers, water wherever they could find it and used the local winds as an extra kicker to torment players. These factors were the signatures of the courses that they were acclaimed for all over the country and all over the world. Dorsey enjoyed their designs, having played some of their courses and learned how to play them pretty well. It was target golf. Not totally about distance, but equally about hitting the ball to the right spots. That didn't make them feel any less diabolical.

Dorsey had driven up for the GRITS match with Wright Strange again. They had become good buddies and traded tales of woe regarding their games. Dorsey never talked to Strange about Jeanette or Carlotta or Pharratt or any of that. He was still interested in keeping Luisa and Alexas and Junior under wraps in hopes that somehow they would help uncover whatever was going on around Jeanette. It was a nice drive and they were early enough to hit some balls and stroke some putts. The distance hadn't kept GRITS players away, it was a full turnout. Even though most of them understood their scores wouldn't be anything that they would want repeated, the reputation of the Course's natural beauty and the challenge made them come out anyway.

Dorsey hit his normal 20 – 30 range balls and dozen or so putts. He hit some extra 3-woods off the turf because he figured that he would be hitting them all day, based on the length of some of the holes. He had swapped out his Ping Zero that he used for his "Texas Wedge" and instead had put in a 7-rescue that he hadn't used for a while. In the practice round, he had a lot of shots from just off the fairway that made it tough to hit an Iron. He had better luck with a Rescue club, but the one he had hit it too far. He reasoned that for 150-160 yard shots from the rough, the shorter rescue might help. As Jimmy Buffett said; "only time will tell." Before getting in the car with Strange, he had recounted his bag to make sure he didn't have too many clubs.

Dorsey made his way to one of the two carts marked 7-A and introduced himself to the driver, George Glazebrook. Since Dorsey had gotten there early, he had immediately strapped his bag onto the passenger side. By this time in the Tour he had given up any pretense of gentlemanly letting the other guy show up late and ride. No way buddy. He hated to keep score and he liked to walk. Let Mr. Glazebrook keep up with all the administration. Dorsey wanted to focus on his play.

When he shook hands with Glazebrook he immediately felt a little bad. Hidden under a Walrus mustache was a sly smirk of a smile. The guy had longish blonde hair and was towards 6'2", probably 225, and a 6 handicap. He turned out to be a Teddy Bear, funny, good golfer, supportive and kind. When they came by the clubhouse after their first three holes he bought a six-pack of Heiniken. Heiniken! Nobody drinks Heiniken on a golf course! He immediately offered one to Dorsey. Dorsey loved the guy.

The other cart was composed of the man, the legend himself, Manny Proudfoot and Casper Hagen, a 7 handicap. Dorsey was not sure what to think of Proudfoot being in his foursome. Trying to analyze the others in the foursome and whatever message that sent was doing him no good. Hagen was a burly 250 pounder with a beard gone white and a golf swing that never repeated itself. After they got going and Dorsey and Glazebrook started yukking it up they didn't interact much with the other cart. Share scores at the Tee Box, hit away and see ya later. Not in a bad way, just that everyone pretty much did their own thing. Dorsey tried to put Proudfoot's presence out of his mind.

First up, hole #7, Par 3, 118 yards. Should be no big deal. The description online mentioned "signature bunkering" and "collection area to the left". Dorsey knew that these were the key elements of the day. All that was required to play well today would be long drives, precise Irons and smooth putting. Argh.

Proudfoot led it out with a shot that found the green for a little while. It trundled into the "collection area", which was not as closely cut as the putting surface. It would be puttable, as long as you factored in any putt would be moving straight up hill, to a cup on a crown where if you hit it too hard it would roll over the green into the bunker and if you didn't hit it enough it would roll back to your feet. No problem.

Casper uncorked a line drive that somehow stayed on the back fringe. Dorsey hit a nice high ball that was a little short, but on the putting surface. Glazebrook hit a textbook three-quarter wedge that skipped twice and stopped about 5 feet past the pin. Dorsey hadn't played with Glazebrook so far, but if this was the way the guy could play, he was very impressed.

Proudfoot's putt came flying up the slope, took a look at the cup and kept on going to the fringe on the other side but stopped short of going in the bunker. He was still away. He lagged that one short but made the 2-footer for his Bogey. Dorsey kept his head, took a nice breath and even though he bladed the putt, it rolled out to 18 inches. He tapped in for his Par. The other two had routine Pars and they moved along.

Number 8, water all the way on the left, but not particularly in play. Overcorrecting on his second shot, Dorsey pushed the fairway 3-wood into thick stuff on the right. Nice chip, 2 putts, Bogey. Proudfoot pulled his drive within a whisker of the rough, chumped the second, on the front fringe in three, 3 Putts, Double. Glazebrook continued to impress with a bold, long high fade that curled back from over the water leaving him only 115 to the pin. Par. And Hagen continued his unorthodox but effective play as well, Par.

Number 9. Long, water, bunkers. Double Bogey for Dorsey, Double Bogey for Proudfoot, Glazebrook Par, Hagen Bogey. Dorsey started to calculate one of the unannounced competitions that he sometimes used with Junior to help him concentrate. They had played three holes and he was three up on Proudfoot. At that moment he defined the mission for the day. Nothing personal, just a way to stay focused. Proudfoot didn't even need to know it.

The course made you focus. You were rewarded if you hit the ball where you aimed, and you would be punished if you didn't. The online site used the terms "native grasses", "correct club selection" and "deceptive greens" as throwaway terms, but they weren't. They were prescriptions that needed to be respected and you could not let your focus waver.

As they swung around to #10, small talk noticeably subsided. Dorsey had accepted the Heineken from Glazebrook gratefully, but was also cautious as to its' effects. Heineken carried more kick that his usual Mountain Lite and they had a long way to go. It tasted good, but Dorsey was wary of enjoying it too much, at least for the moment.

Pars all around on #10. Dorsey dumped a dumb one in the water on #11 for his first Triple of the day. Proudfoot pulled off a decent Bogey, so Dorsey gave up one, and was 2 up for the round. Glazebrook and Hagen both Bogeyed #11 too, so Dorsey didn't feel but so bad. Dorsey had a good Bogey on the Par 5 #12 but Proudfoot pulled off a nice Par, with a sweet wedge to about 12 feet and a two-putt. Dorsey was only up one for their unstated match. Glazebrook and Hagen both made Pars. Number 13 had trouble "long and right" and Dorsey found it. He really smacked his fairway 3-wood and hit it a little too good, on a low screaming trajectory over the green, back right. It was in some really thick stuff, but he horsed it out, and made a nice 2-putt to save Bogey. Good job. Proudfoot didn't have all the drama Dorsey was going through and made an easier Bogey. Dorsey still up one. Glazebrook stumbled a little with a Bogey and Hagen made Par look easy.

On the 13th green, as he waited to putt, Glazebrook had put the toe of his shoe next to his ball, bent and picked up the ball to clean it. Without moving, when it was his time to putt, he replaced the ball to the spot by the toe of his shoe, then putt, missing and tapping in. As the group walked off the green, Proudfoot moved closer to Glazebrook and said "Y'know, you didn't mark your ball back there. That could be a two-stroke penalty."

Glazebrook, to this point a gentlemanly Teddy Bear had not said much of anything to Proudfoot, going along quietly, holding the pin when it was his turn, raking traps when appropriate and offering encouragement to the others. He stopped in his tracks and gave Proudfoot a look. "Manny, I did so mark my ball. My toe never moved, and the ball was replaced where I picked it up. The rule says that the ball needs to be replaced where it was picked up, not that I have to use a special marker or anything remotely like that." He seemed to have gotten wound up quickly and stood still, with his hands on his hips, waiting for Proudfoot to reply.

"Well, I think you should use a ball marker. You don't see the pros using the tips of their shoes do you?" said Proudfoot.

Glazebrook gave him a turn of his head and his body shifted closer. "Manny, you only give me 6 strokes out here and then you want to take

2 away? For what? Have you ever considered giving up some of those strokes that you keep for yourself? Are you just so vain you have to see your name on your leaderboards? Remind me again why I even play your stupid Tour. You have it rigged so that no decent golfer even stands a chance. I'm tired of seeing me finish behind hackers like you every time out. Don't talk to me about rules and fairness when you have the whole thing stacked for you and your buddies."

Proudfoot stood for a minute, then walked on to his cart. No more was said, and the tension hung heavy in the air. The carts moved quietly to #14, the 138- yard Par 3. Hagen hit first on #14 and hit a nice ball to the middle of the green. Proudfoot skulled one into the trap that dominated the left side. Glazebrook motioned Dorsey to hit next. He took several deep breaths, stayed down, hit the 6-iron smoothly and was rewarded with the "plunk" of sound when it landed 18 feet left of the pin. Glazebrook took his sweet time but hadn't quite shaken off the exchange with Proudfoot and found himself in the same bunker with him. It was awkward to see the two men sorting out who was away, not stepping in each other's lies and generally trying not to acknowledge each other. Glazebrook handled it better, with a nice spray of sand leaving him 6 feet for his Par, which he made after marking his ball with a plastic ball marker. Proudfoot took two to get out, then 3-putt for a Triple Bogey. Hagen and Dorsey tidied up their Pars and moved quietly to the carts.

The edge had come off of Dorsey's fabricated competition with Proudfoot, but noted to himself, not out loud, that he was now up by 4. On #15 Dorsey hit it hard, then hit it hard again. He was still 20 yards short, and though he hit a decent chip, still left himself 15 feet, missed that one and had to settle for a Bogey. Somehow even though Proudfoot was shorter on both of his first two shots than Dorsey, his chip kept rolling and rolling toward the pin. He was left with a 2-footer, which he made for an amazing Par. Dorsey was only up 3.

They had played 9 holes to this point. Dorsey broke with his custom and added up the scorecard. Glazebrook had finished his third beer of the six-pack. He was still fuming. Dorsey made it clear that he didn't need another one right then, so Glazebrook popped his fourth as

Dorsey added the scores. For the nine that they had just played, Dorsey had shot a 45. A good score for this course. Proudfoot had shot a 49, Hagen a 39 and Glazebrook a 38. Then why was everyone so quiet?

Number 16 is a Par 5 and the group had to wait for the fairway to clear. Glazebrook sat in the cart and drank his Heineken, and Hagen was fussing with his clubs and his bag. Dorsey couldn't help himself, he slid up next to Proudfoot, because he didn't want to totally miss the benefit of a captive audience. Since he figured Proudfoot was still ruffled after the exchange with Glazebrook, he decided what the heck, go for it "Manny, I've been looking for a chance to talk to you about the Jeanette situation."

Proudfoot snapped to attention as if he'd been slapped. "What Jeanette situation?"

Dorsey stayed cool and looked him in the eye. "The situation that somebody or a group of somebodies from your Tour is out to hurt her. That situation." He didn't lose eye contact. He didn't want to let this opportunity slip by.

Proudfoot sighed and moved back a step. "My Tour. My Tour. Sometimes I think that this Tour was the worst idea I've ever had. I have been close to Jeanette and Tom for 30 years. I invited Jeanette to do her thing with the Tour because I wanted to support her. I've heard the rumors like everyone else. I don't know what I can do about it. Do you?"

Dorsey almost felt a little sad for Proudfoot, because he seemed genuinely hurt. But Dorsey wasn't ready to back off either. "Well, it appears that some of the main suspects in the foul play may be your key guys. A lot of fingers are pointing to George George. Ridgeline seems more interested than he should be. Marvin Pharratt is a long-time Tour member. Maynard Ferry and you are close. Don't you think you should be working to get to the bottom of things?"

By this time, the course had opened up and Dorsey's group could have hit, but so far no one had. Hagen and Glazebrook were taking in the exchange between Dorsey and Proudfoot with rapt attention. Proudfoot's shoulders seemed to droop another level. "Dorsey, you haven't known me long. This is your first year on the Tour. What you need to know is that I don't control those guys. They do as they please.

They've helped me for years, but I don't have any leverage over them. Or their wives for that matter. Is George George capable of poisoning a dog? Maybe. Is Carlotta Ferry a jealous woman? Probably. Is Marvin Pharratt a lost schoolboy? I guess so. But anyone who thinks that I tell them what to do or not do is kidding themselves. They're grown folks. They may not be acting like it, but that's the way it is. I suggest you be careful of what you accuse them of. They can have mean streaks. I suggest you think twice what you accuse me of. I'm fond of Jeanette and have been her biggest supporter, though lately I've begun to wonder how smart that is."

Nothing more was said between the two. Dorsey moved off toward the tee box and waved Glazebrook ahead to hit. Hagen hit next, then Dorsey, and finally Proudfoot. The round continued in relative silence. Number 16 produced two Bogeys, by Hagen and Glazebrook and two Doubles, by Dorsey and Proudfoot. Dorsey and Proudfoot both Double-Bogeyed #17 and #18. The life was out of the round. Glazebrook stopped for another six-pack of Heineken as they went by the clubhouse and Dorsey bought his own six-pack of Mountain Lite. After all, Wright Strange would be driving him home.

Dorsey rallied a little with Pars on #1, #3 and # 5. Proudfoot kept to himself and Dorsey didn't pay any attention to his round. He was able to get back in the groove with Glazebrook as the alcohol had the desired effect. They played the last four or five holes giggling and laughing a little more. There was no question a pall still hung over the group and for whatever reason Dorsey continued to feel a little sorry for Proudfoot.

When it was all added up, Dorsey had shot a 92, which he considered a good score on a long hard course. Proudfoot posted a 102, and Dorsey felt a little bad about that too. Hagen had a decent 79 and Glazebrook pulled off a very respectable 76. None of the group was in the money. By the time they made it back to the club house, things were already breaking up. It had been a long drive in the morning and the round had taken it out of them all. Dorsey imagined that Proudfoot, Jeanette and the others had gone through their normal routines, but he didn't have the stamina for it. He was tired and his buzz from the Mountain Lites was beginning to wear off. He found Wright Strange, whose head was hanging, having shot a 104 for the day. They both silently nodded toward the parking lot and made their way out.

The drive home was long too. They didn't talk much as Dorsey reflected on the fun he had with Glazebrook, but also the exchange between Glazebrook and Proudfoot. He continued to feel as if he had ambushed Proudfoot himself, though that hadn't been his intent. He had wanted answers from Proudfoot but the answers he got left him just as confused as before. Who, what and why were things going on with Jeanette? Who could stop it?

# Chapter 23

## All Hell Breaks Loose

"In golf, when we hit a foul ball, we've got to go play it"
Sam Snead, to Ted Williams, comparing golf to baseball

October 8
4:45 PM – Jeanette's house – Raleigh Court

Coolish evening. Misty and heading towards dark. As the streetlights came on, they reflected in puddles in the street. Pretty dark for this time of day, but it would be a full moon.

Jeanette was bushed. It had been a long day to the New River Course and back. The round had taken the guys forever. Though everyone was too tired for much of an after-party, she had to stay and do her thing. The 50-50 Raffle had only brought in $37 for Alzheimer's, and she hadn't sold a lot of snacks either. Her take was $67 for a 10-hour effort.

Martin had dropped her off at the Park-and-Ride in Salem. She had made it home and parked out front. Since it was getting dark, she didn't always like to pull around to the alley and go in that way. Besides, Greenwood was the prettiest street in Raleigh Court and she liked to take it in sometimes after a long day. She stood leaning on the car door for a moment, taking in the street, the lights and the quiet. She bundled all her stuff into her hands and arms, locked the car, trudged up the concrete stairway to the yard, then up the wooden steps to the porch.

As she fumbled for her keys Brucie began to bark incessantly and her cell phone vibrated in her purse. Since she could only do one thing at a time, she got the door open, made it into the foyer, dropped her keys and purse and turned on the foyer light. She reached down to pat Brucie before heading through to the kitchen, hit the backyard light and let him out. Within seconds he began to bark again, clearly after something. She could only hope that it was raccoon or a squirrel and not a skunk.

As she reached for the kitchen light, something clobbered Jeanette from behind. At the same instant that she felt something across the back of her neck, the same something shattered the glass panels in the kitchen door, right where her face was. As she went down, her right hand grabbed for anything to stop the fall and found shards of glass instead. Later she would learn that she had shredded three fingers on her right hand and almost cut to the bone. The cuts would take time to heal. But for now, blood went everywhere.

As Jeanette struggled to figure out what was going on and to regain her footing, she felt a dull blow in her back just below her shoulder blades. This time she went flat face down. In the instant she hit the ground trying to get a handle on what was happening, the back door came inward, slamming into her head, almost knocking her out. Whoever was coming in the back door gave it another big push, sending her backwards into whoever had been behind her. Since she was lying at the assailants' knee level, they fell on top of Jeanette and began alternately hitting her with fists while seeming to try and pull out her hair or gouge out her eyes.

Jeanette was still face down with the other person on top of her when someone lunged through the back door and landed on top of the attacker. She couldn't get up with both of them on top of her and couldn't get a look at who either of them was. The kitchen light was still off so this whole thing was being conducted with only the backyard light coming through the broken glass and the foyer light from the front of the house.

Then Brucie joined the action. He leapt on top of whoever was on top of Jeanette which made the whole scrum a 400-pound rolling mess. Brucie did manage to get between Jeanette and whoever the other two were and she was able to almost get up from her behind and get to her feet. As the two intruders rolled around and slugged and pulled at each other, Jeanette had made it to the entranceway to the living room and had a clear view when two other entrants came bolting through the front door. She could see that they were women.

After a moment of getting their bearings, these two made it to the kitchen and one of them flipped on the overhead light. Brucie turned his attention to them and caught one of them by her shirt sleeve, nearly ripping the shirt off entirely. Luckily for the intruder, Brucie just missed getting a mouthful of flesh.

Jeanette's confusion had just begun as she realized that the woman Brucie had by the shirt was Fawn Ridgeline. The woman now pulling some guy off the other woman was Jamie George. The other woman, the first one, the one who had clocked Jeanette in the back of the head was Carlotta Ferry. And that the one who must have come in from the back door was Marvin Pharratt! What the hell?

To top it off, within seconds, Jeanette looked up to see another figure coming through the front door. It was a man. It was Junior Loaf. What Dorsey hadn't known up until this time was that Junior and Jeanette had started going out some. After their meeting at Great Falls, they began to get together for a beer or dinner a time or two or three. It was not accidental that Junior was here. He had come to pick Jeanette up and maybe go to the Village Grill for the steak quesadilla. They would sit out by the fire station on the porch and continue to get to know one another. So far, their time together had gone smoothly and easily. They had found each other at a good time.

Junior took one look at what was going on and flew to Jeanette's side. He and Brucie cordoned off a space between Jeanette and the other four bodies in the kitchen. By this time the kitchen felt very small. Chairs were overturned, the table was pushed against the sink, area rugs were scattered, the blinds were ripped from the back door, the windows were busted and there was an impressive amount of blood on the door, the window and the floor.

Junior and Jeanette managed to stand up and get in the entranceway to the Living Room. Brucie was in front of them, snarling and looking formidable. The back door was partly open but blocked by the chairs and trashcan that had become wedged against it in the melee. With everyone in the room heaving for breath, some on hands and knees, some on one knee, all with wild eyes, Junior this time said it out loud; "What the hell?".

An object between Carlotta and the table caught his eye and he quickly picked it up. It was a Ping 6-iron. It was the object that Carlotta had hit Jeanette in the back with. It was the same object Carlotta had broken the kitchen window with when she swung it at Jeanette the first time. Junior knew who the 6-iron belonged to. He had every intention of returning it to its' owner himself.

Fawn and Jamie clearly wanted to make a break for it but Brucie, Jeanette and Junior stood between them and an escape. Pharratt was on both knees with his palms upturned and a shaken look on his face. Carlotta was still on her butt but had managed to maintain her look of rage and was the only one who looked like they still wanted some more. Junior reached into his pocket for his cell phone, the 6- Iron firmly in his grip, ready to swing if need be. He held the chair in front of him while he dialed. He was the only one who knew who was on the other end when he spoke calmly. "Look man, we need you at Jenette's place RIGHT NOW! Call Martin. Call Finn. But call them on your way. We need you here RIGHT NOW! As he pushed the red button to end the call, he took a breath and dialed 911 to begin another call.

Still at Jeanette's house – 9:30 PM

Martin and Detective Finn had left some time ago. The Police had stayed a while, took pictures and statements. Pharratt, Carlotta, Fawn and Jamie had skedaddled before the cops had even made it. Junior hadn't been happy about it, but he hadn't had the energy to fight them either. Carlotta had still been in a rage and looked like she was just getting warmed up. She took Fawn and Jamie by the arms and demanded that Junior and Jeanette and Brucie step aside to let them out. They did. Pharratt had followed in their wake, moving the remaining chair and the trash can so that he could slink out the back door while the others huffed out the front.

Luisa had bandaged Jeanette's hand. Everyone, especially Luisa, had pleaded with her to go get some stiches. She had steadfastly refused.

The bleeding had stopped, and the bandage looked clean. She could wiggle her fingers and it didn't hurt that much. It could wait until tomorrow for a final determination.

One cool thing was that the "Nest" had caught it all. The vibration that Jeanette had felt when she was first coming in had apparently been Pharratt. He had jimmied the back door to get in before Jeanette. Brucie had slowed him down and made him retreat out the back. Brucie had gone after him when Jeantte first let him out. He was by the back door with Brucie lunging at him when Carlotta made her entrance through the front. His story was that he only wanted to see Jeanette, that he meant her no harm, and hey, he had been the hero at Great Falls and that he had been the hero saving Jeanette again tonight.

Carlotta, Fawn and Jamie had all come in Carlotta's Dodge. They had primed themselves with Cosmopolitans all afternoon and had set out to teach Jeanette a lesson once and for all. They hadn't calculated Pharratt being in the mix, had forgotten about Brucie and didn't reckon on Junior at all. Junior and Jeanette identified the lot of them and told the Police what they knew of what had gone on.

The Nest did a great job, first catching a glimpse of Pharratt, since he was partly in the kitchen and had turned to get out ahead of Brucie. It caught Jeanette as she came into the house and deposited her stuff in the drop zone in the foyer, then turned toward the kitchen, Brucie and Pharratt. It caught Carlotta as she steamed in in all her fury. The images were in color, so her orange hair, orange face and lousy disposition were well highlighted. Then the Nest reset while Jeanette, Carlotta and Pharratt went at it. It came back to life when Fawn and Jamie came through the door a few minutes later. It also got Junior clearly. His entrance would later provide comic relief since when he came in, his face registered a full range of emotion and confusion. His tape was a keeper. Jeanette gave the web address and passcodes to Finn and the Police so that they could review them at their leisure. Technology did come through in the form of some hard evidence. Not that there weren't loose ends. Those could be sorted out later.

Dorsey, Luisa, Jeanette and Junior Loaf sat scattered across the living room and den. There were empty beer cans and wine bottles left around. The light from the kitchen seemed unnaturally bright and unnecessary. Music was on, but it was barely audible, and no one was much listening anyway. It was Springsteen, but you could hardly make it out. Brucie lay at Jeanette's feet at the base of the couch.

No one said much, and Dorsey finally struggled to his feet. He reached for Luisa's bare feet sticking up from the armchair where she was slouched sideways. Junior was in a chair at the kitchen table, chin resting on his hands. He hadn't moved in quite some time.

As Dorsey made for the door he tapped Luisa's foot again and said lowly, "c'mon honey, let's get ourselves home." She began to unfold from the chair to get to her feet and find her Birkenstocks. Halfway to the door Dorsey turned to Junior and said; "c'mon man, let's let Jeanette get some sleep". Junior didn't move. After a few moments Dorsey tried again; "Junior, c'mon man it's late, let's get out of here." No reaction, no movement.

Dorsey looked from Luisa to Junior and started a shrug of his shoulders. Jeanette chimed in "Leave him be Dorsey. I would feel safer if I had some company tonight". Dorsey swung his attention to Jeanette, across to Junior and then to Luisa.

Luisa met his gaze with a shrug of her own. Dorsey followed up looking between Jeanette and Junior "Is everybody sure?"

Still no reaction from Junior but Jeanette piped up assuredly "Yeah Dorsey, we're sure." Still no reaction from Junior. Dorsey turned to Luisa. Again, a shrug, as she reached for his arm to lead him out the door. Dorsey turned one last time to check out Junior who still hadn't looked up.

Luisa led Dorsey out the door and down the walk. They didn't speak until after he had opened her door and walked around and climbed in his side. As he turned the key he leaned toward her with a question. "I didn't see that coming. Did you?"

Luisa turned to Dorsey and kissed his forehead. "Men are always the last to notice these things. Let's go." They headed home, Dorsey as equally confused as he had been since he joined the GRITS Tour.

# CHAPTER 24

## The Reckoning

**"Baseball reveals character. Golf exposes it"**

Baseball Hall of Famer Ernie Banks

Thursday October 18
2:30 PM Blue Bells Dining Room

Proudfoot had gotten support from the Blue Bells staff to cordon off
the Dining Room from customers and even staff. A front table had been
arranged where Proudfoot, Detective Finn and Jeanette sat. Proudfoot
and Finn had notepads in their hands. Finn and Jeanette each had
stacks of documents in front of them. Jeanette's stack was pretty big.

Community Outreach Officer Don Francisco was there as well, seated
off to the side by himself. Since the bruhaha at Jeanette's house, this
had Officially become a Police Matter. Since Detective Finn wasn't still
actively a Detective, Don Francisco's presence made it all legal. Dorsey
would note later that all through the meeting, Don Francisco never said
a word.

There were two rows of chairs facing the front, with an aisle down
the middle. The chairs were clearly to delineate appropriate seating
for different factions, much like you would a wedding party. Or the
Hatfields and McCoys or Democrats and Republicans, but certainly
indicating a separation in interests. On the left side of the "aisle"
were Marvin Pharratt, Maynard Ferry, Carlotta Ferry, Randy and Fawn
Ridgeline, Jamie and George George. On the other side were Dorsey,
Luisa, Junior, Alexas and Steve Martin. The room was tense, and no eye
contact was taking place. Ridgeline sat ramrod straight in his chair, his

eyes shifting slowly from side to side.

Proudfoot stood and started to speak, addressing the left side of the room "I have something to say that you are probably not going to like. I suggest that it is in your best interest to hear us all out because there could be repercussions if you choose to ignore what we have to say." He stopped and looked at each face to his left individually, then back at his notes.

Dorsey did a double-take when he looked up at Proudfoot. Without his golf hat, Dorsey noticed for the first time his shock of black, long, combed back hair. His face was more tanned and more lined than Dorsey had ever paid attention to. His features were chiseled, and he stood with his arms crossed, his shoulders back and his feet apart. Dorsey saw a more regal demeanor than ever before. Proudfoot stood before the group as an enigmatic representation of the best of Osceola, Sitting Bull, and the baddest of them all, Red Cloud. It was an amazing transformation.

Proudfoot continued; "I am very disappointed in what has gone on here. You have all let me down, the GRITS Tour down, and you certainly have let yourselves down." He paused, then continued at a measured pace. He looked to his right, at Jeanette, and cleared a catch in his throat. "This woman has spent a lot of her time and energy trying to do something good. Her efforts have reflected well on her and have lent an aura of respectability to herself and the GRITS Tour." At this point Carlotta Ferry began to stir to her feet but the stern tone in Proudfoot's voice made her stop with her butt hanging in midair. "Carlotta, you would be making a mistake to leave. Detective Finn here has some charges pending for you. If you don't want to listen and instead want to head for the door, I suggest that as soon as you get outside you call a lawyer". With this, Carlotta retook her seat. The oversized wad of gum protruding from her left jawline was getting a furious workout.

Proudfoot continued, looking at the group to his left "All of you are hereby advised that you are no longer welcome as it pertains to the GRITS Tour. As Officers you are out. As players you are suspended. As spectators you are not welcome."

With this George George rose to his feet. His eyes were squinty, and he had an oversized toothpick sticking out of his mouth. Dorsey couldn't help but notice that the guys forearms were HUGE. "Manny, I've given 16 years to the Tour! This is the thanks I get?"

Proudfoot met his eyes with a black gaze "It seems that your "service" has only been self-serving lately. As of now you are no longer associated with the Tour." Proudfoot paused again and looked down the table to his right. "Detective Finn has something to say to each of you."

Proudfoot took his seat. Finn stood with his notepad in hand and said to the group on the left; "The stack of papers that you see in front of Jeanette are all complaints sworn out against each of you. She only has to sign them and hand them back to me and I will be able to present them to a judge for certification." Now the room was hushed. "Before I name the complaints individually, let me first say that all of these will be entered as felony complaints. They all potentially carry penalties that include jail time." He definitely had their attention now. He took a breath, then began to read from his pad, looking to each face as he addressed them one-by-one.

He started with Randy Ridgeline, "Obstruction of justice. Conspiracy to commit a felony." Ridgeline's face went white, but he kept his thoughts to himself. Finn moved next to Fawn Ridgeline. "Conspiracy to commit assault. Assault against a domestic animal. Assault. Breaking and Entering. Trespassing, Grand Theft" When her head jerked up at this, he stared back at her and said simply "The money purse". Fawn lowered her head.

He looked over Ridgeline's shoulder to Pharrat and met his eye, "Stalking. Breaking and entering. Assault. Assault against a domestic animal." Even from across the room Dorsey could see Pharratt's Adam's Apple bob up and down.

Finn moved back to the front row, to George George "Conspiracy to assault. Conspiracy to harm a Domestic Animal. Threats to Assault." He then looked across to Jamie George "Conspiracy to harm a Domestic Animal. Conspiracy to Assault. Assault. Breaking and entering. Trespassing. Grand Theft"

He then moved to Maynard Ferry "Conspiracy to Assault." Then to Carlotta "Conspiracy to harm a Domestic Animal. Conspiracy to Assault.

Assault. Breaking and entering. Trespassing. Grand Theft for you too."

It was the quietest room Dorsey could ever remember being in.
Finn moved to the left side of the room, peeling off individual stacks of documents and placing them in front of each of the parties on that side of the room. Finn looked toward Proudfoot and sat down with a nod indicating he was relinquishing the floor.

Proudfoot stood and addressed the left side of the room again. "The papers that Detective Finn has just handed out are restraining orders for each of you. They are signed, sealed and delivered. They are registered with Roanoke City Courts. If any of you get within a mile of Jeanette after you leave this room today, you will be automatically arrested and face charges. "

He picked up the stack of papers in front of Jeanette. Since everyone was sitting close, it was easy to see that the documents looked like more Official stuff. He took his time showing them to the group before he spoke again; "Jeanette is here to make you what I believe is a too-generous offer. She is of the opinion that dragging you all through the courts is something that may be more than she wants to undertake. She feels that the animosity that would generate may keep this whole thing alive longer than she wants to keep it alive. Jeanette is an amazing woman who feels that if we can all put this behind us with minimal damage, maybe even something good can come of it. Detective Finn and I aren't quite as convinced as she is that this is the right way to go, but we're willing to defer to her wishes for now. These additional complaints can sit on a shelf in Detective Finn's office for a while until we see how this plays out. The complaints are good as long they are entered within the next year. We're willing to let Jeanette give her plan a try for now. Detective Finn will still have the last word." He stopped again to let his words sink in.

"Jeanette is suggesting that if everyone of you follow the Instructions I am about to give you, then she might be willing to think more kindly of you for now, and provided you leave her the hell alone, may be persuaded to let this all pass." Again, he took his time.

Never one to take the easy route, George George spoke up "Instructions! What kind of instructions?" Again he waved those massive forearms.

Proudfoot just stared him down "George, you and all of you, need to listen carefully. Detective Finn and I are prepared to see if Jeanette's plan works. If it doesn't we're fully prepared to go with Plan B and serve all of you with felony charges. So maybe you prefer the alternative. It's your choice."

George grumbled under his breath and came back with "What about the Tour?"

Proudfoot responded, shaking his head as he went on; "I did not create the Tour with the idea in mind that a bunch of fat Hackers would create little fiefdoms and lord it over a bunch of other fat Hackers. You've made it into something that it never should have become. I didn't set out to make it worldly or big, but you have managed to make it petty and small." Looking directly at Ridgeline and George he said, "You guys need to get a life." After pausing he added "Maybe we all need to get a life." His face was flushed, and his voice was cracking. He turned away from the room and stood with his back to them, with his hands wiping around his eyes.

When he looked back around, he was looking at the women, Carlotta Ferry, Fawn Ridgeline, Jamie George. "And you women. You went after her because she was prettier than you. Somehow you conjured up the idea that she could be attracted to YOUR husbands? Really? Have you looked at your husbands lately?" With this he added another headshake; "So, you got together and decided to tear her down. To rip into her because she was trying to do good and in your own black little hearts you couldn't imagine just doing something for the good of it. That would never occur to you." Proudfoot took another breath; "You never stopped to realize how much she might be hurting, having just lost her own husband. You only thought that she might upset your own pathetic little apple carts. You never thought to offer her a hand. That joining her and supporting her might make you better people in the process. Instead of just thinking of yourselves could you not see that a sister could be in need?" Proudfoot turned back to the wall for a moment and stood with his back to the group, his shoulders rising and falling, his hands on his hips. It made for an imposing view, with his narrow waist, broad shoulders and slicked back black hair. Dorsey was mesmerized, having never seen this side of Proudfoot.

After a moment he turned back around, took a breath and went on; "Golf is a game of Character" Proudfoot said, looking again at the group to his left. "You have perverted the good that Golf stands for. In a small way I had hoped that the GRITS Tour would stand for those things too. But now you have made the Tour sordid and sullied, and probably the butt of jokes in the future. To be true to Golf, you don't take Mulligans. You hit them as they lie. You putt them all out. You call penalties on yourself and you attest to your score. In a tiny, tiny way, the GRITS Tour was supposed to honor those ideals. It was supposed to be fun. You have turned it into something dirty and sinister. You have singled out this poor woman and picked on her because you could. You have taken what she was doing to make things better and tried to make her pay for it. No good deed goes unpunished…"" With this, he turned away from the group for a moment, wiping his eyes and clearing his throat.

As Proudfoot turned back around his gaze was sure and his voice was clear. "The "Instructions" are this; You all are banned from the Tour as I said before. We don't want to see you around. And the Tour is fining each of you $ 1,000. Each of you. You are to honor the restraining order and leave Jeanette alone. Anything that contradicts the spirit of any of this will compel Detective Finn to file the charges that he is holding for now. That will be his decision, not Jeanette's."

George George of course couldn't help himself; "Fined! Who are you to fine us? And what are you going to do with the money, put it in your own pocket?"

Proudfoot glanced at his notes and stated calmly; "The Fine is to keep this all in the forefront of your minds. It's none of your business what I might do with it. I might use it to spruce up the Tour. I might give it to my favorite Charity." As he said this last part, he glanced toward Jeanette; "And if paying me a fine doesn't seem fair? I don't care. But if I were you, I'd pay it, shut up and be glad I was getting off easy." With this, George sat down and shut up.

Proudfoot scanned his eyes across the group to the left and said with a sad shake of his head "Your Tour is over for this year. I'll think about it over the winter as far as next year goes. Based on what I've learned from this year, I think I'm going to make some pretty big changes assuming the Tour goes forward at all. I think that there is more that we can accomplish with the Tour than we have to this point. If I go forward with it at all, I intend to aim higher." Of course no one in the room had any idea what that meant, but based on the look in his eyes, no one had the urge to ask at that time either.

Proudfoot looked across the room once more before bringing the proceedings to a close; "That's it. No negotiation. You would be wise to not discuss this outside of this room. If it gets out of this room, you could force Finn's hand to have no choice but to file the complaints. If you don't like it, tough. In any case, I'll be glad to accept the checks made out to GRITS from each of you. That's it. This meeting is over."

# CHAPTER 25

## Valley Country Club

**"I don't care to join any club that's prepared to have me as a member."**
Groucho Marx

Valley Country Club
October 29
Par 71 – Boxwood 36 – Cherry Tree 35

Distance / Slope / Rating Gold Tees
Cherry Tree 2778 67.6 / 118
Boxwood 2598 67.1 / 118 Combined 5276 yds

67 degrees at tee off, 71 by noon. Leaves turning with oranges and reds and burgundy colors. A perfect day for football, but since it was a Monday, a perfect day for golf.

It was an amazing, crisp clear day for Golf. Even arriving just after 7 AM Dorsey had to park way out, just inside the grounds near the entrance gate. He put on his shoes and slung his bag over his shoulder, making the trek to the cart area. Coming around the clubhouse, he was astonished at the sight before him. The entire practice range, putting area and porches were abuzz. Volunteers in Purple swarmed everywhere. There had only been 11 days since Proudfoot had made his stand at the Blue Bells meeting. Ridgeline, George, and Ferry were not in attendance today. Nor were their wives. Community Outreach Officer Don Francisco had supplied a Security Detail to ensure that all remained calm. Proudfoot had moved mountains to reshape the Tour in the preceding days.

First, Proudfoot had reached out to the Valley Country Club

management and pulled some strings. They in turn had pulled some strings of their own. Rather than simply set up for the usual 120-man field, they were now serving a buffet breakfast on the deck overlooking the 18th green, free to all comers. There were two dozen women, wives or significant others of the GRITS Tour, serving, making Bloody Marys and Mimosas ($5 apiece). One-half hour before Tee off, The Valley CC Pro would conduct a raucous Putting Contest ($10 entry) with at least 25 participants lined up to take their shot. Proudfoot had decided that for the Tour "Aiming Higher" would mean aiming to do some good. This event was all about Alheimer's. Purple was everywhere. If the players had thought they had seen enough of it earlier in the year "they hadn't seen anything yet."

Purple and white Bunting hung from the balconies all around #18. The carts were decorated with Purple and White. Anyone in attendance who was NOT in Purple was encouraged to pick from the (specially priced) selection of shirts, hats, shorts, socks and gloves on the racks and tables outside the Pro Shop. Valley Country Club had called in favors from their vendors and Purple keepsakes were available in abundance. Cups, ball markers, napkins, sunglasses, even purple "Plus Fours" were available for purchase. It was a tsunami of Purple, all for the cause.

Luisa, Bunny and Alexas had set up what amounted to a Command Center at Jeanette's cottage on Greenwood Lane for the past 10 days. They had concocted color-coded spreadsheets of numbers gleaned from the rosters of every club in the Valley that they could get their hands on. Calls had gone out that were not so much solicitations as directives. They did not plead for donations so much as fulfill orders.

Several times Dorsey or Junior had been in mid-pitch only to find the phone receiver taken away from them by Luisa or Bunny or Alexas. The tone of the call would shift abruptly to a short-form admonishment to double the gift, be sure to add dessert to the meal certificate, forget about expiration dates, or otherwise up the ante. The vendors rolled over easily once one of the three women got on the line. Luisa or Bunny or Alexas would wrap up the call with specific details "How can you get that to us, can you deliver it?" or "When can we have someone pick that up?". Dorsey or Junior or Steve Martin or Proudfoot might then be dispatched to "go get it and hurry, we'll have more for you by the time you get back!" If it was fairly routine and not of key significance, Alexas would dispatch one of her Golf Interns to "go pick this up for us and hurry back please." Amazon would have been impressed with the efficiency with which the three women ran the operation. It should have had a name, like "Operation Overlord" or "Desert Storm", but there hadn't been time for that. They just had to get on with it.

Sponsorships had been sold for every hole, with a Purple sign listing the company or individual who had stepped up to help ($250 per hole). Long drives and closest to the pins were already set up ($10 entry per). Individuals could buy Mulligans ($5) and extra putts ($10). On the Par 5's "Tiger Drives" were for sale, where you could move your ball ahead 300 yards and play from there ($10).

Alexas would be stationed at the Par 3 ninth hole on "Boxwood" which would become the 18th hole for the day. Valley CC had 3 separate nine-hole courses and Proudfoot had decided to play Boxwood as the finishing nine to showcase Alexas. It would serve as a "Beat the Pro" opportunity and allow for a gallery to look on. Anyone willing to take on Alexas could pony up $20 and try and hit a shot better than hers. If they did, they got a free round at Valley CC. If they didn't have a better shot than hers, they got razzed by the crowd of onlookers for "losing to a girl." Proudfoot and Alexas liked her odds.

Alexas had also recruited her Junior golfers to set up the same challenges ($5) on every Par 3 on the Course. Trying their luck against High Schoolers would prove to be very tempting for a lot of players. Alexas was pretty sure the High Schoolers had the edge there as well. Every course on the GRITS Tour had kicked in Free Foursomes to help bump up the proceeds for the GRITS season-ending gala.

Luisa had set up a selection of her Art for the Silent Auction. Most of what she had brought was from the Virginia State Park selection that she had painted to honor the Park's 80th year anniversary. She had also brought a set of the Grandin Road paintings she had done the previous year. That morning Luisa had come out and painted the 9th at Boxwood, the Par 3 over water that would be the finishing hole. She would sign any and all paintings sold today, and all proceeds were going to Jeanette.

Bunny had set up a luncheon fashion show to be conducted while the Tour was playing their round. For the $30 fee, participants would get lunch and the show. The $30 figure was picked because that's what the players were paying to play their round. Davidson's, Garland's, Punch and F Geoffrey Ltd had all contributed. There was a nice selection of the latest fashion, set up conveniently for purchase. If your size wasn't in, no worries, it would be delivered to your home within 2 days, guaranteed.

Each Player found a goody-bag in the front seat of the cart courtesy of Bunny's husband (The Godfather), Alexas' husband (Racquetman) and some gifts that Dorsey had been able to round up from some of his cronies. Sleeves of golf balls, tees, sunscreen, Golf Towels, and coupons from local golf stores were included. Maybe not much, but a first for the Tour, and a nice little touch.

Mike from "Best of Roanoke" was on hand to shoot team pictures or whatever group you wanted and provide prints ($20 each) – all for the cause. The Hotel Roanoke, Mill Mountain Zoo, Local Roots, River and Rail, The Wasena Tap Room, and Five Points Sanctuary had all come across with prizes. The Silent Auction tables would be open until 4 that afternoon. Wheeler's Fast Serve cleaners had a gift certificate for the Raffle, as did the Coffee Pot, The Texas Tavern and the Roanoke Weiner Stand. The guy from the produce stand on Brambleton Avenue had even showed up. He had small bowls of cut-up cantaloupe to hand out with wooden toothpicks. He had cold apples on ice. Dorsey stuck a banana in the glove box on the cart for later and grabbed a bowl of cantaloupe. It was tasty. No business in the community wanted to be left out of this one.

After saying his "hi-howdy's" to everyone he could, Dorsey had made his way to the practice ranges. He hit his normal 18-20 shots on the range and stroked a dozen or so putts. Warming to the spirit of the day he found himself a Bloody Mary and got set to play. For some reason, even with the action and buzz going on around him, he felt strangely calm and at peace.

At 8:55 Proudfoot appeared on the deck above the 18th green with his "Mr. Microphone" in hand. He stepped out first to polite applause, then turned and pulled Jeanette to his side. The place went crazy. There were over 250 men, women and children spread out in carts, around the practice green, on the decks, and in the grass queued up to buy Raffle Tickets. Proudfoot had to wait for the cheering to stop, then wait again as he tried to speak. Jeanette beamed at his side, her hands flapping up and down under her chin, indicating that she was breathless. After the third ovation, Proudfoot was able to get the crowd quiet enough so that he could speak.

"Thank you. I thank you. Jeanette thanks you. Alzheimer's thanks you."

He had to wait for the cheers to stop before he could continue.

"All civilized people everywhere thank you."

This set off a long loud round cheering.

"My first announcement is that today's round will be played under "Paradise Rules!" Pick 'em up, clean 'em, find a good spot to hit from" The crowd cheered when they heard this. "And if you feel like giving out a "Gimme", do It! Let's have fun today!" The crowd whooped it up on this news.

"Well, I don't want to hold back progress. The Purple Raffle tickets today are as good as $5 cash. You can spend then for drinks, spend them for the games on the course, and spend them for the Silent Auction. He held up two giant wheels of Purple Raffle tickets, one in each hand "And we're not gonna run out!" The crowd again went nuts. "There's an ATM in the lobby of the club if we need one and if that doesn't work, we'll take IOU's and get it from you tomorrow! So, go out, have fun, dig deep, spend some money and let's show Jeanette how we REALLY feel!"

The scene was like the beginning of LeMans, the Indianappolis 500, the Kentucky Derby and the Super Bowl all in one. Carts spun out toward their assigned holes, Volunteers ran to their stations and Club Officials sprinted onto the course with clipboards and Walkie-talkies in hand. The final event of the GRITS Tour was off and running in a memorable direction.

Proudfoot had cooked the Tee assignments and foursomes to recognize events that had led up to this day. Dorsey and his group were 1-B. The group on 1-A was hand-picked as well.

1-A was Dooley Hopper, Briscoe Sisson, Chandler Hoffman and Steve Martin.

1-B was Dorsey, George Glazebrook, Dana Blades and Junior Loaf! Even though Junior was not an official member of the GRITS Tour, Proudfoot had made him an Honorary Member for the day in recognition of his contributions over the past few weeks. After all, his intervention had saved the day at Jeanette's cottage the night she was attacked by Carlotta and her group. Junior was a hero!

Proudfoot had pulled another slick trick for this group too. He had felt that playing the holes 1-18, in order was the best way to play the course. So, no "Shotgun start" for these two groups, they would start on #1. Also, to ensure that they had smooth sailing, there were no groups assigned to hole #2, or #3 ahead of them. And no one on #18 behind them. This way, they could play their round with no one to wait on, and no one to push them. They were all decent golfers, and played quickly, but Proudfoot thought that the little extra cushion might be nice.

This had meant bunching up some groups on other parts of the course, and some holes were stacked with A, B and C groups. But with all the games on the course, the "Beat the Pros" and the freedom of Bloody Marys and beer on the course, it was likely to be a five hour round anyway.

Proudfoot had reached some new conclusions about what the Tour should mean and what it might accomplish. The lessons learned from the petty behavior from some of his cohorts had opened his eyes to the fact that the game was meant to be fun. Play by the rules, sure. But some days there were bigger things to be achieved.

After assessing his foursome, and the one teeing off ahead of him, Dorsey couldn't help but smile. He was surrounded by a great group, in a bubble of comfort and all he had to do was enjoy the day. When he thought more about the setup, and the relaxation of the atmosphere, one other item became clear; He and Junior were basically in a Match Play situation. Dorsey wasn't going to say anything, but from the first shot on, he was going to do his best to beat Junior. It would be fun to be in his own head.

The first hole on Redbud is 303 yards up a hill. Dorsey pulled his drive to the left, but it got a good kick and bounced just inside the rough in the fairway. Dorsey was 132 yards out, stayed down on his (newly recovered) 6-Iron and knew he had hit it well. When he got to the top of the hill, he jumped for joy, as he was 12 feet away, and below the pin. After fidgeting and fussing waiting for the rest of the group, he stroked the putt smoothly and was rewarded with that distinctive sound when a putt hits the bottom of the cup. He couldn't help the goofy grin on his face as he realized he had his first Birdie of the day. He felt relaxed and light as a feather. The sun felt warm on his face and life was good. Junior didn't slack off either and made a nice 2-Putt Par.

Dorsey hadn't said anything about their "Silent Match" and reminded himself to not get too carried away. Seventeen holes to go. And just like that he stumbled. Number 2 is a 151-yard Par 3 and Dorsey hit too much club. So now after 2 holes he already had his first Birdie of the day, and his first Double Bogey. Junior hit a nice 5-Iron, nice lag putt, nice tap in. Dorsey was one down after 2. "Pay attention!" he silently screamed at himself.

They both Parred #3 and both Bogeyed #4. Dorsey had a very nice par on the Par 5 fifth, and Junior had a sloppy three-putt for his Bogey. All square. Both parred #6, both parred #7. Dorsey Bogeyed #8, but Junior chumped a chip, then 3-putt. Dorsey up two. Dorsey bogeyed #9 and Junior missed a 4- footer for his Bogey, settling for a Double. Dorsey up three after nine holes. He had shot a 41 on the front nine and Junior had a 44. Both good rounds so far. Dorsey couldn't believe how relaxed and calm he felt. He had gotten a Mountain Lite from the tent after #6, and it had tasted good. Now he reminded himself to cool it, that he was playing well, and that today could be his day.

Glazebrook had shot a 38 and Dana Blades had matched him. They got to chitchat with the group from 1-A when they got to the Par 3 7th. Sisson and Hoffman were each 2 over at that point and Martin was 3 over. Dooley Hopper was 4 over but looked like he was having a good time. He was making good friends with the beer providers but playing well at the same time. Everyone agreed it was a great day to be alive.

Dorsey tried to stay within himself. He Parred #10, Bogeyed #11. On #12 he just plain swung too hard. It was far and away his worst swing of the day. He leaned back and hit a high sidewinding slice that barely stayed in the course. He found the ball, but it was dead to the world. He tried to chop it out and didn't get it all the way to the fairway. He was huffing and puffing when he hit his next one in the trap in front of the green. He hit a weak sand shot and 2 weak putts. It was an 8. Everyone had stood around watching as he slashed his way through the last few strokes.

Dorsey sulked off the green like a spoiled teenager and headed for the shade. Fortunately, the shade produced a beer tent and he helped himself. As he tipped the beer back, Junior Loaf moved right into his face, two feet away. "Hey man, you're bringing us all down. You wanna stay here and have a couple of those? Or do you want to finish the round?" Dorsey was ready to throw down his beer and tell Junior what he thought of him. The smirk in Junior's eye changed his mind. Instead of taking out his play on Junior, it suddenly hit him that Junior was right, he was being a total jerk.

Dorsey burst into laughter, spitting his mouthful of Mountain Lite into the sky. He walked toward the group with his hands out "Guys. Sorry about that. Can I buy you all a beer?" The three of them shook their heads and started pulling their clubs for the next tee shot. It was forgotten.

Ok, an 8 on #12. So, Par, Bogey, Triple. Junior had gone Bogey, Bogey, Bogey. Dorsey had lost 2 shots to Junior. Neither of them had even acknowledged that they were in a 2 man match yet. "Get it together man!" echoed in his head.

A Bogey 5 on #13 somewhat steadied the ship. A beautiful 6-iron on #14 gave him an easy 2-Putt par. Junior hit his own 6-iron to 2 feet and tapped in for Birdie. (Whoa!). Dorsey was 3 down to Junior on the back, even overall. They both made nice Pars on #15 and Bogeys on #16. Dorsey chumped a wedge on #17 for his Bogey, but Junior three-putt for his own Bogey. All tied, 18th hole. Who would have it any other way?

Dorsey had made a habit early in the Tour of not looking at his scorecard during a round. Looking at this one as they made the turn had been an accident, and it had almost cost him, in being too casual, maybe drinking an extra beer that didn't help. He knew his score was pretty good. He didn't know exactly how good. He knew he only had the Triple against him on this side, and he had made some Pars. He knew he and Junior were tied overall, but he didn't know what the actual score was. He pulled his 6-iron and got ready to play the last hole of the season.

There was a huge crowd around the Tee Box, and a bigger crowd on the hillside beside the green. And another crowd on the balcony overlooking the holes coming into the Clubhouse. They were excited, pumped up, and not a little bit fueled by Mountain Lite and whatever. Dorsey did not feel nervous at all. To the contrary, he felt great. Everything that had gone on throughout the season had vanished. He felt elated that this day had come, and that he had been a part of it. There wasn't a cloud in the sky, either in his mind, or in his real life.

Time to "Beat the Pro!" Alexas hit first. The crowd was firmly on her side. Everyone in Dorsey's group had ponied up $20 in Raffle Tickets, so they were all in to "Beat the Pro". Alexas flashed a beautiful smile framed by her golden tan and took her place on the tee box while the crowd grew quiet with respect. It was a beautiful, high arcing shot. It landed just below the pin, bounced once, rolled a little and settled to 4 feet below the pin. The crowd went crazy. The guys in Dorsey's group gulped and stepped away, trying to figure out who had to follow that.

Glazebrook had Birdied #17 and Blades had Birdied #16. They would hit in that order. Junior had Birdied #14, so he would follow them. Dorsey would hit last. Glazebrook hit a nice shot, but above the hole to 10 feet. No cigar. Blades shot looked great in the air, but his was a little long too, to 8 feet. Junior took his sweet time and hit a decent shot, but it was to the right of the pin, not bad, but 15 feet away. An easy 2-putt Par.

Dorsey picked out his long-lost friend, his 6-iron. He could see the individual faces lining the tee box, and the looks on his fellow players faces as well. He could pick out the shades of Purple on the spectators on the balcony. He could see Luisa's sweet face smiling at him and cheering with the others. His hands felt calm and his mind was clear.

Dorsey walked slowly to the tee box, making sure his breathing was slow and steady. His hands shook a little as he placed the tee in the

ground, but he took another breath as he stood behind the ball and
looked at the green and the hole, 142 yards away, across the water. He
went through the routine that he always did, picking out a spot from
behind his ball, then keeping his eyes on it as he moved to the side. He
lined up the club with the target and bounced a couple of times on his
knees to be sure he was loose. He shrugged his shoulders just a little
before he pulled the club back. He kept his head down in his backswing
and thought only "smooth, smooth". He stayed down and balanced
as the ball left his club and only looked up when it was gone. The
ball was climbing through the sky, high and straight against the blue
background. He followed the flight until it came down just sort of the
pin, barely missing Alexas' ball as it bounced once, twice, rolled, AND
WENT IN THE HOLE!

The next 20 or 30 minutes were lost on Dorsey. After he saw the shot
go in, he stood bouncing up and down with his 6-iron over his head.
The crowd went wild, and he almost ended up in the pond in front
of the green in celebration. He made a run as if to jump in and but
overestimated the distance. By the time he realized he was too close and
about to fall in, he had to hop on one leg on the bulkhead around the
pond to stop himself. The crowd loved this too.

It felt as though everyone in attendance slapped him on the back and
gave him a fist pump. Junior chest-bumped him and Glazebrook and
Blades grinned big goofy grins at him. Someone yelled from the crowd
"Drinks on Dorsey!" But he didn't care. In that moment after a long
season and a long year, he was happy. Truly happy.

For the record, Junior had shot a 44 / 38 for an 82, a very good score.
He didn't get any strokes, because after all, he wasn't even really on the
Tour at all. Dorsey had shot a 41 on his first nine holes. With his hole-
in-one, he had shot a 40 on his final nine holes. So he had shot an 81,
more than 10 strokes better than his best score on the Tour all year.
With the 22 strokes that Proudfoot gave him, it was a 59! Only 5 people
had ever shot a 59 on the PGA Tour. So there.

He vaguely remembered the rest of the party at the Clubhouse inside.
He remembered another Mountain Lite or so and giving his Raffle
Tickets to Junior. He learned later that Junior had won a free round for

four at Great Falls. He vaguely remembered Proudfoot shushing the crowd and Jeanette crying. He thought he remembered everyone in the place hugging Luisa, Alexas, and Bunny. He seemed to remember Proudfoot announcing that the proceeds for the day weren't all counted yet, but they were somewhere over $36,000. Proudfoot had added to the $6000 collected from the banned group, so that GRITS contributed a total of $10,000. Alexas, Luisa and Bunny had accounted for over $10,000 just in the "Beat the Pro", Art Auction and Luncheon. Jeanette's earlier yearly goal had been $22,000. Before today, including the fiasco at Hanging Tree, she had collected $4600. So yes, today had been a big one.

When Dorsey finally pulled away and agreed to follow Luisa home, he had walked down the driveway with his clubs over his shoulder and thrown them in his trunk for the last time for a while. As he pulled out of Valley Country Club, his mind felt uncluttered He felt good about himself. And about what could be.

Made in the USA
Columbia, SC
15 March 2019